The Tyrian League

D.J. MacHale

THE EQUINOX CURIOSITY SHOP

Dedication
For Mike (o) Monte

The Tyrian League

BOOK ONE: Donovan 6

FOREWORD

I have been asked time and again if I'll ever write another *Pendragon* novel. Of course I'll never say never to anything…

…except maybe in this case. In my mind, Bobby Pendragon's story is such that it wouldn't make sense to continue it. *Pendragon* depicted a unique challenge (Saint Dane) that brought together a special group of individuals (The Travelers) who had to deal. Without giving away any spoilers for those who haven't read it (and why haven't you???) I can't imagine trying to come up with a way to justify bringing those individuals back together again. I could probably contrive some kind of scenario where the ending wasn't really the ending, but to me, that cheapens the story. I already dipped my toe into using an alternate timeline scenario with *The SYLO Chronicles* and would just as soon stick with a single calendar this time around, thank you very much.

This is an age where storytellers are constantly going back to the well to resurrect/reboot old IP because they know it's a safe bet due to a built-in audience of fans. Don't get me wrong, I'm a fan as much as the next person and I love reading about or seeing favorite characters make a comeback…no matter how disappointing it usually ends up being. But the downside to that is it reduces the number of new and unique ideas being created.

That doesn't mean they're not. There are plenty of talented writers creating wonderful new material, but it's difficult for them to find an audience because they're competing with a powerful adversary: nostalgia.

But I'm not one to shy away from a challenge. Introducing, drum roll please: *The Tyrian League*.

Let me say right up front, in many ways this story will feel familiar to *Pendragon* readers. Not in content, but in style. I loved writing about Bobby's grand adventure, and missed telling exciting stories about young, bold adventurers on a world-hopping quest to defeat an invincible villain while grappling with their personal demons. You know…*Pendragon*.

That's where the similarity ends. You're going to meet an entirely new cast of characters here. Donovan, Issa, Bodie, Kobain, Kellen, and many others who populate this saga. There are new worlds to explore and battles to wage. Of course, this story isn't simply about overcoming a generic evil, it's about exploring what that evil is, why it exists, and the kind of threat it presents. Hopefully, it'll make you think a bit while you're busy hanging from cliffs.

It felt good to jump back into this arena and create the kind of adventure I loved writing so much with *Pendragon*. But it's not about me, it's about you getting caught up in a story that I hope will get your blood pumping, your brain working, and maybe your heart aching just a little bit.

That's what good stories are all about.

As Donovan would say: Let's not forget that.

And so we go!
D.J. MacHale

PROLOGUE

The silver orb lifted off with silent power, rising from the depths of a seemingly abandoned building where it had been concealed. The large sphere smashed through the flimsy roof and quickly gained speed as it rose into a cloudless sky.

The sight was both triumphant and horrifying.

Watching from the ground, the handful of people who had sent the vessel on its way fought to control their emotions. They were afraid the craft would be intercepted. Or worse, shot down. But as it flew higher, the fear of disaster gradually melted away and the reality of what they had done began to sink in.

Though every detail of the launch had been carefully planned, not one of them truly believed it would happen. Only hours before, the idea of going through with this drastic plan seemed impossible. But things changed. Quickly. They went about their tasks quietly and efficiently while trying not to let their minds spin toward the horrible reality of what they were about to do.

The one thing that kept them going was that they believed they had no choice. The launch was a last desperate attempt to save their lives, the lives of their loved ones, and to create a better future for every last person on the planet.

There would be a heavy price to pay for their bold move, for sure. They would be hunted down and made to suffer for what they'd done. That was the least of their concerns. Their thoughts were focused on the precious cargo on board. Sending it to the heavens was the most difficult task any of them had ever done, or would ever do.

Without a word, they joined hands. It was a gesture of mutual support and understanding that their lives would never be the same. If there was any comfort they could take, it was that the craft carried the promise of something they were in desperate need of.

Hope.

The nightmare was back.

It had been haunting him for as long as he could remember. It wasn't the normal kind of nightmare. There were no monsters or maniac killers or a horrifying realization that he'd shown up at school wearing only underwear.

This nightmare was about numbers. Floating numbers. The setting would be different, but the numbers were always the same. His dream would start out with him doing something normal, like tossing a football or eating pizza. There was never anything about the situation that foretold what was about to happen.

Then, without warning, the numbers would appear, floating around whatever dreamscape his mind had created. There were equations and strings of digits, and strange symbols that drifted about like random debris in a pool. There were words as well. Some were recognizable but it was mostly gibberish. As his dream-self walked through the sea of numbers and nonsense words, the figures would part to let him by. He could reach up and touch them and even brush them aside. They'd float away for a moment, then gently return to whatever sequence they'd originally been in.

Then the ground would shake, as if a violent earthquake were charging up from below. The numbers would shift and go out of focus until the shaking reached a climax. The nightmare always ended with him being rudely shocked awake.

Crazy things happened in dreams. But two things boosted these particular dreams to the level of disturbing. One was that they kept happening. But why? What was in his brain that made him have the strange experience time and again? He could go months without having the dream, then he'd be hit with it four nights in a row. He dreaded falling asleep for fear he'd have to walk along the same, odd, digit-cluttered path. He told adults about it, but they blew him off. Or ignored him. Eventually, he stopped trying and suffered in silence.

The other troubling thing was that when he woke up, he always had a headache that was so intense he couldn't get back to sleep. Ordinarily he didn't get headaches. It was only when he had the dream.

The nightmare.

The foreshadowing.

CHAPTER 1

I don't get mad. I get even.

That's not entirely true. I get mad sometimes too. Usually right before I get even. So, I guess the truth is I get mad and *then* I get even. Yeah, that about sums it up.

I found the guy's car where he always parks it, behind the high school gym. I don't know if he's got a normal home, but kids say he sleeps in a storage closet near the art department at school. They'd seen the evidence: a sleeping bag, tossed Shake Shack burger wrappers, and a putrid body-odor that floats near that closet like an invisible, noxious cloud. Loser. His car was an ancient Buick. It was probably a deep burgundy once, but after a few decades in the sun it had faded to a luxurious shade of diarrhea brown. I'd feel sorry for the guy if he wasn't such a dirt bag. Because of him, there was a good chance I was going to get kicked off the football team and suspended from school. I've been guilty of a lot of stuff in my fifteen years, but in this case, I was totally innocent.

Life isn't always fair, and it was about to get very complicated for one lying, thieving asshat of a janitor.

It was a clear, warm night. The sky was filled with so many stars I felt as though I could see to the far side of the universe. It was a sparkling umbrella of endless possibility. Each spec of light stood for a different life. A different world. If I were being philosophical, I'd say that it was humbling to gaze up and consider mankind's minor place in the endless, celestial stew.

But I wasn't being philosophical. I was too busy being pissed off. I wanted revenge, and maybe a little bit of justice. But mostly revenge.

I knew how to hot wire a car, especially older models. I learned it from one of the many foster fathers I'd known. I guess the one who taught me that particular skill wasn't exactly the best role-model, but the skill was about to come in handy. The car door was open, probably because the lock was busted. I tossed my backpack onto the passenger seat and was about to duck under the dashboard to root for the ignition wires when a thought hit me. I reached overhead, pulled down the sun visor, and the car keys fell into my lap. The guy was a loser *and* an idiot. And a thief and a liar, let's not forget that.

I jammed the key into the ignition, and hesitated. This was the moment. There would be no going back from here. Was I doing the right thing? Was I truly solving anything? Or was I being just as bad as this guy? I had to stop, take a breath, and decide if getting revenge was the smartest thing to do.

Abso-freaking-lutely!

I turned the key, and the old engine groaned to life. The radio was on and blasted out "Freebird." Figures. I moved to turn it off, but the song fueled my adrenaline rush. Play on Skynyrd.

"Whooo!" I screamed as I threw the car into gear and peeled out.

Yes, I knew how to drive. More or less. That skill was taught to me by my last foster father. I think he was hoping I'd get myself to school, but he was dreaming because I didn't have a driver's license. Or a car. But hey, it was another life skill that I was about to put to good use.

The parking lot was empty, so it was easy enough to maneuver around. My plan was to drive the car up to the front entrance of the school, pop the trunk and abandon it there, but as I drove past the open gate that led to the football field, I got another idea. It probably wasn't the wisest thing to do, but neither was getting revenge. I should have been happy with just making sure justice was served.

But where was the fun in that?

I spun the wheel, jammed the gas pedal to the floor and drove through the wide-open gates that led to the football stadium of Davis Gregory High. I bounced over the track, drove under the goal posts and charged straight for the fifty-yard line. It was nearly midnight and though the place was empty, I had to make this happen fast. If anybody saw me, it would kill the mission and get me into even more trouble.

It was a grass field. Perfect. When I reached midfield, I cranked the wheel hard and accelerated. The car spun as the tires dug into the turf, spewing grass and dirt. After doing a three-sixty I let up on the gas and the car lurched to a halt.

"Whoo!" I screamed in adrenaline-fueled triumph. I followed that with a quick air-guitar riff to "Freebird" and killed the engine. It was time to be somewhere else, but first I grabbed my pack and took out a bottle of bourbon I'd pinched from my current foster father. I unscrewed the cap and sprinkled the amber liquid around the car, letting it sink into the stained cloth seats. It made the car smell like a drunk's tongue. Perfect. I jammed the bottle back into my pack, yanked out the keys, threw open the door and…

…came face to face with a girl.

"What the hell!" she shouted with surprise. Or anger. I couldn't tell which.

I was momentarily frozen. I knew her. Her name was Issa something-or-other. She was a year or two older than me and judging from the fact that she was wearing tights, a t-shirt and was out of breath, she'd probably been using the track for a moonlight run.

Just my luck.

"This looks bad," was all I could think to say.

"Uh, yeah," she replied with a heavy dose of "duh."

"I know you," I said. "Issa, right?"

She didn't answer because she was too busy gaping at the six-inch deep massive donut I had skillfully carved into the turf.

"What're you doing here?" I asked.

"Training for Cross Country. This is the only time I can…wait, what am I doing here?"

"Before you get all judgy, check this out."

"You realize this is a police thing," she said, nervously.

"I'm counting on it."

I hurried to the back of the car and popped the trunk.

"Observe," I said and gestured to the open trunk like a model on a TV game show.

She gazed into the trunk to see a treasure trove of stuff. There were IPads, jackets, sneakers, earbuds, backpacks and a bunch of other items that didn't belong in the trunk of a puke brown junker of a car.

"Where did you get all that?" she asked, incredulous.

"I didn't. This is Kralovenic's car."

"Who?"

"The creep janitor who sleeps at school. He's the one who's been stealing stuff out of kid's lockers. From the looks of it he's not just stealing from school, either. He drives around, selling this stuff out of his trunk like a rolling Wal-Mart."

Issa's mouth hung open. She was still trying to process it all.

"How did you know it was him?" she asked.

"Because he tried to sell me a watch. Only it was *my* watch that was ripped off from my locker last week. I should have turned him in but that was the second thing I thought of."

"What was the first?"

"I decked him. One shot. Pop! Knocked him flat on his butt. But then I was the one who got in trouble. I told the assistant principal why I did it, but he didn't believe me. Story of my life. So I'm giving him the proof. Ta da!"

"Did you have to do it like this?"

"Hey, the guy ripped me off. Then tried to rip me off again. And I still don't have a watch. Three strikes. He's done."

"I think that's only two strikes."

"Whatever. The guy's history. If you don't mind, I'd like to be somewhere else when the cops get here."

I walked away quickly, headed for the gate. Issa was right behind me.

"It's Donovan, right?" Issa asked. "Donovan Park?"

I stopped short and she nearly ran in to me. I turned quickly so we stood nose to nose. Truth be told, Issa was pretty hot. She was Asian-American. Korean, I think. She was as tall as me, with long, jet-black hair that she tied back into a ponytail. And she was an athlete. There was a whole "Lara Croft" thing going on, or maybe I was just fantasizing. But she knew my name, which was kind of cool, unless she was going to rat me out. Then it would be better if she thought my name was Jason or something.

"You gonna tell the cops it was me?" I asked.

"Do you always take revenge on people you don't like?"

"Only the ones who deserve it."

"Remind me not to cross you," she said. "And no, I won't tell anybody."

"Thanks. You're kind of cute."

"I'm older than you."

"That doesn't make you less cute."

Suddenly the sky was lit up by what looked like a rogue firework. Or a shooting star.

Issa and I both followed its trail as it blazed across the night sky directly overhead, creating a long streak of orange light that quickly burned out and was gone. Though it was faint, I heard the distant sound of a sonic boom.

"That was cool," I said.

Issa was still gazing up at the sky, looking way more concerned about the celestial lightshow than I was.

"Shooting star," I said. "It's not like we're being invaded."

She shot me a quick, dark look as if I'd said something wrong.

"Get out of here, Donovan," she said, all business.

She backed away, turned and ran.

"You're worried about me, I like that!" I said, calling after her. "Do me a favor? Call nine-one-one. I want them to find the car before Kralovenic does."

Her answer was to pick up the pace and sprint toward the far end of the field. She was fast, too. Seeing her flee like that gave me an uneasy feeling. I thought we were having a genuine moment, but then she saw a stupid shooting star and panicked. Why? What kind of freak does that? Maybe she was running home to make a foil helmet.

Whatever. Didn't matter. I had taken my revenge. The next day I was going to get an apology from the school, let back on the football team and maybe even get a medal for being a hero who cracked the case of the loser locker thief. Yes, it had turned out to be a good night.

Except for that strange shooting star. What was it? And why did it scare the crap out of Issa?

CHAPTER 2

I was relieved to see that the school ground-crew had done a pretty respectable job of filling in the donut I'd gouged into the fifty yard line of the stadium field. Good thing, too. We had practice.

"Lightning! Lightning!" I called out to my guys on defense.

That meant I was going to blitz. I loved blitzing. It was basically a green light to cause mayhem.

The quarterback came to the line and gave me a nervous look. I smiled back at him. He knew he was in trouble. Man, I love football. I'm a middle linebacker which means I get action on every play. Hitting people is a rush. Where else can you knock somebody stupid and not get in trouble for it?

It had been a perfect day. The cops found Kralovenic's car and though he denied having torn up the field, they charged him with reckless vandalism, or something like that. He was so hung over he wasn't even sure if he'd done it or not. The booze-smell in the car cemented it for the cops. And oh yeah, they arrested him for having all the stolen property. Let's not forget that.

I was off the hook for having decked him; un-suspended and allowed back on the team. It was almost as though I had planned the whole thing. Which come to think of it, I had. They only thing I didn't get was a medal for having solved the crime spree. I guess you can't have everything.

But I did get my watch back, thank you very much.

And now I was with my team at practice, looking across at Bodie Willard, our quarterback, knowing I was about to take his head off.

Sometimes life can be sweet.

"Ready...go!" Bodie called.

He took the snap and dropped back to pass. I went after him, slicing between the guard and the tackle who hadn't set up fast enough to block me. I had a clear shot at Bodie and took it. Before he could release the pass, I drove my facemask straight into his chest, knocking him off his feet and flat onto his back.

The coaches blew their whistles instantly.

"What the hell, Park!" Bodie screamed.

I quickly jumped up and helped him to his feet.

"I'm sorry man," I said in my best fake-apology voice. I even brushed some grass off his shoulder pads, but Brodie shrugged me off.

"This isn't live, Mutt!" he said with a snarl.

I hated that he called me that. It was a nickname that was used by exactly one person. Him. I wanted to deck him again.

"You're right," I said, trying to sound genuinely apologetic. "I'm sorry."

I wasn't sorry. Not even a little. Besides liking to hit people, I wasn't a Bodie-fan. The guy was a typical quarterback: tall, strong, fast, blonde and probably pretty smart. I've heard he's good looking too, but I'm not the best judge of that. I, on the other hand, was more of a typical linebacker. Medium height but wide and strong for my age, which was a good thing because I was younger than the other guys. Nobody ever accused me of being handsome but it's not like I'm cracking mirrors either.

"If you do that again…" Bodie warned, letting the threat hang there so I'd get all nervous, as if there was any chance of that.

"Park!" Coach Ornato called. "This isn't live!"

His words said one thing, but his smile said another. He appreciated a good hit. But this wasn't a live scrimmage. Meaning everything was full speed right up to the point of the tackle. But it's hard to fight through a block, grab a runner and not drop him. It's unnatural.

Especially if the guy with the ball was Bodie-Freaking-Willard.

I jogged back to our huddle and got a few fist-bumps from my guys on defense. I may have been younger than everybody else, but I was the leader of that squad. It wasn't like I was all rah-rah, I was just good and played hard. That got me respect.

In the huddle I said, "He's gonna pass again, so I'm gonna blitz again."

There were chuckles all around. I had no plans to let up on my boy Bodie.

As we broke the huddle and went to the line, my eye caught a group of Cross-Country girls jogging around the track. Leading the pack was Issa. She glanced toward us, so I gave her a big wave. She ignored me. That was okay. She was out of my league, but she sure was cute. And cool because she didn't tell anybody about what I'd done the night before. Let's not forget that. I owed her.

Bodie brought the offense up to the line. He shot me a quick glance which meant I was in his head. I liked making guys like him sweat. He had it all going on and not just on the football field. It felt good to drop a little reality bomb onto his perfect world.

"Ready…go!" Bodie barked and went back to pass.

This time I faked it as if I were going to drop into pass coverage. It froze the offense line, so I looped around the tackle and used my speed to get to Bodie from his blind side. As he cocked his arm to throw, I wrapped him up and threw him to the ground.

Whistles blew. Bodie jumped to his feet and in a mad-crazy fit of anger, he threw the ball at me, drilling me in the stomach.

"Asshole!" he screamed.

I'm not saying I didn't deserve it, but it hurt. So I charged him. The two of us locked up, throwing punches that were useless because we were in helmets and pads.

The rest of the team cheered us on.

"I'll kill you!" Bodie shouted in a rage.

I don't think he meant that literally, but maybe he did. We both fell to the ground. Bodic sat on my stomach while throwing punches that glanced harmlessly off my helmet. I smiled back. That only made him angrier. I grabbed his face mask and yanked him off me. Seconds later I was on top of him with my knee in his chest.

"You're over your head, Junior," I said.

The coaches descended and pulled me off. Other coaches yanked Bodie to his feet and held him back because he was still hot.

"This is football," I said, laughing. "Tackling's a thing."

"It's not a live scrimmage!" Bodie hissed, spraying spit.

Coach Ornato, our Head Coach, stepped between us.

"Are you two serious?" he said, incredulous.

"He's out of control," Bodie yelled.

"You're both out of control," Coach Ornato replied. "What're you doing, Park?"

"Sorry, Coach," I said. "It's hard holding back."

"But you will, or you'll be gone. Same goes for you, Willard."

"Me? But I didn't—"

"Shut it!" Coach Ornato snapped. "You're supposed to be leading this team. What're you gonna do if something you don't like happens in a game? You gonna get all pissy and throw a fit?"

Bodie deflated. The fight had gone out of him.

"No," was all he could mutter.

"We're on the same team, gentlemen, remember that," Coach Ornato announced. "After practice you're both on the dummies. Now huddle up."

As we all went back to our sides of the ball, Bodie glared at me.

I gave him a smile and a wave.

I love football practices. They're grueling, but they make sense. And when you have energy like me, all the sprints and agility drills and strength exercises help to burn it off.

And I loved to hit people. Let's not forget that.

Maybe best of all is that every second spent at practice meant less time I'd have to be at home. If "home" is what you could call it. I'd been bounced between foster homes my entire life. I never knew my biological parents, just a string of people, some decent some not-so-decent, who would take me in for a while to get whatever fee the state paid them for the privilege. I didn't hate any of them. I didn't care enough to feel anything, one way or the other. When I was little I hoped one of these families might adopt me, but that never happened. I guess I can't blame them. Who would want a kid who was always bouncing off walls and picking fights with other kids who thought they were better than him? I'd wear out my welcome by getting suspended from school for being disruptive or because I punched one of their real kids when they called me a name or by setting the kitchen on fire.

That last thing was an accident, I swear. I didn't know you couldn't put metal into the microwave.

It always ended the same way. The fed-up foster people would call child services, a sympathetic social worker would pick me up and by the end of the day I'd be placed in another temporary home to start the dance all over again. It eventually became clear that none of these homes would be final.

My current deal had me with a single guy, which was kind of weird. But he wasn't a perv or anything. Mr. Leo was okay. There were two other younger guys in the house and we each had our own bedrooms, which was sweet, and made it easy to sneak out. Mr. Leo took in a load of guys over the years. I heard stories about how a lot of them stayed with him long enough to graduate. I'd already been with him for a couple of months and dared to think it might last to the end of high school.

Still, it wasn't really "home." Not that I knew exactly what that meant. I'd been through so many, and even more schools. It was tough making friends that way. So I pretty much kept to myself. Football saved me. It helped to keep my brain calm, which kept me from doing stupid stuff. So other than punching out a nasty, thieving janitor, I'd managed to stay out of trouble for a pretty long time.

When practice was over, Bodie and I had to pay the price for our fight. Being "on the dummies" was a hated punishment. While the rest of the team hit the locker room, we had to collect all the heavy tackling dummies and practice pads, lug them under the stands and lock them in the equipment shed. It was brutal, especially since we had to work while everyone else was in the showers. Doing the dummies added a half hour to an already grueling practice.

Bodie and I didn't say a word to one another. It's dumb to say I resented the guy. I barely knew him. But it ticked me off that he had this perfect life and didn't even know it. Or appreciate it. I think that's what bugged me about him. He had no idea how lucky he was.

After we loaded in the last tackling dummy, I closed the shed door, locked the padlock, and turned to see Bodie standing there with his hands on his hips.

"What's your deal?" he asked.

"No deal. I just like football."

"You could hurt somebody. You're dangerous."

"It's a dangerous game," I said with a shrug.

He pointed a threatening finger at me and said, "Back off. I'm not gonna let some mutt ruin my chance at a scholarship."

The hair went up on the back of my neck.

"Scholarship?" I said with a laugh. "Hate to tell you, Junior, you ain't that good."

Bodie stiffened, but all he did was give me a cold glare and walk away, pulling off his jersey and shoulder pads. I jogged after him, caught up, and kept moving past.

"What'sa matter, Junior?" I asked. "Tired?"

"Yeah, of you," he shot back.

I called him "Junior" because he was Bodie Willard Junior. A real richie-rich name. Such a tool.

I pulled off my shoulder pads and saw that Bodie had picked up the pace and jogged past me. It was an obvious challenge, and I wasn't going to let it go, so I ran. When he saw that I was about to catch him, he turned on the speed. Suddenly we'd forgotten how tired we were. The two of us ran, side by side, juggling our shoulder pads and helmets, racing for the locker room. It was dumb, I know, but I don't like to lose.

It became a flat-out sprint. You'd never know that we had just been through two hours of practice and another half-hour of heavy equipment-lugging. We got to the locker room door at the exact same instant and touched it together. A tie. We dropped our gear and stood there with our hands on our knees, gasping for air.

I looked to Bodie and laughed. Bodie laughed too. We both realized how dumb it was to race like a couple of eight-year-olds.

I picked up my pads and yanked the handle of the locker room door, but it wouldn't open.

"Aw no!" Bodie exclaimed. "They can't be gone already!"

"It's not locked, it's probably just--"

I looked down to see a shiny, metal wedge stuck under the door.

"--jammed."

I kicked the wedge with the heel of my cleats. It was shoved in so tight that it took a couple of solid shots to work it loose. This time the door opened easily.

"What idiot did that?" Bodie said and cut in front of me to step inside first.

The door led directly into the varsity locker room. What I expected to see was a room crowded with guys getting dressed. That would be normal. What we saw instead, wasn't.

"Holy shit--," Bodie said with a gasp.

The room was full of guys, all right. But they weren't getting dressed. The floor was covered with the bodies of unconscious kids. Or dead kids. They were in various stages of dress, as if whatever happened was sudden. Bodies were strewn across the floor in awkward poses. Arms and legs were twisted at odd angles. Some guys had fallen on top of others.

I think we both went into brain lock because we just stood there and stared. Nothing about what we were seeing could be explained, at least not in a way that made sense or had a happy ending.

Bodie knelt down next to one kid and held two fingers to his neck to check for a pulse.

"He's alive," Bodie announced.

Across the room, somebody groaned.

"Coach!" I exclaimed.

We both ran to Coach Ornato, leaping over bodies to get to him. He was lying outside of the door to his office. I dropped to my knees and helped him to a sit up.

"You okay?" Bodie asked.

Stupid question because the guy obviously wasn't even close to okay. I had to hold him up or he would have fallen right back down.

"My head…" Coach Ornato mumbled.

"What happened?" I asked.

"Came out of my office," he said, slurring his words. "Boys were on the ground, there were men, dressed in black, spraying gas."

That explained why everybody was knocked out. I took a deep breath to see if I could smell anything, which was a completely dumb move if poisonous gas was floating around, but I wasn't thinking straight.

"Who's that?" Bodie asked.

He pointed to the doorway on the far side of the room that led to the larger, PE locker room. There was a man out there, dressed from neck to toe in black, with a black ski mask covering his face. He was walking slowly over more fallen bodies, holding a device down low to each kid as if taking readings of some kind.

"Hey!" Bodie yelled and waved to the guy. "In here!"

I pulled his arm down.

"Shut up," I hissed quietly. "That's the guy!"

The dark figure tensed up and looked our way. It didn't take a genius to realize we were in trouble. Even Bodie figured it out.

"Oops," he said.

The guy was wearing a filter-mask over his nose and mouth. Before we could react, he made a quick move as if to fling something our way. I didn't see anything come out of his hand, but it was real because it gave off a hum as it flew closer.

"Look out!" I screamed.

Bodie dove away. I was stuck holding the coach, which saved me. Whatever the guy threw hit Coach Ornato because I felt him tense up as if an electric charge had gone through his body. He gasped and went limp.

Bodie scrambled to his feet and went for the door to outside.

I let go of the coach and followed Bodie as another electric charge flew by my head and pinged off a metal locker. It was so close, the hair stood up on my neck. I jumped outside and slammed the door shut just as another charge hit it from inside. I had the smarts to kick the metal wedge back under the door to keep it from opening.

"We need help," Bodie declared, breathless.

"You think?"

He took off running along the side of the school building and I was right behind him.

It was late afternoon. The parking lot was empty.

"We gotta call nine-one-one," Bodie declared. "Do you have your cell phone?"

"Seriously?" I said. "I don't own a cell phone, and if I did I wouldn't keep it in my practice pants."

"We'll find a phone inside," he said with authority.

We reached a set of glass doors, but they were locked.

"Is that guy a terrorist?" Bodie asked.

"Guys," I corrected. "Ornato said there was more than one."

My eye caught movement inside. I looked through the glass door to see another dark figure flinging something toward us.

"And there he is," I said and dove into Bodie, knocking him to the ground. We both hit the pavement as the door shattered, raining bits of glass down on us.

"Move!" I commanded.

We scrambled to our feet and ran, headed back toward the football stadium. The school grounds never felt so quiet and empty. There wasn't a car to be seen, except for one.

"We'll take my car," I said.

"You've got a car?" Bodie asked, incredulous.

"Sort of."

Parked behind the stands was the formerly burgundy Buick that belonged to the thieving janitor, right where the police left it after towing it from the field. I ran to the driver's door.

"This wreck is yours?" Bodie asked with surprise.

"You don't like it, stay here."

I got in as Bodie rounded the car to the passenger side. I reached up to the visor and pulled it down. No keys.

"Damn!" I shouted.

"Looking for these?" Bodie said, holding up the keys. "They were on the seat. Not too smart, Mutt."

I grabbed them, stuck them in the ignition and cranked the engine. The ancient clunker wheezed like it was struggling to turn over and I feared I might have messed something up when I took it for a spin. I turned off the ignition and waited a second.

"Do you seriously not own a cell phone?" Bodie asked.

I turned the key again. The engine groaned for a painful three seconds, then turned over.

"Yes!" I declared with relief.

"No," Bodie replied soberly. He was pointing forward.

One of the dark figures was standing in front of the car, calmly gesturing for us to get out. I looked into the rearview mirror to see another one standing behind us, a few feet back.

"What do they want?" Bodie asked with fear.

"Whatever it is, they ain't getting it from me."

I threw the shift into reverse, jammed on the accelerator and the car sped backward. Its tires squealed and spewed smoke. The car may have been old, but it had serious horses under the hood. The terrorist behind us barely had time to dive out of the way. I drove backward, careening across the empty parking lot, then hit the brakes and skid to a stop. As I shifted into drive, two more projectiles hit the car. One pinged off the fender, the other hit a rear side-window, shattering it.

"Go!" Bodie screamed.

I hammered my foot to the floor. The car whined, complained, but responded. In seconds we were accelerating across the empty parking lot, headed for the street.

"What are they shooting at us?" Bodie asked fearfully.

"I don't know, but we've got a bigger problem."

"What's that?"

"I'm a bad driver."

Bodie buckled his seatbelt.

Weenie.

I took a tight turn out of the parking lot and bounced over the curb. The harsh sound of metal scraping across cement meant we were probably leaving a chunk of Kralovenic's exhaust system in the parking lot.

"Go to the police station downtown," Bodie ordered.

"Too far. I told you, I'm a bad driver."

"Then I'll drive."

"I'm not stopping, and you don't want to be caught driving this car."

"Why not?"

"It's not really mine."

"So what? After what happened you think the cops are going to care?"

I turned off the main road and onto a suburban street lined with homes.

"My house isn't far," I said. "We'll call the police from there."

"Okay," Bodie said, relaxing. "That'll work."

We drove for a few seconds in silence. It was the first chance we had to think about what had happened.

"If we hadn't been on the dummies..." Bodie said, letting the thought trail.

"Yeah."

"Why would terrorists attack us?" he asked.

"It could have been a robbery."

"What do you steal from a high school locker room? Jocks?"

"I don't know!" I screamed. "Jeez, stop asking questions. They could be d-bags taking hostages for ransom. Or a couple of freaks who got all worked up on-line about hating school and wanted to do some damage."

"Yeah, you hear about stuff like that, but you never think it could happen to you."

With that somber thought, we drove in silence until Bodie grimaced.

"What is that smell?" he asked curiously while sniffing the air.

"Bourbon," I said with a smirk.

"No," Bodie said, frowning. "It smells like…like—"

I smelled it too.

"Smoke!" I exclaimed.

Up ahead, black smoke billowed from the windows of a small house.

"Oh man," Bodie said. "Somebody's house is on fire."

"Yeah," I said, soberly. "Mine."

I pulled to the curb across from the house where I'd been living for the past few months. Mr. Leo's house. It was a plain, white, two-story place with a small front lawn; a split-rail fence; a basketball hoop in the driveway; and flames licking out of every window.

We got out of the car in a daze.

"I hope nobody's home," Bodie said.

"They aren't. Mr. Leo gets home late, and the other kids go to after school programs."

"So then how did a fire start?" Bodie asked.

Good question.

A far off-siren cut through the sound of the crackling flames. Help was on the way.

Somebody whistled at us. We both turned to see…

…standing next to Kralovenic's car was one of the bad guys. At least we knew who started the fire.

"No!" Bodie yelled and turned to run away.

He didn't get far. The guy shot his arm forward to fling something. The humming sound was unmistakable. I could hear it, whatever *it* was, whiz past me. The invisible missile hit Bodie in the back. He stopped suddenly, stiffened, and fell to the ground, unconscious.

It didn't scare me. It pissed me off.

"What do you want?" I said, trying to sound as though I was too tough to be scared.

The guy gestured for me to follow him.

"Like hell," I yelled. I had had enough. I charged for the guy, ready to take him out like an enemy ball carrier.

The dark guy didn't flinch. He flung his arm forward. I heard a brief hum, then felt as though I'd been hit by a truck. My body went rigid, and I hit the ground. At least I think I did because I was already unconscious.

My last fleeting thought was a simple one: *Why?*

Then the lights went out.

CHAPTER 3

I woke up, just enough to decide I'd rather be asleep. My head felt like a couple of chimps were knocking it around like a tetherball. As consciousness slowly crept back, I realized that I was lying on something hard. Maybe the ground. I couldn't tell. Whatever it was, it wasn't comfortable. I rolled over. Big mistake. I fell off whatever I was on and hit the floor with such a rude jolt that there was no chance I could go back to sleep. *Now* I was on the ground. My whole body ached, and it wasn't from football. It took a few seconds for me to remember why.

It was the guy in black. The terrorist, or whatever he was. He hit me with some kind of energy-bolt that knocked me into next week. For all I knew it really was next week. Memories came rushing back: the bodies strewn across the locker-room floor; escaping in Kralovenic's car, Mr. Leo's house on fire.

I really, really wanted to go back to sleep.

I cautiously cracked open one eye and was hit with a bright burst of light and color that made my head pound even worse.

Looming above me was a massive stained-glass window. The colorful mosaic was a dramatic depiction of a yellow, rising sun against a blue-green background. The actual sun shone through the glass, making the mosaic sun look as though it was shooting out sharp yellow beams of light, directly into my aching head.

I wanted to rub my eyes but that was a no-go. My hands were tied behind my back. Uh oh. Maybe my theory about those bad guys kidnapping us for ransom wasn't far off. Panic started to tickle my brain. Mr. Leo was a good guy, but he couldn't pay a hefty ransom. Maybe Bodie's family could. He was rich. Maybe that's who the kidnappers were after. Everybody else could be collateral damage.

Bodie. What happened to Bodie?

I rolled onto my back and looked up to see what I had fallen from. It was a long, wooden bench. Somebody else was up there who had on football cleats.

"Bodie!" I called out. Ouch. It made my head throb.

The cleats twitched.

"Watch out," I said. "You're lying on a—"

He groaned, rolled over, and fell off.

"—bench."

He landed right in front of me.

"Ow," he bellowed. "What the hell?"

He was thirty seconds behind me and going through the exact same process: Wake up; register pain; fall off bench; grunt in more pain; crack open eyes to invite still more pain; realize hands are tied behind back; focus; see stained glass window. Total confusion. Now we were both up to speed.

"Go ahead, ask the question," I said.

"What question?" Brodie replied in a daze.

"I think you know."

"Where am I?" Bodie grumbled.

"That's the one. I think we're in a church."

Beneath the imposing stained-glass window was a wooden podium where somebody would stand to give a speech. Or to preach. The bench we'd fallen off of was a church pew. Many of them stretched back, row after row. If this was a church, it was a plain one. There were no statues or religious symbols, only the dramatic rising sun window that shot us with warm, painful light.

I struggled to sit up, which wasn't easy with my hands tied and my head feeling as though it was stuck in a bucket of molasses that somebody was hitting with a hammer.

"I think we've been kidnapped," I said. "Your parents better be rich enough to pay the ransom for both of us."

Bodie sat up and said, "My head hurts so bad I could puke."

"Do it on the way out," I said with no sympathy. "They tied our hands, not our feet."

We both got to our knees. The room swayed, but I didn't give in and stood up on wobbly legs.

"Gentlemen!" came a booming voice.

Somebody had entered the room and was standing beneath the stained-glass window, backlit by the yellow light. It was a woman, I think. She was tall, with long, wavy hair that fell to her shoulders.

"Whoa, dramatic," I said.

"I trust you're feeling better," she said warmly.

I wasn't, but whatever.

I'm guessing she was in her forties. She wore a dark suit with pants and high heels. Around her neck was an electric-blue scarf that was so bright it glowed. She had a deep voice that was unusual for a woman. At least in my limited experience. What stood out most about her was her long hair. It was brilliant red. With the stained-glass sun glowing behind her, she looked other-worldly.

She held a silver tray with a fancy glass pitcher filled with water, and two glasses.

"I know you're thirsty," she said kindly. "This will help with the headaches as well."

She walked to a small table that was in the center aisle between the pews. She seemed to glide rather than walk, and gracefully rested the tray down.

"I must apologize for the restraints, Donovan," she said. "But you do have certain, aggressive tendencies."

"You know me?" I said with surprise.

"We've never met," she said. "But I've been looking forward to this moment for quite some time." She picked up a glass of water and held it out to me.

I didn't take it.

"I promise you," she said. "It's nothing more than water."

Her eyes were locked on mine. They were so brown they seemed black. It was like being hit with a couple of dark lasers. She wasn't somebody I wanted to piss off. At least not yet.

"Uh, a little help?" I said and turned to show her my tied wrists.

"Of course," she said with a chuckle, as if she'd forgotten.

She put the glass back on the tray, then walked to me and grasped the plastic tie that bound my hands together.

"You won't do anything foolish now, will you?" she asked.

"Me? Nah."

Total lie.

With one quick, violent move, she snapped the plastic tie as if it were made of paper.

I looked to Bodie. His wide eyes meant he was as shocked as I was by her strength. He tried to break his own plastic tie but couldn't.

"What about me?" he asked.

"Let's become friends first," the woman said. She picked up the glass and held it out to me.

"Don't drink it!" Bodie shouted.

"If she wanted to hurt us, she could have done it while we were knocked out," I said. "And I'm thirsty."

The woman smirked and raised an eyebrow as if to say, "good point."

I took the glass, looked at it for a second, then gave Bodie a questioning look to ask if he wanted to drink. Bodie answered with a "why not?" shrug so I lifted the glass to his mouth. He downed it all.

I watched him closely and asked, "You feel okay?"

"Seriously?" he said, peeved. "I was the guinea pig?"

"Well…yeah."

The woman picked up the other glass and handed it to me. It was heavy. I wondered how much damage it would do if I winged it at her head.

"Please don't," the woman said, as if reading my mind.

She nodded toward a doorway near the front of the church. Standing in the shadows, barely visible, was a guy dressed all in black who could have been one of the marauders from school.

I drank the entire glass of water with a few gulps and slammed it onto the tray.

"My parents will pay any ransom you want," Bodie said, boldly. "That's what this is about, right? Money?"

"I appreciate your pragmatism," the woman said with a chuckle.

"I get things done," Bodie replied with arrogance.

"I'm sure you do, but this has nothing to do with money. Or with you, for that matter. I'm here for Donovan."

"Me?" I said with surprise. "If you think anybody's going to pay a dime to save me, you're dreaming."

"As I said, this isn't about money."

She was enjoying herself, which made everything seem even more crazy.

"What do you want with Park?" Bodie asked. "He's nobody."

In any other situation, I would have smacked him for that.

"Park," the woman said thoughtfully, as if trying it on for size. "Such a perfectly plain name."

"Yeah? What's *your* name?" I asked, annoyed.

"I am Vail Kobain."

"Vail Kobain?" I repeated. "What is that? Like, Russian?"

Bodie said, "If you don't want money, why are we here?"

He was trying to be all threatening. It wasn't working. This lady was used to having things go her way. It also didn't hurt that she had a couple of thugs watching from the shadows who would pounce if things went south.

"You hurt a lot of people to get me here," I said.

She picked up the tray and moved it to the podium, out of our reach. So much for using the glass as a weapon.

"No one has been injured. Your friends were simply unconscious for a short time, just as you were. By now they're awake and no worse off."

"What do you want?" I asked.

A door opened in the back of the church. Bright light blasted in creating a silhouette out of the person who had opened it.

"Excuse me," a girl called out. "Is this the Church of Regenesis?"

Kobain turned cold and said, "I'm afraid you're too early for the service."

The silhouette walked forward, headed for the center aisle, and us. She moved slowly, as if nervous about being in a holy place.

"I know," she called out, meekly. "I was hoping to join. I've heard so much about Regenesis. I thought it would be a good idea to come before a service and talk to somebody."

I squinted to get a better look at the girl. There was something strangely familiar about her.

"I understand, child," Kobain called out, impatiently. "You are most welcome, but this is not a good time."

"But I'm here now," the girl replied. "Won't you talk to me for a few minutes?"

Kobain waved her hand, and the two dark marauders slipped into the sanctuary. These were definitely not altar boys.

"I'm afraid I must insist that you leave and come back later," Kobain said coldly.

The girl stepped forward into the warm light that shone through the stained-glass window. She was dressed in running tights and a warm-up top with a small green backpack slung over her shoulder. Her long black hair was tied back in a tight ponytail.

I let out a gasp but didn't say a word.

Bodie wasn't as smart.

"Issa?" he exclaimed.

Kobain tensed up.

Issa rolled her eyes. "And there goes the surprise," she said with a sigh. "Run!"

"What?" Bodie responded, confused.

The two marauders charged for us.

"I said run!" Issa screamed with more force.

I gave Bodie a shove and we took off running toward the back of the church, past Issa.

The guys in black flung humming projectiles. Issa quickly shrugged off her backpack, went down on one knee and held it out like a shield. Sharp, metallic sounds rang out as she deflected the missiles. This was no ordinary backpack.

Kobain stood by her podium looking as calm as if she were about to give a sermon.

"This only delays the inevitable, young lady," Kobain called to Issa.

The marauders stopped throwing things at Issa and charged for her.

Issa threw the pack at them. As it flew, its strap extended like a lasso. The shield had become a weapon. It wrapped around the first marauder's ankles, tripping him up.

The second marauder changed direction and lunged at her.

Issa was ready. She ducked, threw her hip out and used the guy's momentum to flip him up and over her back. He flew head-over-butt and landed flat on his back with a pained grunt.

Bodie and I stopped at the back end of the aisle, watching in awe.

The first marauder freed his ankles from the backpack strap, looked up, and took the full brunt of Issa's foot as she kicked out and crushed his nose.

Whoa. Issa was a badass.

With blood streaming from his flattened nose, the marauder stumbled backward. Before he hit the ground, Issa spun toward the other marauder who was back on his feet and attacking. With a move that was so quick and smooth it looked like she'd been practicing it for years, she grabbed the small table with the water pitcher, sending the tray and the glasses crashing to the floor. She swung it like a baseball bat, catching the attacker square in the ribs. The table legs broke, probably along with a few of the guy's ribs. Both marauders were flat out on the floor, dazed and beaten.

Issa was barely out of breath. She looked to Vail Kobain who hadn't moved from the podium. If the woman was upset by the violent turn of events, she sure didn't show it.

"Well done," she said with genuine admiration. "But you realize this is futile."

"Is it?" Issa said, cocky.

She scooped her pack off the floor. The strap had retracted, and it was back to normal. She backed away up the aisle to where we stood like a couple of dumbfounded idiots.

"Service is over," she said to us and pushed us toward the exit.

"I'll be seeing you again soon, Donovan!" Kobain called out.

"Don't bet on that!" Issa called back.

"You gonna explain this?" Bodie asked Issa.

"Not right now," she said and shoved us out of the front door into the bright sunlight of a late summer Connecticut afternoon. "We're not out of this yet."

CHAPTER 4

The church stood on the corner of a busy commercial suburban street. It was the kind of building you'd pass by a million times and never think twice about. There was nothing churchy about it. It was a three-story box stuck between a Subway Sandwich shop and a UPS shipping center. The only hint that it was a church was a small brass plaque near the door that read: *CHURCH OF REGENESIS.*

"I know this place!" Bodie declared. "It used to be a garage."

"Now it's somewhere we don't want to be," Issa said. "Get in the car."

Parked at the curb was a dark blue Kia. Bodie went for the front passenger seat, but I got there first and boxed him out. He gave me an annoyed look and jumped in back. Issa got behind the wheel, fired up the engine and peeled out.

"Can somebody please get me out of this?" Bodie whined, twisting to show the plastic tie that was around his wrists.

"There's a knife in there," Issa said, pointing to the glove compartment.

I flipped open the door and took out a heavy hunting knife.

"Whoa," I exclaimed. "Bold."

"Just use it!" Bodie yelled.

He turned around awkwardly while I reached back and cut the plastic.

"Thank you," Bodie said sarcastically, as if annoyed I hadn't done it an hour ago.

I jammed the knife back into the glove compartment as Issa maneuvered through traffic, going faster than the law allowed.

"A Kia?" I said. "This was the best you could do for a daring rescue?"

She gave me a sideways look and laughed. The joke wasn't all that funny, but it broke the tension.

"Drive us to my father's office," Bodie commanded. "He'll call the cops. Those assholes will be done by dinner."

"Not possible," Issa said.

"Why not?" Bodie asked, peeved.

"Because I've got to lose the car that's chasing us."

I twisted around to see a black BMW dodging through traffic, trying to catch up.

"I'll say it again," I said. "A Kia?"

"Will you please tell us what's going on?" Bodie asked with growing panic.

"Right now I'm trying to keep us alive."

She jammed her foot down on the gas and sped through a traffic light that had just turned red. It was a daring and perfectly timed move as crossing traffic blocked the BMW.

"You've done this kind of thing before," I said.

She gave me a sly smile.

"Now I owe you twice," I added.

"Remember that," she said.

Something about that answer made me uneasy. There was a whole lot going on here that I had no clue about. I wasn't so sure I wanted to know any of it.

Bodie said, "Take a right here and head to the police station."

Issa ignored him and blew through the turn.

"Did you not hear me?" Bodie exclaimed.

"It's okay, we're there," Issa declared.

"Where?" I asked.

She turned into an empty parking lot that was in front of several industrial looking warehouse buildings. She didn't slow down as we moved deeper into the complex.

"I don't think they saw us turn," Bodie said. "We'll hide behind one of these buildings then drive to the police."

"We could do that," Issa said. "We won't."

We flew past many more buildings, none of which looked occupied.

"Is this like a shortcut?" I asked.

"Sort of."

She made a sharp left toward a building and drove through an open garage door that led to an underground parking garage. As soon as we got inside, the big garage door closed slowly.

"Did you do that?" Bodie asked.

He didn't get an answer.

Issa drove with authority through the vast, empty parking garage as if she knew exactly where she was going. About halfway through we came to a steel wall that went from floor to ceiling, with a single door in the dead center.

Issa screeched to a stop and killed the engine.

All went deathly quiet.

"We're here," Issa announced.

I looked around to see…nothing.

"Where exactly is here?" Bodie asked.

We all got out of the car.

"Go home, Bodie," Issa said. "You were in the wrong place at the wrong time."

"What about me?" I demanded.

The sound of squeaky-hinges echoed across the empty garage as the door in the steel wall swung open. A man popped his head out.

"How'd it go?" he asked in a raspy voice that sounded as though he needed to clear his throat.

"It went," Issa replied.

The guy looked to be in his fifties. He hadn't shaved in a week. Or three. He had blonde-gray hair that covered his ears and looked as though it hadn't been brushed since that last shave. His red flannel shirt was untucked over baggy jeans that hadn't been washed in a while. Or ever.

"Who's the other kid?" he asked.

"Collateral," Issa replied. "He's not coming."

"Might be better to take him," the guy said. "Could be dangerous if he's been tagged."

"Tagged?" Bodie exclaimed. "Call the police."

The man laughed, but it quickly turned into a coughing fit.

"Nothing the police can do, fella," he said between hacks.

At least it cleared his throat. A little.

"If I'm the one they want, bring 'em on!" I declared. "I'm not hiding from anybody."

"Yes you are," the guy said. "For a while, anyway."

I had no idea what he meant by that, and I didn't care. I backed away from the group and said, "I'm outta here. You coming, Junior?"

Bodie opened his mouth to answer but was cut off by the sound of a violent, metal-on-metal collision. A heavy-duty SUV burst through the closed garage door we had just come through. The huge, industrial door blew down like it was made of plastic. The vehicle charged in, followed by two more SUVs and the BMW that had been chasing us.

"How did they find us?" Issa said with a gasp.

On the opposite end of the garage another door burst open as two more SUVs blasted in.

"Time to go," the man said and ducked back through the door.

"Inside, " Issa commanded. "Both of you."

"I don't want to run from these guys," I said.

"Yes you do," Issa shot back, dead serious.

The two sets of cars were getting closer, fast.

"What's in there?" Bodie asked. "Is it like a safe room?"

"Exactly," Issa said. "Move!"

She shoved us both toward the door.

I won't lie. Seeing those big cars charging toward us was frightening. I never back down from a fight, but the odds were not good. I had to trust Issa. She'd already saved me twice, so I gave in, and we went through the door. Issa slammed it shut behind us and the room went pitch dark.

"They'll get through that door," Bodie said, nervously. "It's not exactly a vault."

"Won't matter," Issa said as she pushed us through the dark space. "We'll be long gone."

"Ow!" Bodie exclaimed as he hit his head.

"Duck down," Issa commanded.

"You could have said that a second ago," Bodie said, peeved.

She pushed us through what seemed like another, narrower door and the sound instantly changed. It felt like we had gone from a large room to a much smaller one.

"Sit here," she ordered. "Hurry."

She guided me into a comfortable, padded seat that was reclined like an easy chair. The old guy took charge of Bodie and eased him into his own chair.

"How can you see what you're doing?" Bodie asked.

"Been doing this a long time," was the man's reply.

"Jeez, your breath!" Bodie exclaimed. "You're drunk!"

"Yes I am," the man said, almost proudly.

Issa worked quickly, running straps across my chest and waist.

"Whoa, what're you doing?" I shouted nervously.

"It's okay," Issa said reassuringly. "It's for your safety."

"Safety?" I asked. "Is something dangerous about to happen?"

"Nah," the man said. "I told you, I been doing this a long time."

Issa finished with me, and I heard the sound of more buckles being latched which made me think that Issa and the drunk guy were also strapping in.

"Ready?" Issa asked.

"Always," the man replied.

"Ready for what?" I asked.

That's when the lights came on.

"Ho-ly…" Bodie exclaimed.

The four of us were strapped into cockpit-like seats in what looked like a small, high-tech vehicle. The old guy was seated in front of us, facing an array of touch-pad controls that were distinguished from one another by a spectrum of different colored lights.

Bodie, Issa and I were lined up behind him, shoulder to shoulder.

"This isn't right," Bodie said. It was the biggest understatement I think I ever heard.

The door we had come through slid shut on its own and locked in place.

"My ears just popped," Bodie said.

"We're pressurizing," Issa said.

A faint hum began, as if engines were powering up. I sensed a steady vibration. The room was coming to life.

A crashing sound came from outside. The marauders had arrived and were smashing at the outside door while we were trapped in this…this…whatever it was.

"Pressurizing?" Bodie exclaimed. "Is this a submarine?"

Issa looked at the man at the controls and the two chuckled. I hate it when people chuckle.

"No," Issa said. "We're going the other direction."

"What does that mean?" I asked.

"Relax and enjoy the ride," Issa said.

For one agonizing moment, nothing happened.

"Wait," Bodie said, near panic. "Is this a—?"

We were all suddenly thrown back into our seats by intense G-forces that only happen when a powerful vehicle launches straight into the sky.

I think I screamed.

CHAPTER 5

THE CHURCH OF REGENESIS

Vail Kobain sat behind an ornate oak desk in a darkened room with her back pressed firmly against the rich, leather chair. Her eyes were closed, her hands flat on the desk's polished surface. She took several deep breaths as if she was lost in meditation.

A gentle tone sounded.

Kobain took one more deep breath and said, "Yes?"

An electronic screen rose from out of the desk, an unusual bit of technology built into the antique piece of furniture. The screen flashed to life, showing the image of a young man wearing a dark brown uniform.

"Good evening, Your Eminence," the man said from the screen. "Glory to the Regent."

There was a long pause as the man waited for a response from Kobain. He shifted uncomfortably.

"Yes?' Kobain finally said with a touch of impatience.

"There was an unexpected development," the man said. "We were moments from capturing the scion when he boarded a small craft that was hidden in an empty building. It was a Jump Ship of Tyrian design."

Kobain stiffened ever so slightly as she opened her eyes.

"Did it lift off?" Kobain asked.

"It did," the man said as his voice cracked with nervous tension.

"And the girl?" Kobain asked. "Was she the pilot?"

"Unknown. We are working to identify her."

"If she wasn't the pilot, there is yet another player we were not aware of."

"Whoever was flying the craft is quite skilled," the man said. "The ship took evasive action and was able to elude our tracking before leaving the atmosphere."

"Which means you have no idea where they are," Kobain said

"But not for long," the man said, ducking the question. "We'll lock on to the craft's signature long before it can reach a channel."

"A Tyrian craft," Kobain said, thinking aloud. "That would mean this mystery pilot is Tyrian as well."

"Undoubtedly," the man replied.

Kobain drummed her fingers on the desk, thinking, while the man on the screen stared at her uncomfortably.

"I believe I know who the pilot is," Kobain finally said. "And now he has a scion."

"We feel certain we know their destination," the man said.

"Of course you do," Kobain said sharply, showing her frustration. "It's the very thing you were ordered to prevent."

The man had no response for an uncomfortably long time.

"We will capture the scion quickly," he finally said, reassuringly, if not confidently. "However, we must consider how this might affect the schedule."

"The schedule will not change," Kobain snapped. "The Covian Solution will go forward as planned. Please relay that to the Ministry."

"Understood," the man said.

"And hunt them down," Kobain added with venom.

"We will, Your Eminence," the man said. "Glory to the—"

"

Kobain lashed out and punched the screen in a fit of anger. The glass shattered and the image winked out. She looked at her knuckles and licked the blood that oozed from a few small cuts. She stood and walked to a coat rack near the closed door. Hanging there was a brilliant blue robe, the same color as her scarf. It could have been the robe of a judge, if not for the bright color. She slipped it on and buttoned it to the neck, then stepped in front of a mirror and ran the palms of her hands over her long red hair to insure nothing was out of place. Satisfied, and totally composed, she took a deep breath and opened the door to leave the office.

Bright light enveloped her as she stepped into the church beneath the brilliant, stained-glass window. It was an awe-inspiring sight, exactly as she intended it to be. The pews were now filled with people of all ages and a mix of ethnicities. There were couples, singles and families. Elderly folks sat in front while younger men stood along the walls, having given up their seats to those who needed them more. Though the church was packed, there was absolute silence. They were all holding their breaths in anticipation.

Kobain slid gracefully into the sanctuary and stretched her arms out wide, as if to corral the entire congregation in a motherly embrace. She smiled benevolently, and with a firm yet warm voice she began.

"Welcome!" she announced. "And thank you. By gathering in this sacred place, you have transformed an ordinary day into a truly warm and wonderful evening. Our congregation has grown so quickly! I'm humbled by your presence, and your faith in the power of the Regent. You are special. You have recognized that yours is not an ordinary destiny. You have vision. You have goals and aspirations far beyond the unenlightened masses."

Everyone had their eyes laser-locked on Kobain. There was barely a breath taken for fear the sound might interfere with the magic of the moment, and the great woman's speech.

"We have come here to walk the path that will lead us to peace, tranquility and yes, the rewards that we so justly deserve. I applaud you. And I beckon you to join me in prayer to praise our most benevolent guide. Glory to the Regent.

"Glory to the Regent," the congregation repeated enthusiastically.

Kobain turned her back to them and faced the glowing stained-glass sun.

"We are Regenesis!" she bellowed in the bold voice of a charismatic preacher. "We have come to worship, to sacrifice and to thank the Regent for all that our efforts will bring. With his grace, the majesty of the universe is ours!"

CHAPTER 6

We were jolted, bumped and rocked but it wasn't much worse than being on a rollercoaster. I wanted to believe that's what it was. A ride. The one thing that told me different was the feeling of having a crazy-heavy weight pushing me into the seat.

This was no Six Flags coaster.

"What…is…happening…?" Bodie said through gritted teeth.

"Hang tight," the old man said calmly. "Won't be much longer."

I closed my eyes, gripped the armrests and tried not to pass out.

"Is this an elevator?" Bodie asked with desperation.

"You could say that," the man replied, then laughed and added, "You'd be wrong, but you could say it."

"Focus, Kellen," Issa said to the man, scolding.

Kellen. That was the drunk guy's name.

Just when I thought my eyeballs were going to pop, the shuddering stopped, and the weight was lifted from my chest.

"I'm outta here," Bodie said and unbuckled his safety straps.

"Bad idea," Issa said, too late.

"Whoa!" Bodie exclaimed.

He floated up from the seat, weightless. He clutched the arm rest as his feet drifted above his head.

"How are you doing this?" I exclaimed. I was still in "this is a ride" mode.

"It's not rocket science," Kellen replied.

He hit a switch on the console. In front of us a panel split in two and slid open to reveal a field of brilliant stars in the black void of space.

"I lied. It *is* rocket science," he added with a chuckle.

"Would you please get back in your seat," Issa said to Bodie, impatiently.

Bodie pulled himself down and buckled in.

"We're in space," I said, though hardly believing those words were coming out of my mouth. "Like outer space. This is real. This is a spaceship. We just took off from Earth and we're in outer space. On board a spaceship."

"That's a lot of ways to say the same thing," Kellen said. "But yeah, you got this all figured out."

I snapped. I was in an impossible situation that I had absolutely no control over that brought on a feeling I wasn't used to. Panic.

"Turn back," I demanded while fumbling to unlatch my safety belt. "Let me out."

Issa reached over and grasped my hand with surprising strength.

"Take a breath, Donovan," she commanded.

Her unwavering glare told me she was in charge. I'm not used to being controlled like that. No matter how hard my various guardians tried to bend me to their will, I wouldn't let them control me. It's probably why I never got adopted. But in this case I did what Issa told me to do. Maybe because I was terrified. Or maybe because she was totally fierce and I didn't want to fight her.

"This is a lot to handle," she said calmly. "We'll take it one step at a time."

Bodie's mouth hung open as if he wanted to scream, but nothing came out.

I nodded and said "Okay."

She let go of my hand and I relaxed back into the seat.

Relaxed? Yeah, right.

"Let's take that first step," Bodie said with a shaky voice. "How is this possible?"

Issa looked to Kellen for guidance.

Kellen gave her a shrug as if to say, "It's your move."

"We're in a Jump Ship," Issa said. It's used for short trips."

I looked around the cabin to try and understand. It was circular and not much larger than a good-sized bathroom. The only controls were the flashing lights on the panel in front of Kellen. I'm no astronaut, but this wasn't normal technology.

"Short trips to where?" Bodie asked.

Kellen hit a light on the controls and a panel dropped down to reveal a three-foot-high window that circled the vehicle. It gave us a 360-degree view of a starfield. In space. We were in outer space. It was awesome and impossible.

Bodie looked behind us and let out a surprised gasp.

I twisted around to look back and had to catch my breath.

Behind us was a breathtaking view of Earth. The blue and brown colors were brilliant, as if it were an artist's perfect vision of what Earth should look like from space.

"It's not virtual reality, if that's what you're thinking," Issa said.

"So we're in a spaceship," I said slowly, making sure to use the right words. "Orbiting Earth, with a drunk at the wheel?"

"I am not a drunk!" Kellen barked, insulted. "I'm a functional alcoholic. And we're not in orbit. We're leaving."

"Leaving?" Bodie blurted out. "Leaving Earth? To go where?"

"One step at a time," Issa said calmly. "Donovan, I have to tell you something that's going to be hard to accept."

"You mean compared to everything else?" I said with sarcasm. "Who the hell are you?"

"I guess you could call me your Guardian Angel. At least for the last year or so. There have been others. We've been watching out for you. Just in case."

"In case what?" I asked.

"In case of the very thing that happened today."

I did a quick, mental flashback to all that had happened since we found the guys knocked out in the locker room. Nothing made sense, especially the bombshell news that space travel was real. There was only one thing that I totally got: this was definitely a lot to handle.

"Vail Kobain," I said. "Who is she?"

"She's a Bishop in the Church of Regenesis," Issa answered.

"Ha!" Kellen laughed, sarcastically. "That is no holy person."

"Regenesis isn't like any religion you've heard of," Issa said.

"It's all made up," Kellen said, sounding bitter. "They suck people in, thinking they're working for some higher power called The Regent as if he's some kind of god who's gonna reward them for their loyalty, but all they're doing is controlling people's lives and taking them for all they've got. Regenesis isn't a church, it's a band of thieves."

"What do they want with me?" I asked.

"And me?" Bodie added.

"They don't want you, Bodie," Issa said. "You were in the wrong place at the wrong time. I'm sorry you got caught up in this."

"No problem," Bodie said with a glimmer of enthusiasm. "Drop me off back home and I'll pretend like it never happened."

Nobody commented.

"I didn't think so," he added, defeated.

"I'm truly sorry," Issa said. "You'll have to ride this out."

"Ride what out?" I shouted. "What does that Bishop-lady want with me?"

"That's the part you're *really* not going to like," Issa said.

"It gets *worse*?" I asked, incredulous.

I got the feeling Issa was searching for the right way to give me some really bad news.

"Just say it!" I shouted, impatiently.

"Donovan, do you believe there's life on other planets?"

I was about to shout out an incredulous, "No!" but backed off.

I looked at Kellen who was focused on the data streaming in front of him. He let out a booming belch. Class guy. I glanced around at what seemed to be a vehicle that had just launched us into space, and to the Earth that was growing smaller by the second. Did I believe in life on other planets?

"I don't know," I said. "The universe is a big place. It's dumb to think we're the only ones who live in it."

"That's good," Issa said. "You're open to the idea."

"Are you saying there's life on other planets?" Bodie asked.

"I am," Issa answered with authority.

Bodie let out a long, nervous breath and said, "I was kind of hoping this was a dream."

"This Jump Ship is proof," Issa added. "Earth technology isn't close to building anything like this."

"How do you know all this?" I asked.

"Because I'm not from Earth," she said casually as if announcing she liked pizza.

"Me neither," Kellen added. "In case you were wondering."

What I thought couldn't get any stranger, had just gotten stranger.

"Seriously?" I said. "You guys are like…aliens?"

"On Earth, yeah," Issa said. "But here comes the kicker—"

"Am I ready for the kicker?" I asked.

"Probably not."

"Doesn't matter. Kick me."

"Okay, you are too."

"I am what?" I exclaimed.

The ship was suddenly jolted as if we'd been swatted by the hand of a celestial giant. The force threw us all against our safety straps.

"Whoa!" Bodie exclaimed. "Was that an explosion? Are we in trouble?"

"Sort of, and yes," Kellen answered. "They must have locked on to our signature."

A flash of blue light erupted outside. Whatever it was, it had serious power because an instant later we were rocked again.

"Who's they?" I asked.

"The Regenesis Watch," Issa replied.

"That church?" Bodie exclaimed. "They're in outer space?"

"They're everywhere," Issa said. "That's the problem."

"Not *my* problem," I declared.

"Yeah it is," Issa said. "It's why you're here."

"I don't care!" I hollered. "It's not my…wait, what?"

"Find the channel," Issa said to Kellen with calm authority.

"Help me," Kellen said, while wiping sweat from his bloodshot eyes.

Issa spun her seat to face a control panel and started hitting the lighted buttons. She knew what she was doing, whatever it was.

"Whoa!" Bodie screamed.

A silver, boomerang-shaped spacecraft cut across in front of us. As it passed it fired off two, glowing projectiles that headed straight our way.

Kellen grabbed a small joystick.

"Here we go!" He announced and jammed the stick forward.

The Jump Ship dove down as the two projectiles flew overhead. I spun around in time to see the two blue lights trailing away behind us.

"Hang on," Issa said.

The lights exploded, sending a wave of energy back our way that hit us hard and spun the vehicle around.

"Shoot back!" Bodie yelled.

"I'd love to," Kellen said. "Jump Ships don't have weapons."

He slammed the joystick and flew to the left. I'm not sure if my stomach came with me.

"How did this go to crap so fast?" Kellen snarled at Issa.

"Good question," Issa said while quickly inputting data. "We'll lose them in the channel."

Her fingers flew over the lighted panel lights while her attention was focused on the data flashing across a screen.

"What's a channel?" I asked.

"Wormholes," Kellen said. "Short cuts through the stars. Without them, interstellar travel wouldn't be possible."

"So we fly into one and get shot to another part of the galaxy?" Bodie asked.

"Yup," Kellen replied.

"I don't want to do that," Bodie said, sounding ill.

"It's either that," Kellen said. "Or deal with them."

He jabbed his thumb over his shoulder. Coming up from behind were four boomerang-craft that were spread out like a pack of wolves stalking a defenseless deer.

"What kind of church is this?" I asked, numb.

"Where's the channel?" Bodie shouted.

"Not always in the same place," Kellen replied. He glanced to Issa and added, "But we're going to find it, right?"

Issa stayed focused. She hit a few more lighted buttons, stabbing the final one with force.

"Got it. Locked." she announced triumphantly.

Kellen breathed a sigh of relief, let go of the joystick, spun his seat around to face us and crossed his arms, suddenly all relaxed.

"What are you doing?" Bodie cried out, exasperated. "Be evasive!"

"It's out of my hands," Kellen said with a shrug. "We're on auto-pilot."

"What if they shoot us before we hit the channel?" I asked.

"Then you'll never know why you're here," he said with maddening calm.

"Here it comes!" Bodie announced, pointing behind us.

Each of the Regenesis Watch craft had released two glowing torpedoes.

Kellen whistled in awe. "They're not fooling around. I'm good, but I can't duck all of those."

"Maybe if you were sober," I said.

"If I was sober I wouldn't have dodged the other ones."

"You're not even going to try?" Bodie asked with horror.

Kellen glanced to Issa. "What do you say, darlin'?"

Issa was focused on her data screen.

"Coming up," she replied.

Up ahead, a huge black void appeared in the star field.

"Cutting it close," Issa said, her voice cracking with uncertainty for the first time.

Behind us, the glowing missiles grew brighter as they closed in on us.

Ahead, the dark hole loomed larger.

"How about you step on it," I said.

"No need. You feel it?"

I did. I was pressed into my seat which meant the Jump Ship was picking up speed, like we were being pulled into the channel.

"We're in," Issa announced with relief.

Kellen spun to face me and said, "I've been waiting fifteen years to say this."

"What?" I asked.

"Welcome home, Six."

All eight missiles erupted.

Too late.

We were sucked into the channel and on our way.

But to where?

CHAPTER 7

odie screamed out a command as we entered the hole in space called a "channel".

"Hang on!" he yelled.

I think he was mostly hollering at himself, but I hung on anyway. I grabbed the arms of my seat, ready for the sudden acceleration that would speed us to the other side of the galaxy. Or somewhere. The idea scared me, but the torpedoes coming up fast on our butts scared me just a little bit more.

The light from the multiple explosions flashed briefly, though we didn't feel a thing. Everything beyond the viewing window went dark. There was nothing to see outside but absolute black. It didn't even feel like we were moving.

"Did it work?" Bodie asked, breathless.

"Did what work?" Issa asked calmly.

"The channel. Aren't we supposed to be flying at hyper speed or warp drive or something?"

"Uh, no," Issa said. "There's no such thing."

"So then how are we supposed to make it all the way to another galaxy in this lifetime?" Bodie asked, confused.

"Because the channel connects us," Issa replied. "Look."

The window suddenly lit up with light from a sea of stars. The glow was so intense I had to blink a few times before my eyes adjusted. Behind us, the dark void that was on the other side of the channel grew smaller.

"So it's just a shortcut?" I asked.

"Didn't somebody call it that before?" Kellen said. "Oh right, it was me."

He finished the sentence by letting out a loud and sour-smelling burp. I was beginning to think he was doing it on purpose.

"Well that was disturbing," I said. "I mean the trip. Not your gas attack. That was exceptional."

"Thank you," Kellen said.

Moving through the channel was no more dramatic than stepping through a doorway from one room to another. But this new room was much different than the one we had come from. The star field ahead was clustered so tightly it looked like a single, massive sun.

"That's not what we see from Earth," Bodie said.

"Because we're nowhere near Earth," Issa said. She pointed to the right where the edge of a massive, green planet was coming into view. "This is Tyria. Fourth planet from the sun of Agoran. It's my home. And Kellen's."

"And yours," Kellen added, looking directly at me.

I snapped at look at him and barked, "Bullshit."

"Is it?" Bodie asked.

"Shut up, Junior. I know who I am," I said, defensively. "And I'm no Martian."

"Correct," Kellen said. "You aren't a Martian."

"Thank you!"

"You're a Tyrian," he added.

"That means nothing to me," I said with disdain.

"There's no reason it should," Issa said. "But it will."

None of what was happening fit my understanding of how life worked. How *my* life worked. I wanted to argue. I wanted to hear this was a cosmic, TikTok prank. But one thought kept tickling the back of my brain: I truly didn't know my own history. At least the first part. I'd always been told that I was abandoned as a baby. Somebody dumped me at a fire station. I kept asking the child services people about my parents, but they had no idea. And it wasn't like I could use Google to hunt them down. There was no information about me anywhere. There wasn't even a note found with me saying something gut-wrenching like: *Please take care of my beautiful son and give him a loving home. He's a good baby, though he'll probably grow up to be a pain in the ass.*

I fought for control my whole life and I wasn't about to stop now. But the fight had suddenly become way more complicated.

"The Regenesis Watch gunships will be coming through behind us," Kellen said to Issa.

"Get us down," Issa commanded.

Kellen pushed the joystick and accelerated toward the planet. The craft cut through the atmosphere and made the transition from space without so much as a bump. I soon felt the weight of gravity. The planet's surface looked kind of like Earth's, with large continents divided by vast oceans. But the shapes of the land masses were completely different.

"Where are we going?" I asked.

"The city of Essen-Tet in the Sandoor Federation," Issa replied. "It's the largest city on Tyria and the center of the Church of Regenesis. It's where Vail Kobain lives."

"Seriously?" I said. "Maybe we shouldn't be going there."

"Like I said," Issa replied. "One step at a time."

The Jump Ship descended through a layer of clouds. The closer we got to the ground, the more details I could make out. We were dropping quickly toward a vast, congested city.

"Look familiar?" Kellen asked.

"No," I said sharply.

"Right," Kellen said. "You were only a baby."

"Kellen, stop," Issa scolded. "Give him time to breathe."

I sensed Bodie's eyes on me.

"What are you looking at, Junior?" I asked, irritated.

"Jeez, back off, Mutt," he said defensively. "I was just looking."

"For what? Antennas? Green skin?"

"No! I was thinking that--"

"What? You're thinking I'm a freak?"

"No. I was thinking about how you've always been an a-hole. Now I'm feeling kind of bad for you."

I wasn't sure if I should thank him for his concern or punch him in the head.

"I'm not an alien," I snapped.

"Well, that's true," Kellen said with a chuckle.

"Thank you!"

"In these parts, Bodie's the alien."

That shut us both up.

Kellen dipped down and flew us through a canyon of tall buildings. They were like big-city skyscrapers but made of stone rather than steel or concrete. It seemed as though they'd been carved rather than built. They looked both ancient and modern, with many smaller buildings surrounding them. It all appeared to be a jumble, as if buildings were stuck wherever there was a square inch of space. Sky bridges connected some upper floors, making it a complicated, spider web of a city.

As we dropped lower, streets came into view. They were narrow and clogged with people on foot or riding bikes. There weren't many powered vehicles, making it look more like an ant colony than a modern city.

The craft swooped low, zipping between buildings, passing some with only a few inches to spare. I tried not to think about Kellen being drunk. We finally came to a stop, hovered in place, then dropped straight down.

I held my breath and braced for the worst.

Issa did too. She grabbed on to her armrests for support.

"Seriously?" Kellen said to her. "You don't think I can do this?"

"Sorry," Issa said.

She let go of the armrests but didn't look any less nervous.

Kellen flicked the joystick, and the craft jerked, making us all grab on to something.

"Oops, sorry," Kellen said with a shrug.

He wasn't sorry. It was totally on purpose.

"I hate this guy," Bodie whispered to me.

The vehicle descended slowly through what turned out to be an opening in a roof. After a moment of darkness, Kellen flicked on the external lights to reveal we had dropped into a large, empty warehouse. I leaned over to get a view of the floor where a handful of people stood looking up, waiting for us.

"Isn't it dangerous to be there while we land?" Bodie asked.

"Nah," Kellen said. "We haven't used combustion engines for centuries. They're safe, as long as I don't land on somebody. No guarantees."

The craft settled with a gentle thump and the whine of the engines died quickly.

"I need a drink," Kellen announced as he unbuckled himself. He pointed a finger at Issa and added, "You know where I'll be. Don't go there."

He touched a light-button, and a small hatch slid open beneath the wrap-around window. It was probably the same door we had entered through in the dark. On Earth. In another reality. Yikes.

"Thank you, Kellen," Issa said. "This has got to be an emotional day for you."

I was expecting an obnoxious comeback from Kellen. Or another savage burp. But he sat there for a long moment, staring down at the deck.

"Let's keep moving, alright?" he said with surprising sincerity.

He threw a quick glance to me, as if to make sure I'd heard him. He then jumped out of his seat, went through the hatch and was gone.

"Moving where?" Bodie asked. "Where are we going?"

"Come with me," Issa said as she unbuckled herself.

"Not until you tell us what we're doing here," I said.

"I will," Issa said. "But we need to secure the Jump Ship in case the Regenesis Watch spotted us."

She ducked out of the hatch.

Bodie grabbed my arm and said, "Don't lie to me, Mutt. Do you know what's going on?"

"I'm as clueless as you are. Something I never thought I'd say."

"This is a bad dream," he said, shaking his head, bewildered.

I pulled away from him and went for the hatch. Bodie jumped in front of me to get out first. It didn't matter what planet we were on; he was still a tool.

A handful of people stood outside the vehicle. Normal looking people. Two arms, two legs, a head. You know, people. There wasn't a lizard-alien in sight. They were all dressed in simple, neutral colored work clothes that could have come from Earth. There was nothing unusual about them, except that they were all staring at us. Or at me. Nobody made a sound. A few were crying, which was weird. But they seemed like happy tears.

I felt like I had to say something.

"Uh, hi," I said and waved weakly.

Not exactly a profound statement like "That's one small step for man…" but it was all I could come up with.

"Greetings!" Bodie announced, while holding up his hand in a dumb alien-meeting salute that he probably got from TV. "Donovan's home!" he declared. "Yay! Is there a pilot who can fly me back to Earth?"

He got no answers. Only blank stares.

"We gotta move," Issa said.

She pushed us to start walking. After a few steps she motioned for us to look back. We turned and--

"Wow," Bodie gasped.

I looked back to see the alien "Jump Ship". It was a perfect, silver sphere. Its smooth surface was only broken by the hatch and the window that wrapped around its diameter. The opening in the ceiling we had come through was closing. Two massive doors slid toward one another. Once they met, they locked together to give the appearance that it was a normal ceiling and not a hangar door.

"We just flew across the universe in a giant pinball," I said, incredulous.

"Here's what's going to happen," Bodie said to Issa, annoyed. "Do whatever you want with Donovan, but I'm going home. Find me a pilot. Hopefully one who isn't hammered but I'll take whatever I can get. We'll get right back in that bowling ball and fly out of here."

"What bowling ball?" Issa asked.

"Don't be cute," Bodie said, annoyed. "The Jump Ship, or whatever you call it."

He pointed back to the ship, but the ship was gone.

"Wait, what?" Bodie said, numb.

"Jump Ships are outlawed for anyone outside the Regenesis Watch," Issa explained.

"So where did it go?" I asked.

"It dropped below on an elevator."

The crowd that greeted us quickly set up wooden tables and chairs while rolling out small, colorful rugs. In seconds, the space was transformed into a busy marketplace that was set up in an otherwise empty warehouse. Some people displayed fruit and vegetables while others set out bolts of cloth or tools. Racks of clothing appeared while another vendor fired up a grill filled with sizzling meats.

More people arrived. Shoppers. They spread out among the vendors to shop and eat, but mostly to give the impression that the market had been open and busy for a while. Within minutes, the empty warehouse had been transformed into a crowded, indoor bazaar.

"Look," Issa said, pointing to a large door on the far side of the building.

Two men wearing dark brown uniforms strolled in. They had priest-style collars, and the rising sun symbol over their breast pockets.

And pistols strapped to their waists.

"Police?" I asked.

"Regenesis Watch," Issa whispered.

The two strolled around the market, checking out the goods, having no idea that a spaceship was hidden under their feet.

"We just made it," Issa said.

She hurried us away from the newly born marketplace. A few seconds before, all eyes had been on me. Now, nobody gave me a second glance. I had become invisible, which might have been exactly what they were going for.

"You need clothes," she said while keeping her eyes on the crowd.

We were still wearing padded football pants, t-shirts and cleats.

"So we can blend in?" I asked.

"That, and I want you to look your best. This is an important day.

"Why's that?"

She gave me a big smile and said, "Because you're going to meet your mother."

CHAPTER 8

I felt like a dizzy boxer who'd taken a few too many punches to the head. There was too much coming at me, too fast.

"I don't want to meet my mother," I said.

Issa seemed surprised to hear that, and didn't know how to react. So she didn't.

"Well we can't stay here," she said.

She pushed Bodie and me out of the warehouse where the Jump Ship had landed, and into the city of Essen-Tet of the Sandoor Federation on the planet Tyria. All words that had no meaning to me only a few hours before.

We were in a narrow alley, away from the crowded streets I'd seen from above. A woman came running up to us clutching a bundle of clothing.

I froze. Could she be?

"Not her," Issa said, reading my mind.

"Hurry," the woman said. "It's all I could scrounge on such short notice."

"Thank you," Issa said while quickly taking the clothes and sorting through them.

Bodie took a pair of pants and held it at arm's length as if it were diseased.

"Not wearing this," he said with disgust. "I don't even rent bowling shoes."

"Understand something, Bodie," Issa said without a hint of sympathy or patience. "If they catch you, they'll probably kill you."

Enough said. We kicked off our cleats and ditched our padded football pants.

The woman looked at the stuff we were taking off with confusion.

"Such odd garments. Is this what people wear on the planet you grew up on?"

"Yes," was my simple answer. I wasn't about to explain football to a lady from another planet. Yikes.

She brought us well-worn pants made of a coarse, black material and long-sleeved shirts made of light-colored cotton that we pulled on over our heads like sweaters. There was nothing about any of it that would stand out in this dreary city of stone. Issa got dressed as well, putting the simple clothing over her colorful cross-country running gear.

The woman also gave us each a pair of lightweight work boots that were well worn in.

"Thank you," Issa said to the woman.

"Whatever you need," she replied.

She reached out and touched my cheek. I pulled back because I didn't know this lady and didn't know why she was touching me.

"Welcome home, Six," she said with genuine warmth.

Being touched like that was a totally strange experience. I guess that's the kind of thing that normal people do to kids all the time, but it wasn't anything I'd ever experienced. For one brief, pathetic moment I kind of wished she *was* my mother.

She gave me a smile, then hurried off.

"What is with this Six thing?" I asked.

"That'll take some explaining," Issa said. "First we've got to get someplace safe."

"No, *you've* gotta get someplace safe," Bodie said angrily. "Take Donovan wherever you want but I want a ride home."

"You'll get one," Issa said. "But we can't just take off in a Jump Ship. We have to be careful. We'll get you home, but not right now."

"This isn't fair!" Bodie cried. "I don't even like Donovan!"

"So walk away!" I shouted.

"Gladly!" Bodie snapped.

"No!" Issa barked. "We stay together until we figure out how to get Bodie home."

"And me too," I added.

"Just come with me," she said, exasperated.

She hurried off and I got the distinct feeling that Issa was losing patience with us. As for Bodie, I wanted nothing to do with him. He was one of those guys who always had things go his way. Good for him, but guys like that don't know how to deal when things go south. Me? I live in the south. I'm used to it. It would have been great to be with somebody who had my back. Bodie wasn't that guy.

Issa led us out of the alley onto a main street, where Bodie and I one look, and both stopped short.

"Is this normal?" he asked with surprise.

The narrow street was packed with people. Crumbling stone warehouse-looking buildings stood to either side, looming above the confusion. It looked like pictures I'd seen of ancient Egypt, but it was oddly modern.

Hundreds of people were gathered to sell things, buy things, or just to weave their way through. There were people of all skin colors, which meant Tyria had different ethnicities like on Earth, but this wasn't Earth, so I had no idea what to call them. There was food cooking on grills and clothes hanging from hooks. Everything was for sale. One man was selling something he called "electric credits;" another clutched his stomach in pain and was searching for medicine. One woman was trying to sell a toy-merchant a clump of her own hair, to be used to make dolls.

The smells were intense. It was a combination of frying meat, dirty clothes and sweat. If any one of these people walked down the Ave in Stony Brook, people would think they were homeless. The sounds of negotiation and arguing created a white noise of mayhem.

I was hit with an overpowering feeling of sadness. As much as I complain about my life, I couldn't imagine living like this.

"This is so much like Earth," Bodie said. "A really sad, dirty Earth."

"They all look so, I don't know, desperate," I said.

"Because they are," Issa replied.

"How do they know English?" Bodie asked.

"Better question is, how do they know English on Earth?" Issa replied. "English is a universal language. It was brought to Earth hundreds of years ago. Tyria is centuries ahead of Earth, technologically. But very few people get the benefits."

"Sure doesn't seem like an advanced world," I said. "Other than the spaceship thing."

"Yeah, what happened?" Bodie asked.

"The Church of Regenesis."

A loud horn sounded that made Bodie jump. I didn't. I was beyond being surprised.

"That's the signal for work shifts to change," Issa said.

People quickly left the market as though they were programmed to obey.

"I want to show you something," Issa said. "It'll give you a better idea of what life is like here."

"What if I don't care?" I said.

She ignored my question and hurried off, joining the crowd of people.

Bodie and I didn't budge.

Issa turned back to see we weren't moving.

"Do you really want to be left on your own here?" she called out.

As much as I hated to admit it, Issa was calling the shots. Until I figured out how to take back control, I had to stick with her. Bodie must have realized the same thing because he went after her. I followed. We moved through the swarm of people. Some were moving with us but just as many were flooding out of the building, headed the opposite way.

"Their shift is done," Issa explained. "Essen-Tet is a manufacturing city. Goods made here are sent all over Tyria and to other planets."

She led us through the doors of a factory-looking building with a sign over the door that read: "FACTORY B." As soon as we stepped inside I was hit with a chemical smell that burned the hairs in my nose.

"What do they make here?" Bodie asked, wincing. "Rat poison?"

"Right now, I don't know. It changes all the time."

She led us to a flight of metal stairs that rose up to a catwalk that ran the length of the huge building and overlooked the manufacturing floor.

"People breathe this all day?" Bodie asked.

"All day, every day," Issa answered.

From up above we got a good view of the work being done. There were several automated assembly-lines, each manned by dozens of people who used hand tools to add parts to large, black cubes that were dotted with bits of colored glass. The workers had to work quickly as the next piece was brought to them on the conveyor. Some added circuit boards while others painted the metal with a dark coating.

"Don't they have robots to do this?" Bodie asked. "I mean, that's how it works on Earth."

"Why bother with expensive technology when you have an unlimited supply of cheap labor?" Issa asked.

"Who does?" Bodie asked.

"Regenesis."

"The church owns this factory?" I asked, surprised.

"And hundreds of others like it. Regenesis is the number one employer on Tyria. If you don't belong to the church, you'll have a hard time getting work. And feeding your family."

We walked the length of the catwalk, gazing down on the horrible working conditions. It's what I imagined it was like working in sweat-shop factories in poor countries on Earth, not in a modern society that conquered space travel.

"People don't complain?" Bodie asked.

"Not if they want to work. And eat."

"I don't get it," Bodie said. "How can you be advanced enough to fly through space, but still make people work like robots?"

"And get paid next to nothing," Issa said. "Starting to get the picture? There's a very big gap between the haves and the have-nots."

"And it's all run by a church?" I asked.

"The strange thing is, many people love the church," Issa said. "They worship this entity called the Regent, who promises eternal rewards for those who make sacrifices in life."

"That's how they get people to work for them?" I asked. "That's crazy."

"That's Regenesis," Issa said. "Technically it's not slavery, but it's slavery."

Her eye caught something below and she tensed up.

"Get down," she whispered with urgency. She grabbed us and we crouched down to kneel on the catwalk.

A small, flying drone was headed our way, floating silently over the heads of the workers. It was a mini-version of the boomerang gunships that attacked us in space.

"It's how they monitor the workers," Issa whispered. "At least that's mostly what they do."

"What else do they do?" Bodie asked.

"Right now I'd guess they're looking for us."

A beam of white light came from its belly that shone on the workers as it passed over them. It was like an eye in the sky, watching. The workers shot quick, nervous glances up at it for fear they might be caught doing something wrong. It moved slowly, floating closer to us. In a few seconds it would pass underneath the catwalk directly below us.

"We're okay, it's not looking up here," I said.

The light suddenly shot up toward the ceiling, as if it had heard me. The three of us crouched down even lower. I don't know why. If that light hit us, it would be over.

I held my breath as the light scanned the walkway to our left, growing closer. It was about to reach Bodie when the light was re-directed back to the floor. I let out a relieved breath, but the snooping device wasn't done. It floated beneath us, stopped and hovered in place. I held my breath, expecting the light to shine up to us at any second. But it was focused on a woman worker on the line. She looked up at it, squinting against the light.

Issa nudged me and pointed to the floor where two men in the dark brown uniforms of the Regenesis Watch marched along the assembly line. Leading them was a woman in a similar uniform who looked like a supervisor. They were on a mission, and it had to do with the woman who was standing at her station in the glow of the drone-light.

I looked to Issa. She shrugged. She had no idea of what was going on.

The supervisor marched right up to the worker while focused on the tech-pad she was holding. The woman worker stood there looking nervous as the assembly line stopped and the light from the drone went out.

"Magda T-Fair?" the supervisor asked brusquely.

"Is there a problem?" the woman asked, though from the quiver in her voice she knew the answer.

"You are relieved," the supervisor said, matter of fact.

"Why?" Magda asked with rising panic. "I've met my quota every day for three years. You have no reason to relieve me."

"You no longer qualify for this position," the supervisor said with no sympathy.

"That's not right!" Magda declared. "Ask anyone. I've never missed a shift, even when I was sick!"

"Pick up your pay at the checker," the supervisor said coldly.

Magda was in a panic. She took a step toward the supervisor but was blocked by the two male Watchers.

"I have a family!" she declared. "Who will feed my children? Regenesis?"

"Why would they?" the woman asked coldly. "You haven't pledged to the Regent."

The supervisor spun and walked away.

Magda tried to follow but the Watchers held her back.

"So that's it?" Magda yelled at her. "I don't want to join your church, so you fire me? Remember what you did here! Because we'll remember when it's your turn to be judged!"

The supervisor kept walking with her eyes on her tech-pad. The drone flew above her, following like an obedient dog.

Magda pulled her arms away from the Watchers. She took a deep breath and stood up straight, as if to show they hadn't beaten her. She looked at the other workers who only moments before had been working by her side. None had tried to help her, and now they couldn't look her in the eye.

"Who turned me in?" she asked.

Every last one of them seemed ashamed about what had just happened, but nobody fessed up, or made eye-contact with her, or offered any sympathy.

"This can't go on," Magda shouted to them. "It won't go on."

The assembly line started up again and the workers took their places without saying a word.

Magda walked off quickly in the opposite direction, holding her head high, with the two men Watchers following close behind.

"Look," Bodie whispered.

On the far side of the factory, another drone appeared, only this one had its light aimed up toward the ceiling, sweeping the catwalks.

"Time to go," Issa said.

She led us back down the stairs and we quickly made our way to an exit. Soon we were back in daylight on the grimy streets of Essen-Tet.

"What was that about?" Bodie asked.

"Someone must have told them she wasn't a member of the church," Issa said. "You never know who's watching."

"And who's a rat," I added.

"If you want to work, you join the church and pay your dues."

"What'll she do?" Bodie asked. "If she can't work how does she take care of her family? How does anybody?"

"Many people join Regenesis just to get a job," Issa said. "But many can't stomach even pretending to be part of that criminal cult. They have to scrounge to survive any way they can, like those merchants back there. One thing for sure is you can't get a decent job if you're not a member of the church."

"And the people go along with it?" I asked.

Issa turned to me, looked me in the eyes and said, "They have, but they won't for much longer. They've been waiting for a long time to fight back. That time has finally come."

"Why now?" I asked.

Issa gave me a big smile and said, "Because you've come home."

CHAPTER 9

THE COVIAN SOLUTION

The boomerang-shaped silver space vehicle sliced through the atmosphere of Tyria and dropped quickly toward the city of Essen-Tet. It soared over the dense metropolis of stone buildings, carefully avoiding the dark plumes of smoke that spewed from tall smokestacks that were scattered throughout the city. Once past these noxious spouts, the spacecraft was suddenly bathed in bright sunlight under clear blue skies. This remarkable change was made possible by massive fans and filters that kept the air clean above the craft's destination.

The Regenesis Compound.

From the sky it looked like a series of pristine, modern structures surrounded by a forbidding, silver-steel wall. Most of the buildings were only a few stories high and weren't made from the same stone as the rest of Essen-Tet. These buildings were gleaming white steel structures that glistened in the sun. They were scattered about in a park-like setting, nestled in acres of perfectly manicured green grass and leafy trees. It was a vast, modern oasis in the center of the bleak city.

Standing in the very heart of the compound was a glorious, forty-story high steel castle with three breathtaking towers. This modern, majestic building was known as The Core. It was the center of Regenesis on Tyria and home to Vail Kobain.

One tower came to a point and was topped by a flag that depicted the rising sun symbol of Regenesis. The second was topped by four massive dish antennas, each pointed to one of the four points of the compass. The third was flat, with a circular landing-pad on top.

The space craft hovered over the flat tower and gently descended. As soon as it came to rest a hatch opened and Vail Kobain strode out. She was met by a short, rotund man who was nearly as wide as he was tall. He was dressed impeccably in a royal blue uniform-like suit with a clerical-collar that squeezed his chubby neck. His round face was highlighted with a moustache that turned up on either end forming perfect curls. His dark hair was parted in the middle and held tight to his head with glistening gel.

He was August C-Bonn, Chief Counselor to the Bishop of Regenesis. Vail Kobain.

Kobain didn't break stride or even look at him. She towered over the diminutive fellow who had to hurry to keep up, taking three steps to every one of hers.

"Welcome home, Your Eminence," he said with enthusiasm. "I understand you successfully established the church on that primitive planet Earth."

"C-Bonn, you have an uncanny knack for seeing only what you wish to see," Kobain replied, coldly.

"I do prefer to focus on the positive," August said nervously.

Kobain stopped abruptly and squared off against him. The little man tried not to shrink under her withering gaze.

"The Regenesis Watch located a scion on Earth," she said, coldly. "They had him. Now they don't. He left that planet in a Jump Ship and was tracked here to Tyria. To Essen-Tet."

"I...I'm aware of the situation," August said nervously. "It was an unfortunate misstep. We didn't know that he was being protected by radicals."

"Misstep?" Kobain said with contempt. "Is that what it was? An innocent mistake? A minor miscalculation?"

August nodded quickly. "Frankly, I'm surprised we were able to locate him at all. So much time has passed. Thank goodness the scanners picked up the signature of the illegal Jump Ship and--"

"Are you saying you should be congratulated?"

Beads of sweat formed on August's forehead.

"N...no, not at all," he said, his voice quivering. "The return of a scion is exactly what we tried to prevent from happening."

"And failed," Kobain said as she stepped forward, forcing the man to back away.

"Unfortunately, yes," August said nervously. "But the scion is being hunted down as we speak. This will not affect the roll out of the Covian Solution. I guarantee that."

He took a quick look back to see he was growing uncomfortably close to the edge of the platform. There was no safety rail and the fall to the ground was a long one.

"You guarantee that?" Kobain said with sarcasm. "And if you're wrong?"

"I...I'm not," August said, his voice cracking. "There's nothing the scion can possibly do to interfere now. We are very close."

"Yes, you are very close," Kobain said.

August had backed up as far as he could go. His next step back would be over the edge into air.

"Please, Your Eminence, let me show you how far we've come," he said, a few octaves higher than normal. "A final demonstration. I've assembled the Ministry in anticipation of your return. They're waiting for us in the--"

"Now!" Kobain barked, making August flinch.

She spun around and stormed off, leaving August with his heels hanging over the edge. He took a relieved breath and hurried after her.

An elevator rose up out of the platform. Kobain entered. August followed her aboard and offered a smile.

She ignored him.

He dropped his smile and stared at his feet.

The elevator descended quickly. After a few seconds, the doors opened onto a long hallway covered in plush, red carpeting. The two walked past artwork and sculptures that had come from many different cultures, countries, and planets. There were oil paintings of ancient monarchs from Earth; kinetic sculptures from the city of Venia on the planet Rist; and robot-like armor from the battle-planet known as Jazeer. The lighting fixtures were gold-encrusted works of art that had come from the ruins of a magnificent castle on the planet Winder-10.

Neither Kobain nor August stopped to appreciate any of it. At the far end they entered another elevator that took them further down into the depths of The Core. This time, the door opened onto a much different space. Beyond a set of sliding glass doors was a cavernous room lined with aisles of computer drives, workstations and monitors. Dozens of technicians wearing dark coveralls sat at desks, their eyes fixed on monitors that streamed data on multiple 3-D planes.

Most were focused on their work and didn't see the visitors passing through. Others who did notice quickly jumped to their feet and bowed their heads in deference to the Bishop of Regenesis.

Kobain didn't acknowledge any of them.

August walked proudly behind her, as if the technicians were paying their respects to him as well.

They weren't.

The two continued to the far side of the massive nerve center and stepped through a steel door that slid open as they approached. This led to a short corridor lined with doors.

August jumped ahead and led Kobain to a door marked simply with a large "F."

"I thought it best to assemble the Ministry so you can all bear witness to what I'm sure will be a most impressive demonstration of the Covian—"

"Stop talking," Kobain said, flatly.

"Yes, yes of course," August said nervously. "When I get excited I tend to, oh, there I go again."

He made a "zipping" motion across his lips then touched his finger onto a pad that triggered the door to slide open. Inside was a small room with no furniture and a single, large window that looked into an adjacent room.

Waiting inside were six people. Three men and three women. All were dressed in similar, royal blue clothing, the color of the church's elite. When Kobain entered, they stood tall and bowed their heads in respect.

In unison, they said, "Glory to the Regent."

Kobain barely acknowledged them with a quick nod.

"Show me," Kobain asked impatiently.

August was giddy with excitement. This was his moment.

"I am proud to tell you all that we now have a fully functioning prototype," he announced to the group. "I don't know what better way to say it than, it works."

August waited for a reaction. Any reaction. But got none.

"Right, well, let's proceed," August said.

He lifted his arm and spoke into a slim communication device on his wrist.

"Bring in the subject," he commanded.

In the room beyond the glass, a door slid open to reveal a woman. It was Magda T-Fair, the worker from Factory B who had been fired from her job. She stood defiantly, with her hands on her hips until she was given a short but firm shove from behind by a technician in a white lab coat. She stumbled into the room as the door slid shut behind her, leaving her alone.

"Can she see us?" Kobain asked.

"No," August replied. "Nor can she hear us, until we want her to."

Magda looked around at the mostly empty room to see a table in the center. On it were two items: a hammer and a large, red rubber ball.

"Let's begin," August said.

Next to the window was a flat, lighted button. August pressed it and said, "Pick up the ball."

This activated a speaker in the next room. Magda heard August's command and looked around with confusion, trying to understand where his voice was coming from.

"Who are you?" she called out. "Why am I here?"

August pressed the button again and said, "Pick up the ball."

"You don't control me," Magda said, her anger growing.

August hit the button. "Pick up the ball and bounce it."

Magda's whole body stiffened with rising fury. She picked up the ball and shouted, "I'm not your slave."

She threw the ball with anger, as if she were throwing it at August. It was a good guess. The ball hit the window directly in front of the little man, making him jump.

"As you can see," August said to the group. "She is not a willing participant."

"Do it," Kobain said calmly.

August spoke into his wrist communicator.

"Commence," he ordered.

A ceiling panel over Magda slid open and a mechanical device was lowered into the room. It was one of the devices being manufactured in Factory B. It was a black, metallic cube that was studded with an array of colorful glass beads. The device hung inside a U-shaped yoke.

Magda backed away from it and said, "What is that thing? We've been building them for months and nobody has the decency to tell us what they are."

August looked to Kobain and chuckled with glee. "She's about to find out."

The metal cube began to spin slowly inside the yoke.

Magda watched it with curiosity.

The glass beads embedded in the device lit up, shooting out laser-like beams of colorful light that painted the room, and Magda T-Fair. The device picked up speed as the lights created a multi-color hatch-work design on the walls, floor and ceiling of the little room.

Magda threw up her arms to protect herself, but the beams were harmless. Slowly, curiously, she lowered her arms and stared at the lights that danced across her face. She relaxed. Her strained expression softened. There was no sound, only the lights.

Magda was in a trance.

Kobain nodded to August.

"The program is set to your voice," August said.

He touched the wall switch again and nodded to Kobain.

"Pick up the ball," Kobain said.

Without hesitation, Magda walked to the ball and picked it up.

"Bounce it," Kobain commanded.

Magda obeyed and bounced the ball a few times.

"Stop," Kobain ordered.

Magda caught the ball and stood there docilly, waiting for her next command.

The people of the Ministry exchanged satisfied glances and smiles. The demonstration was going very well.

Kobain wanted more. She nodded to August who spoke into his wrist communicator.

"Continue," he said.

Behind Magda, the door she had entered through slid back open. Beyond it stood a young boy. A toddler.

"Mommy!" the boy called and ran to Magda.

He threw his arms around his mother, hugging her close.

"I want to go home," he said, fighting tears.

The boy wore dark goggles, preventing him from being effected by the lights.

Magda didn't hug him back or look at him. Her focus was on the lights.

Kobain glanced back to the people of the Ministry, gauging their interest. They were all laser-focused on the scene taking place in the next room.

Kobain nodded to August. August hit the speaker button.

"Pick up the hammer," Kobain said with no passion.

Magda looked down at her son, then to the table that held the hammer. She pushed the boy away and walked, as if in a trance, to the table. She grasped the hammer and lifted it, feeling its weight.

"Now kill him," Kobain said coldly.

One woman of the Ministry gasped in shock. All six tensed up. None had expected the demonstration to go this far.

"Mommy?" the boy asked, confused. "Why won't you talk to me?"

"Your Eminence," one of the men said, nervously. "I believe August has made his point."

Kobain ignored him. She kept her eyes on Magda T-Fair as if willing her to go through with the brutal command.

Magda turned to her son.

"Are you mad at me?" the boy asked innocently.

Magda's blank expression turned to one of rage. Her face contorted into a hideous grimace.

She raised the hammer, and charged toward her son.

"Mommy don't!" the boy cried while backing away in terror, his arms over his head to protect himself.

"You Grace!" the minister cried out.

"Stop," Kobain said calmly.

Magda froze instantly. Her blank expression returned. She lowered her arm and held the hammer loosely at her side.

The light show stopped.

The little boy burst into tears and ran to hug his mother. This time his mother hugged back. She dropped the hammer and clutched the boy close to her chest as both sobbed.

"I'm sorry," she sobbed. "I'm so sorry."

Kobain turned to the people of the Ministry and focused on the man who had spoken out.

"If any of you do not have the faith, or the conviction to make the hard choices necessary to support Regenesis, there is no place for you in this Ministry. Or in this church."

"I beg forgiveness, Your Eminence," the man said and bowed his head in shame. "It was a moment of weakness that will not happen again."

Kobain kept her eyes on him for an uncomfortably long time, then turned to August and said, "How soon?"

"Dozens of units will be completed within days, ready for shipment and deployment," he said with new-found confidence.

"Then I suppose you were right," Kobain said.

"I was?" August said with surprise. He wasn't used to receiving praise from the Bishop. "About what?"

"The scion's return may be no more than an annoyance."

"Yes, of course. We have nothing to worry about. We no longer have to concern ourselves with--"

"That isn't what I said," Kobain shot back.

"It isn't?" August said, once again off balance.

"He is an annoyance that must be dealt with. Find him."

"Consider it done, Your Eminence."

CHAPTER 10

odie and I hurried to keep up with Issa who was leading us quickly along a sidewalk headed for somewhere. We didn't know. I think she was deliberately not telling us for fear we'd refuse to go along. But it wasn't like we had any other options.

When we turned the corner onto a wide boulevard, we were faced with a sight that was completely out of place in this crummy city. Sitting in-between two drab towers made of stone was a modern, blue-silver building made of steel and glass. It was maybe ten stories high and more like the kind of building you'd expect to see on an advanced planet like Tyria. A small, two- seater flying car took off from the roof and shot down the street.

"Uhhh," I exclaimed, dumfounded. "What is that?"

"Regenesis calls them Privilege Manors," Issa said. "If they feel you've served the church well, they'll let you to live in one. All expenses paid. They're new and clean and totally tricked out with technology. The only thing better than living in one is to get a house inside the Regenesis Compound."

"This is more like it," Bodie said in awe. "I could live there."

There was a truck parked outside that had no wheels. It didn't need them because it hovered a foot above the pavement. A few guys wearing dark coveralls were unloading furniture and carrying it into the building. A family stood in front (Mom, Dad, two little boys) looking all sorts of excited like they'd just won the lottery.

"So not everybody's life sucks," Bodie said.

"It's a tease," Issa said with disdain. "Like dangling a carrot in front of a hungry horse to get him to obey. Every once in a while they throw a bone to a few people. It's all about giving everyone else hope that one day they might be chosen to live there. But it's false hope. For every person who moves into a Privilege Manor, there are five thousand others who live in poverty. It's just another way they control us."

"That's pretty cruel," I said. "Unless you get chosen."

"You're starting to get the picture," Issa said.

"Uh oh," Bodie said. He was pointing to something further down the boulevard.

A silver drone was half a block away. It flew ten feet in the air, shooting a beam of light toward the ground that swept back and forth as if scanning for something. Or somebody.

"You don't think it's looking for--" The beam of light shot forward and hit me square in the eyes.

"--me."

It had found its prey.

"Move!" Issa commanded and gave me a shove.

The three of us sprinted down a narrow side street until we hit an intersection. We turned the corner and huddled together near the building.

"Split up," Bodie said, breathless. "We have a better chance of getting away from that thing on our own"

"Bull," I said. "You want it to go after me and not you."

He didn't argue.

"Splitting up is a bad idea," Issa said. "You have no idea where you are."

"I know enough. We'll meet back at the marketplace," Bodie said and took off running as if he hadn't heard her.

"He's an idiot," I said.

"You go too," Issa commanded. "I'll distract it."

"What if it sees you?"

"That's the idea. Find the marketplace."

"But—"

"Go!"

I took off, running in the opposite direction from Bodie.

Issa stepped into the alley, waved to the drone to get its attention, and ran off in a third direction.

Yup. Badass.

I had no idea where to go. Hiding seemed like a good idea, so I went for the first door I came to and ducked inside. Hopefully, the drone was focused on Issa and didn't see where I went. Better yet, maybe it went after Bodie. Not that I wanted anything bad to happen to him. Not usually, anyway. But Regenesis didn't care about him, so he was a good decoy. I had no idea what Regenesis wanted with me, but after seeing how those a-holes operated, I didn't want to find out.

I entered a long, narrow hallway with closed doors to either side. Paint chips had fallen from the grimy walls and garbage was everywhere. This was no "Privilege Manor." I went for the first door and was about to open it when the outside door was blown open by a violent explosion. The force of the blast hit me so hard I was knocked forward and slammed into the wall. When I looked back at the destruction, the silver drone floated in through the smoke that billowed around the destroyed doorway.

So much for decoys.

I sprinted deeper into the building. I wanted to confront the thing to find out why it was after me, but seeing how it blew down that door to get me didn't give me a whole lot of confidence that it would go for a friendly chit-chat.

I reached the end of the corridor, turned right and poured on the speed. I made it to the end of the hallway, blasted through the last door and found myself outside in a narrow alley. I went left and kept running. Seconds later the door was blown open behind me. The drone was freaking relentless.

Running through the alleys of Essen-Tet was like weaving through a maze. This was not a city designed on a grid with right angles and parallel streets. The stone buildings were built in such a random way that I had to keep twisting and turning through curves and intersecting alleys to try and lose that thing. I dodged piles of garbage; a couple of greasy looking dogs eating something that hadn't been dead very long; and puddles of water that smelled like rot. I don't know how far I ran but after a while I figured I'd shaken it. Maybe Bodie was right. Splitting up was the right thing to do, though I'd never admit that to him. My thoughts went from trying to get away, to finding my way back to the marketplace.

I turned down another dark, narrow alley that I thought would get me headed in the right direction, but after having taken so many twisting turns, I couldn't be sure. A few yards later I reached an open courtyard and discovered that I'd given Bodie too much credit. Splitting up was a very bad move.

Bodie stood on the far side of the courtyard with his back to a wall. Hovering in front of him at eye-level, was the drone.

If he could have pushed through the brick wall, he would have, that's how scared he looked. That drone was deadly. One shot and no more Bodie. I glanced around the courtyard looking for something to attack it with but there was nothing.

Bodie took a step to his left.

The drone mirrored him.

He took another step. The drone moved too.

"What do you want?" he yelled at the thing.

"The scion," came an eerie voice from the drone. Oddly, it sounded like a woman. Maybe that Vail Kobain lady.

"The what?" Bodie asked.

"Where is he?" the drone asked.

"Who? Donovan? I don't know. He could be anywhere."

The drone fired a charge of energy that hit the wall dangerously close to Bodie's head. The charge sent chunks of stone flying everywhere. Bodie cowered and covered up, terrified.

"Where is the scion?" the drone repeated with icy calm.

"I don't know!" Bodie cried.

"The next shot will be aimed at your head,' the drone said.

Bodie's eyes went wide with fear.

"I'm right here!" I shouted.

Bodie saw me and let out a relieved breath.

The drone spun and floated toward me, slowly. Now I was the one in its cross hairs.

"What do you want from me?" I yelled. "I don't care about your church or your factories or that lady who calls herself a Bishop. I just want to go home and forget I ever saw this place."

The drone floated closer.

"I don't know who you think I am," I said defiantly. "But you got the wrong guy."

The drone stopped about five yards from me. Was it possible? Did I actually make it understand that I had nothing to do with any of this?

"You are a scion," the drone said.

"No I'm not," I said. "What's a scion?"

A light on the underbelly of the drone flashed on. I squinted and took a step back, but the light didn't do any more than blind me.

"You will be brought to The Core for extraction," the drone said.

"Extraction?" I said. "What the hell does that mean?"

The light turned from white to blue. I felt a tingling sensation. The light somehow made my entire body go numb and my head went light. I thought I might pass out.

A familiar voice called out, "Donovan, don't move!"

A second later, boom! The drone exploded.

My head cleared instantly, and I covered up to protect myself from the spray of debris that came from the shattered machine. What had happened? As the echo of the explosion died down and smoke drifted past me, I saw the wreckage of the drone lying on the pavement.

"Yes!" Bodie exclaimed in triumph. He pointed skyward.

Issa was on the roof of the building above me. She was on one knee, still pointing the silver pistol she had used to shoot down the drone. Once again, my guardian angel had saved me. She put the pistol in her backpack, hooked one strap on to something and rappelled down the side of the building as the strap extended. She hit the ground, yanked on the strap and it zipped back into the pack.

I wanted one of those packs.

She headed toward me with Bodie following her.

"From now on we stay together," she said to Bodie.

"What's your problem?" Bodie said, back to his confidant self. "It all worked out."

"And whether you like it or not, I'm calling the shots," she added. "You will do what I say without question."

She was pissed and I didn't blame her. Bodie had nearly gotten us both killed.

Issa looked to me and asked, "You okay?"

"Hey, what about me?" Bodie asked. "I'm the one who got shot at."

"I'm fine," I said. "Thanks again, again. That makes three."

"We gotta go," she said and strode past me.

"No," I said firmly.

She turned back to me.

"No?"

"I'm not going anywhere until you tell me what this is about."

"Don't be stupid, Donovan. There's probably another drone headed this way."

"And I want to know why," I said defiantly. "You brought me here, the least you can do is tell me why."

Issa looked as though she wanted to argue but couldn't find the words.

"You're confused," she said patiently. "I get it, but things are happening fast."

"Yeah they are, and before I go another step, I want the truth."

"Me too," Bodie added.

Issa was torn. She had a plan, and I wasn't going along with it. Too bad. She could figure out a new plan.

"All right," she finally said. "But it shouldn't come from me. I was a toddler when you were born. You need to hear it from somebody who was there. I'll take you to him."

"Good," Bodie said. "Let's go before another drone shows up. Follow me."

He turned away from us and strode boldly out of the courtyard into the alley.

"He has no idea where he's going," Issa said.

"That's never stopped him before."

We hurried after him. Issa took the lead, moving past Bodie with confidence. She looked like a high school cheerleader who also happened to be a ruthless commando. Yeah, kind of hot.

We walked quickly through the filthy city for a good half an hour. Issa kept making turns and doubling back to make sure nobody was following us. With all the mis-directions we must have covered a couple of miles.

Every so often a flying motorcycle would zip by us carrying one of the Regenesis Watch goons. Good thing we always heard them coming so it gave us time to duck into a doorway or an alleyway to hide.

"They're not all looking for me, are they?" I asked.

"No," Issa said.

I relaxed.

"Not all," she added. "But probably most."

I stopped relaxing.

Nothing I saw changed my opinion of Essen-Tet. Other than a few unique "Prestige Manors" that stood out like bright lights in a dark room, it was a depressing ghetto filled with people who lived horrible lives. Issa said it hadn't always been this way. Could it all be the doing of this church? How could these people let that happen?

I was getting ready to balk when Issa stopped at the door of a rundown building.

"You're not going to like most of what you hear," she said to me.

"I wasn't expecting to," I said.

"Let's do this," Bodie said and strode for the door.

"Wait," Issa called out.

"What?" he asked impatiently.

She walked to the next door over.

"This is where we're going," she said.

Bodie gave me a blank look. Idiot.

"Maybe you should tap the breaks a little, Junior," I said and followed Issa.

When she opened the door, I was hit with a sour smell that I recognized instantly. One of my foster fathers was, to put it simply, an alcoholic. When I was five he used to bring me to his favorite dive bar because he couldn't leave me alone in his house. At least I learned how to tap a beer keg. Yet another important life skill I picked up.

The sad barroom was empty except for a single, droopy looking bartender who looked ninety years old.

"I guess we missed Happy Hour," I said. "Or maybe this is as happy as it gets."

"It's sure ain't the Star Wars cantina," Bodie said. "Space travel is more fun in the movies."

"Try to have an open mind," Issa said to me. "About what you're going to hear, and who you're going to hear it from."

The sound of somebody retching came from behind a closed door next to the bar. Whoever was in there was having a seriously bad day.

"Definitely not Happy Hour," Bodie said.

The sound of a toilet flushing followed. A few seconds later, the toilet flushed again.

"Double flush," Bodie said. "Not good."

The bathroom door opened, and the sick drunk stumbled out.

"Oh jeez," I said. "Really?"

It was Kellen A-Quiss, our drunk space pilot. His face lit up when he saw us, then he let out a rafter-rattling belch. He was much worse off than before. While we were running from killer drones, he was sitting in this fine establishment getting completely hammered.

"So soon?" he said, while holding on to the door frame for support.

"I think it's best for Donovan to understand the situation before meeting his mother," Issa said. "It'll make it easier."

"Easier?" Kellen said with a snide laugh. "That's a joke."

He staggered to the bar and slapped it. The droopy bartender reached for a bottle.

"No!" Issa shouted. "I need your head clear for this."

"Why?" he said with a big, goofy grin. "My head hasn't been clear for years."

Issa scowled, then nodded to the bartender.

The old guy grabbed a brown bottle and poured a shot of clear liquor.

"Are you going to tell me about my parents?" I asked.

Kellen downed the shot, slammed it onto the bar and said, "I'm going to tell you about The Tyrian League."

CHAPTER 11

FIFTEEN YEARS BEFORE

ourteen people were gathered in the dusty basement of an apartment building below the streets of Essen-Tet.

"We need to understand how important this moment is," Kellen A-Quiss announced to the group in a strong, clear voice. "We've been over it multiple times, but now it's for real."

It was a dark place where they had been secretly meeting for months, planning for this very moment. Some never thought this day would come. Others felt it couldn't come soon enough. For all of them, the idea that once seemed like a far-fetched dream was about to become reality.

"I'm confident we'll succeed," Kellen said. "But we have to be prepared to do what's necessary if we don't."

Kellen scanned the sober faces. There were six couples. Seven if you counted Kellen and the woman who stood next to him. Her name was Misha T-Soo, and she was the most important piece to the puzzle they were assembling.

Kellen was a charismatic leader. People were drawn to him because of his confidence and commitment to bringing back the life they once knew. A life where people had choices. Where hard work and talent were rewarded, and everyone had an equal chance at happiness. A life where people didn't live in fear.

A world without Regenesis.

He created the Tyrian League to make things right.

"I don't mind saying, I'm nervous," one man said. "We're putting our faith in Misha's, what does she call it? Her Chrysalis? How can we be sure it will work?"

Misha T-Soo was a slight young woman with intense, dark eyes that missed nothing. Though in her late twenties, she looked no older than a teenager. Her brilliant, analytical mind quickly shot her up the ranks of Regenesis to become a senior programmer who helped develop the church's vast computer network. She was an invaluable member of the church.

A church she hated.

Her parents refused to join and went from being respected physicians to working hard labor in a Regenesis-run factory. Both died from exposure to toxic chemicals, leaving Misha alone. And angry. She wanted revenge and chose to get it using the best weapon she had, Her intelligence. She joined the church to damage it from within.

Misha was like a deadly virus, waiting for the chance to infect her host.

She developed an actual virus she called the "Chrysalis." When released into the Regenesis computer network, the insidious program was designed to paralyze communication, knock out power to every Regenesis institution and silence the energy-firing weapons of the Regenesis Watch. When the Regenesis security systems and firewalls engaged to fight back, it would only strengthen Misha's virus. The very systems meant to prevent such an attack would feed it and help it grow.

Regenesis would go dark.

"I have full confidence in the Chrysalis," Misha said in a soft yet confident voice. "My concern is what happens after it cripples the grid."

"We're ready," Kellen said. "Over a thousand people are outside the Regenesis Compound right now, staging a peaceful protest. The moment Regenesis goes dark, the protest becomes an invasion. The Regenesis Watch will be overwhelmed by the swarm. We'll invade The Core, arrest Vail Kobain and that will be end of Regenesis on Tyria."

"And if we fail?" one woman asked.

If we fail, there's no telling what Vail Kobain will do," Kellen said. "The Regenesis Watch will find us. I'm certain of that. I don't think we'd be executed; we'll just wish we were. If it comes to that, we all know what we have to do."

Everyone exchanged nervous looks.

"I know, it's horrible," Kellen said. "But would there be any other choice?"

There were reluctant nods of acceptance all around.

"We've done incredible work," Kellen said. "The Tyrian League will go down in history as the founders of our freedom. We should all be very proud."

A wan-looking man stood up and said, "That sounds good, but let's not go erecting any statues just yet."

That got a nervous chuckle from the group.

Kellen stood and raised a small glass of bright-green liquid.

"To us," he announced. "To the future, and to the Tyrian League."

Everyone raised their own glasses and downed the fiery drink.

"It's time," Misha said to Kellen.

She gave a shy smile to the group and went for the door.

Kellen looked to the assembled and said, "Have faith."

There were a few nods and smiles, but mostly everyone looked worried.

Kellen followed Misha out of the basement room and closed the door. Before she could climb the stairs, he took her arm to stop her.

"Hey, you okay?" he asked.

"Honestly?" she said. "I couldn't be better."

The two hugged. They had met when Kellen was a pilot who flew junkets between planets. He didn't pay much attention to Regenesis because they didn't stop him from doing what he loved most. Flying.

That changed when he met Misha.

He was hired to fly her between Regenesis facilities on different planets. At first he saw her as a robot-like genius who was dedicated to Regenesis. But through her, he learned the truth about the church. She showed him work camps, factories, and prisons. When she finally opened up to tell him how her parents died in one of those factories, her true mission came clear.

She wanted to bring Regenesis down.

Misha had opened Kellen's eyes and together, they created The Tyrian League. It was a band of rebels who would fight for their freedom. The day had finally come to reveal her true intent to Regenesis.

In the basement, the two held each other for a long moment, then Misha pulled away.

"You have the authorization pass?" she asked, all business.

Kellen held up a small tablet, the size of a deck of cards.

"Delivery will be on time," he replied. "As long as the Watch doesn't take the package."

"They won't," Misha said. "You have the chip, correct?"

"Oh no!" Kellen exclaimed with mock horror. "I left it on the sink at home!"

Misha gave him a playful shove.

"I'm trying to think of everything," she said.

"You have."

Misha looked into Kellen's eyes and said, "You made this possible. Thank you."

"We'll celebrate tonight, in Vail Kobain's apartment."

The two hugged one last time, then Misha hurried up the stairs. Kellen watched her go, thinking he was incredibly lucky to know and love the woman who would bring down Regenesis. He imagined a very bright future together and was anxious for it to begin.

A mile away, a crowd gathered outside the imposing steel wall that surrounded the Regenesis Compound. Hundreds of people sauntered up and stood on the sidewalk across the wide boulevard that separated the compound from the rest of Essen-Tet. There was nothing dramatic or unusual about it.

Inside Gate B, armed officers of the Regenesis Watch glanced toward the growing crowd with no concern. They knew these protests were harmless and in the end, futile. No amount of angry shouting could stop the overwhelming power of Regenesis.

What they didn't realize was that these protests were meant to lull them to sleep. They wanted the guards to become so used to these gatherings that they'd be ignored. Once a week the people would appear at the gate, chant for a few hours, then disperse. It was routine. It was boring.

It was a loaded trap that was about to spring.

The crowd of protesters grew to triple the size of any other. The Watchers didn't take notice. Nor did they realize that in spite of the fact that it was a warm, sunny day, many of the protestors wore long coats. They needed the coats to hide their weapons. Metal clubs. Once the Regenesis grid went dark, the Watcher's energy-firing weapons would go dead. The metal clubs would be more than effective when the rebels charged the compound.

Misha T-Soo arrived at Gate C as she had done every working day for the past three years. Entering the compound was an ordeal. Everyone had to pass through a scanner that would detect any suspicious item they were carrying.

She didn't have the Chrysalis. Though it was the size of a grain of rice, it would surely have been detected and taken from her. The revolution would have ended before it began. The Chrysalis had to be brought into the compound a different way.

The Regenesis Compound was a different world than the rest of Essen-Tet. It was a community of large, stunning mansions that were the homes of the Ministers of Regenesis and the elite leaders of their many businesses. The gorgeous buildings were scattered throughout the parklike setting of grassy lawns, ponds, and colorful flower gardens. Beyond the populated area were acres of dense forest, clean rivers and vast fields of grass.

It was an Eden-like city within the city.

Misha passed through the security checks and took her familiar route to The Core where she worked. The three-towered castle was in the dead center of the immense compound. Getting there meant a ride aboard a sleek monorail train that was quick and silent. It was designed that way so as not to disturb the important residents.

Like Misha, most of the people who worked in The Core lived outside of the compound and were only allowed in to do their jobs. Each day as they rode the monorail and looked out of its windows, they were teased by the possibility of becoming a member of the church's inner circle and live in such splendor.

On her way to the monorail, Misha passed a floating tram that was filled with visitors from the city. It was a common sight. Regenesis ran daily tours of the compound for anyone who wished to view this special world. A tour-guide stood in front, speaking to the group through speakers.

"Welcome to the Regenesis Compound," the guide said brightly. "For the next thirty minutes you will be treated to a glimpse of the special world that was built with the grace of our Regent. One day, with hard work and sacrifice, you too could become part of this community. The choice is yours. Glory to the Regent."

"Glory to the Regent," the people in the tram repeated.

In spite of this promise, Misha didn't know of anyone who actually got the chance to move from outside the compound, to inside its walls. The tease, and false promise, only made her hate the church more.

After a ten-minute journey on the monorail, the train stopped at the massive, modern castle that was the center of the Regenesis church on Tyria, and the home of Vail Kobain. The Core. Misha's routine was to enter the building and take an elevator down to the floor that held the expansive sea of computers that the church relied upon for everything from controlling the assembly lines in their factories; to checking on the comings and goings of employees; to providing the energy that powered the weapons of the Regenesis Watch.

Power was transmitted through the air by the dish antennas that were on top of one of the towers. The ability to transmit power was the number one source of wealth that Regenesis drew upon to run its empire. The technology was sold and installed on multiple worlds that were under Regenesis control.

Misha worked in the center of this sea of technology. She arrived at her cubicle, logged on to her station, and waited.

On the other side of Essen-Tet, Kellen had a schedule to keep. He had taken a job as a messenger who made deliveries throughout the city. His transportation was a high-speed, motorcycle-like aerobike that traveled a few feet off the ground. He would zip through the crowded city streets, delivering parcels to the various companies owned by the church. He was a popular driver because he was fast and efficient. Some called him reckless, but he knew no other way. For him it was either full-speed or stop.

He was well known to the Watchers who patrolled the gates of the Regenesis Compound. He'd bring them gifts of smuggled green-ale from the planet Wivven and made the offer to bring them along on one of his interplanetary journeys. They liked him, which is exactly what Kellen wanted. He wasn't a messenger because he enjoyed it. His true calling was to fly. But he spent a year staying home on Tyria, working as a messenger to gain the Watcher's trust so he could make one single delivery on a very important day.

That day was today.

Kellen zipped through city streets, taking tight corners, trying to keep his heart from racing. He wore the dark blue jump suit of the messenger company (owned by Regenesis) along with a black helmet. He needed to go through the paces of a normal day, though there was nothing normal about the silver cannister tucked in the saddle bag of his aerobike. He rounded the last corner to see the wall of the compound looming ahead. It had never seemed so huge. Impenetrable. He flew directly to Gate D, just as he had done dozens of times in the past.

"Morning!" was Kellen's friendly greeting to the Watcher who was holding up his hand to stop him. "You're missing all the excitement."

The Watcher approached Kellen who straddled his floating aerobike as it hovered a few inches above the pavement.

"What excitement?" the Watcher asked.

Kellen reached for the small, electronic pad that held the forged authorization pass that said he was to deliver a parcel to a senior programmer named Misha T-Soo. He'd delivered dozens of packages to her, and to others, over the last year. They had all been totally legit.

This one wasn't.

"There's another protest going on at Gate B," Kellen said. "A big one. I don't get those people. What are they trying to prove?"

The Watcher scanned the pad with a wand to insure the credentials were in order. They were, thanks to the woman who worked in dispatch who also happened to be part of The Tyrian League.

"They must not have anything better to do," the Watcher said. "Move ahead slowly."

Kellen knew the routine. He floated forward through a metal frame that scanned every inch of him, and his bike. The Watcher checked a display screen, looking for any suspicious or banned items.

"I think they'd be better off going to work instead of complaining about how much they hate their lives," Kellen said.

His voice was calm, but he kept a wary eye on the Watcher for any sign that he might have noticed something out of the ordinary with his orders.

"What's that?" the Watcher asked.

"What's what?" Kellen asked innocently.

"In the left saddle bag."

Kellen's heart raced. That was where he had the silver cannister with the Chrysalis.

"Oh, right," Kellen said. "Almost forgot."

He reached into the saddle bag and pulled out a black thermos.

"From Wivven," Kellen said. "Got it from a friend who made the run yesterday."

He held the cannister out to the Watcher.

"Be cool," Kellen said. "The church doesn't like people drinking something they didn't produce themselves."

The Watcher took a cautious look around to make sure curious eyes weren't watching, then grabbed the thermos.

"Careful what you say," the Watcher said.

"Right. Good advice."

"Thanks A-Quiss," the Watcher said. "I owe you."

"Nah, just doing a kindness for a friend," Kellen replied with a big smile.

The Watcher waved him on. Kellen gunned his bike and flew into the compound.

Outside of Gate B, the crowd of protesters grew. Though they acted like nothing unusual was happening, the energy from nervous tension was building. If all went according to the plan, Regenesis would soon go dark. Every last person was aware of the schedule. Many grasped their hidden weapons, ready to throw off their coats and rush to the gate.

The Watchers felt the tension. It radiated from the crowd like furnace heat, though none could have guessed why. As a precaution, a Lead Watcher contacted his command center to request that a few more guards be sent to the gate.

Inside The Core, Misha stared at her monitors, pretending to be thinking of anything other than what was about to happen. On her desk was a portable drive the size of her pinkie. It would soon become a weapon she would use to introduce the virus into the grid. Misha picked it up and rolled it between her fingers.

Kellen shot across the compound following the monorail track and zipped up to a service entrance of The Core. He was met by another Watcher, who checked his authorization. He scanned the pad with barely a look and waved him on. Kellen flew to the entrance and parked. He took off his helmet, put it on the bike seat, grabbed the saddlebag and headed for The Core. He had to hold back a smile. Getting past this final Watcher meant that the year spent as a messenger hadn't been wasted.

The Regenesis Watch had been lulled to sleep.

He was in.

So was the Chrysalis.

The route to the elevator was familiar. He walked with purpose but didn't hurry, passing several Watchers and other staff that worked in the belly of Regenesis. He couldn't help but wonder how they would react to the takeover. How many would stay loyal to the church and fight back? Which of them would welcome the overthrow of the cult? Who would pretend to welcome the change, only to re-group and support Vail Kobain afterward? As much as the Church of Regenesis had made life unbearable, there were those who still believed that their suffering would somehow be rewarded. They wanted to live in the compound, or at least be given an apartment in a Privilege Manor.

The elevator brought him down to the tech floor where the sea of computer stations sat beyond sliding glass doors. The day shift was always the busiest, with dozens of programmers scurrying about or focused on their computer screens. Kellen walked through the doors with purpose and didn't get a second glance from anyone. He made his way through the high-tech labyrinth until he arrived at cubicle 39-A. The station of Misha T-Soo.

She was sitting at her desk, staring at a screen of data though he was pretty sure her mind was somewhere else.

"I have a delivery for Misha T-Soo," Kellen said, all business.

Misha tensed up. Though she knew he was coming, hearing Kellen's voice made it real.

"Great," Misha said lightly as she spun around to face him. She gave no hint that she knew who Kellen was, other than a messenger delivering a parcel.

Kellen was just as casual in case there were any curious co-workers listening. He reached into his saddle bag and pulled out the silver canister. It was a cylinder the size and shape of a small thermos. He held it out to Misha and the two made eye contact.

"Do I need to sign for it?" Misha asked.

"Nah," Kellen replied. "But I've been asked to stay until you've installed whatever it is to make sure there are no problems. If it doesn't work I'll have to return it."

"It'll work," Misha said with confidence.

"I'm counting on it," Kellen said.

He gave her a playful wink.

Misha took the cannister that she herself loaded that morning and spun back to her desk. She unscrewed the cap and peered inside. There was a brief moment that she feared the chip wouldn't be there, but of course that was just paranoia. The chip was there, locked in place by a strip of plastic on a soft cushion of foam, just as she'd placed it that morning. Misha took it out and was surprised to see that her hands were shaking. Though she was confident the Chrysalis would work, they wouldn't know for sure until it was uploaded to the grid.

She cautiously pulled the tiny chip out of the cannister and placed it into a slot in the portable drive. With a satisfying CLICK, it was locked in and ready to be introduced to Regenesis.

"Now what could that be?" came a strange voice.

Misha and Kellen spun to see a visitor. It was August C-Bonn, a junior programmer who had been assigned to Misha's group. He was a short, round little man who Misha felt wasn't especially competent, but her supervisor insisted that she keep him around. Misha didn't complain, but she never gave him challenging work. Worse, August spent more time looking over other people's shoulders and asking questions than he did on his own job.

"It's a diagnostic program," Misha said without missing a beat. "To clean up some of the sketchy code in the battery drivers."

"Really?" August said. "I wasn't aware of any problem."

"Then you haven't been paying attention," Misha shot back curtly.

She spun back around and reached the drive toward the input port.

"Stop," August commanded.

Kellen had to hold himself back from punching the annoying little man.

"I know you feel as though I'm over my head here, Miss T-Soo, and maybe I am. But you should know that in addition to the pedestrian work you've assigned me; I've made it my business to be fully versed on every aspect of the work this division is doing."

"Can we discuss this another time, August?" Misha said, barely controlling her jittery nerves.

"Now is the perfect time," August said firmly. "As I said, I'm not quite the incompetent you think I am, and I know nothing about a diagnostic program designed to clear up sketchy code in the battery drivers."

Kellen tensed up. What began as a minor annoyance had suddenly gone critical. He slowly reached for the empty cannister on Misha's desk.

"And definitely not one brought in by a messenger from outside The Core. So tell me, Miss T-Soo, what is it exactly that you're about to introduce to the grid?"

"That's it!" Kellen shouted.

With one quick move he hit August on the side of the head with the metal cannister. The fat man stumbled and fell to his knees.

"Do it!" Kellen commanded.

Misha fumbled with the drive and reached for the input dock...

...only to be pulled back by a Watcher who arrived with August and had been hovering outside the cubicle.

Another Watcher appeared and held his stun-gun to Kellen's head.

"You've always been considered a security risk because of your family history, Miss T-Soo," August said from his knees as he rubbed his aching head. "But we took a chance on you because you proved to be such a brilliant programmer."

"We?" Misha asked. It was dawning on her that August C-Bonn wasn't the person she thought he was.

"You've treated me with nothing but disdain," August said as he struggled to his feet. "I didn't take offense because my true job is with security. I was assigned to watch you, Miss T-Soo. Nothing you've done gave me cause for concern, until now. What exactly will that device do to our system?"

"I told you," Misha said. "It's to clear up some useless code."

"Is it now?" August said, skeptically. "Then you won't mind letting me take a look."

August held out his hand for the drive that held the Chrysalis.

Misha threw a nervous look to Kellen.

August saw this and said, "Or perhaps it contains something a bit more insidious?"

"Close your eyes," Kellen said calmly to Misha.

"And who are you?" August asked Kellen.

Kellen had no intention of answering. He flipped the cannister over and pressed a button on its bottom.

The others looked about, momentarily frozen, not sure of what was happening or what to do about it.

Kellen tossed the cannister to the floor and a silent explosion of energy erupted that knocked everyone off their feet. The two Watchers, August, Misha and Kellen were thrown to the floor. Several others in nearby cubicles were knocked down as well. Since there was no sound, most other people on the tech floor weren't aware that anything had happened.

Kellen's body went numb, and his head spun. He fought to re-focus and crawled to Misha, who was in worse shape than he was. Through sheer force of will, he staggered to his feet and lifted Misha up. He grabbed his saddle bag and the two stumbled out of the cubicle.

"Can we use another port to input the Chrysalis?" Kellen asked, though he couldn't hear his own voice because his eardrums had been pummeled by the energy surge.

Misha didn't answer. Her legs moved, but she was too dazed to think.

"Misha!" Kellen barked. "Can we upload to the grid through another port?"

People looked up from their workstations, watching in wonder as the two staggered past them.

"Yes," Misha mumbled. "But it will take time to set up."

"Never mind," Kellen said and pulled Misha toward the exit.

"Stop them!" August screamed as he crawled from Misha's cubicle on his hands and knees.

None of the technicians responded. It was all happening too fast.

August got to his feet and shouted, "In the name of the Regent, stop those two!"

Too late. Kellen and Misha had made it through the doors and into a waiting elevator. The elevator doors closed, and they were gone.

"Destroy the chip," Kellen said.

Misha was quickly regaining her senses. She opened the drive and plucked out the Chrysalis.

"I'm sorry," she said. "I had no idea C-Bonn was a Regenesis spy."

"Doesn't matter," Kellen said. "We can't let them get the Chrysalis or we're done for good."

She took the tiny chip in her fingers, sighed, and snapped it in two.

"Not good enough," Kellen said.

He took the chip pieces from her and swallowed them.

"We have to get back," Kellen said. He took out his tablet and texted a message.

The crowd outside of Gate B was growing restless. Nothing had gone wrong, which meant something had gone wrong. The designated time that the Chrysalis was supposed to have shut down the grid had come and gone. What had happened? Was it only a delay? How long should they wait? There was one thing everyone knew for certain: if the grid didn't shut down, they could not storm the compound. No matter how ready they were to attack, they had no chance if the Watcher's weapons weren't silenced.

Then, in unison, the communicators that everyone carried came alive. They all received a simple, pre-determined text message from Kellen. The message they were expecting and hoping for was the word: "STRIKE." That was the signal to move on the compound. Instead, the text they got was the word: "SLEEP." It meant the attack was off.

There was frustration, confusion and disbelief. Some hoped it was a minor setback, and they'd soon try again. But that feeling wasn't shared by many. Most felt only crushing defeat.

Silently, reluctantly, the group dispersed.

The Watchers at Gate B viewed them with confusion. The crowd was huge, but the protest never took off. The people left without so much as a single angry shout. Strange.

The feeling in the basement meeting room of the Tyrian League jumped from confusion to disbelief, to disappointment, and settled on despair. When the "SLEEP" text came through, one woman gasped. Another cried. Most everyone exchanged horrified glances. They had put their faith in Kellen and Misha but for whatever reason, they had failed. Now the group was faced with the horror of going through with the alternate plan they had all agreed to, but never thought would happen.

"Can we do really do this?" one man asked.

No one answered. They were all searching their souls, questioning themselves and trying to get their heads around what their failed mission would lead to.

"They'll hunt us down," one woman said. "The better question is, can we live like that?"

They all knew the answer.

Another woman wiped away tears and said, "We have to prepare. There's no telling how much time we'll have."

"What if Kellen and Misha don't make it back?" one man asked the group.

"Then two of us will take their place," the woman replied.

Nobody volunteered.

"Let's hope it doesn't come to that," the woman said.

At the Regenesis Core, the elevator carrying Kellen and Misha rose to the ground floor. Kellen reached into his saddle bag and pulled out another cannister.

"My bike is outside," Kellen said.

Misha nodded in understanding.

The elevator doors opened to reveal Vail Kobain.

Misha gasped in surprise.

The Bishop of Regenesis stood with her hands folded in front of her, looking remarkably calm. Behind her stood a Watcher with a stun gun aimed at Kellen.

"Good afternoon," Kobain said with a slight smile.

Kellen held up the cannister threateningly.

"This will hurt," he said.

Kobain showed no fear but backed away from the open elevator.

Kellen nudged Misha and the two stepped out.

"Such tragic poetry," Kobain said. "The child suffers for the misdeeds of her parents."

"The tragedy has nothing to do with me," Misha said.

"And who might you be?" Kobain asked Kellen politely.

"One of many," he replied.

"Again, such tragedy," Kobain said with a sigh.

Kellen let go of Misha and grabbed Kobain's arm.

The Watcher lifted his weapon and shouted, "Step back!"

Kellen held up the cannister.

"If I activate this, she's done," Kellen said.

"It's all right," Kobain said to the nervous Watcher.

The Watcher hesitated, then took a step back while keeping his weapon aimed at Kellen.

"I don't believe you're capable of murder," Kobain said. "Or suicide."

"Believe what you want," Kellen said. "We're leaving. And you're coming with us."

Kobain shrugged, as if she didn't care one way or the other.

Kellen nudged Kobain to start walking. The group moved together, headed for the doors through which Kellen had entered only minutes before.

The Watcher followed, beads of nervous sweat dripping from his forehead. Other Watchers ran from deeper in The Core.

"Stay back!" the Watcher called to them. "He's got a weapon."

The others froze. Seeing the Bishop in danger shook them. It didn't help that they didn't have a show of force since many of their team had been sent to Gate B.

"What happened to your parents was unfortunate, Miss T-Soo," Kobain said calmly. "You should know that their sacrifice was in service to a greater good."

"You offer no greater good," Misha said with disdain. "Your cult exists only to exploit and profit. Your so-called Regent isn't God. It's money."

"And that allows us to provide so much to so many," Kobain said.

"You've created a society of slaves that benefit only a few," Misha said. "It will not last."

The group moved out of The Core, headed toward Kellen's waiting aerobike. A few Watchers lifted their weapons, but Kobain raised her hand to warn them off.

"Then help us, Misha," Kobain said. "You have a gift. Use it to help Regenesis become the positive force you believe it should be."

Kellen pushed Kobain away and mounted his bike. Misha got on the seat behind him.

"If that was possible it would have already happened," Misha said.

"Such a waste of talent," Kobain said with a sigh, then turned to the Watcher and said, "Kill them."

Kellen hit the ignition button on the cannister and flipped it toward the Watcher.

Kobain and the Watcher dodged away.

Kellen throttled up and flew off before the cannister hit the ground.

The Watcher took aim but didn't get the chance to fire as the intense pulse of power erupted from the cannister, knocking him off his feet.

Kellen and Misha flew for the gate ahead of the explosive wave of power. The surprised Watcher that Kellen had given the Wivven ale to fumbled for his weapon. Kellen sped directly at him. The Watcher couldn't take aim fast enough and had to dive out of the way.

"Hang on," Kellen said.

Misha wrapped her arms around his waist, locked her hands together and pressed her cheek against his back. Kellen accelerated and flew through the gate, headed for the maze of city streets.

The Watcher at the gate wasn't done. He landed, rolled and stayed focused. He raised his weapon, took aim at the speeding aerobike, and fired.

Kellen felt Misha's body stiffen up. The jolt surprised him, but Misha didn't loosen her grip, and he didn't risk stopping.

There was nothing more important than to get back to the Tyrian League and put the back-up plan into motion. He drove the aerobike through the streets of Essen-Tet on the edge of recklessness, dodging pedestrians as if maneuvering through a dense forest. A crash would have been tragic, but he had to get back before the Regenesis Watch came after them.

After ten minutes of white-knuckle flying, they arrived at the sad apartment building that was home to the Tyrian League. No sooner did Kellen's aerobike appear from around a corner than a garage door opened. He flew inside and the door slid closed. Finally, he brought the bike to a stop inside the empty garage.

His heart was racing from the high-speed ride.

"That was intense," he said as he gulped for air.

Misha's arms were still around his waist, her hands still locked.

"It's okay," Kellen said. "I'm sorry if I scared you."

Misha didn't respond.

Something was wrong. Kellen grasped her hands and pulled them apart. She didn't resist but stayed pressed against his back.

"Misha?" Kellen said.

He got off the bike while still holding one of her hands.

Misha slumped forward and fell on the seat.

"No, no, no!" Kellen cried.

He scooped her up, lifted her off the bike and rested her down on the floor, gently laying her head in his lap. Kellen pressed two fingers against her neck, checking for a pulse.

Several of the Tyrian League team ran into the garage.

"What happened?" one man yelled. "Did the Chrysalis fail–?"

They registered what was happening and froze where they stood.

Kellen held Misha close, hugging her to his chest. Tears trickled down his cheeks. No one said a word. It was clear that the tragedy of this day was still unfolding.

Finally, Kellen looked up to the others with red, swollen eyes.

"We were going to do this together," he said, his voice cracking with emotion.

"And now?" the man asked softly.

Kellen looked to Misha. It seemed as though she was sleeping peacefully. He took a deep breath, gathered his strength, and looked to the others.

"They feared she was a security risk. They had a spy watching her," Kellen said. "We didn't get the chance to make the upload"

The others let out sighs of frustration and anger.

"We destroyed the Chrysalis so they couldn't get their hands on it," Kellen said. "Now they'll be coming for us. We have to follow the plan."

"Can you do it?" the man asked.

"I don't have a choice," Kellen said. "Can you?"

Less than an hour later the group was gathered in the basement room. Only now there were thirteen. They had prepared and practiced for this moment. A moment they hoped would never come. Everything was in place, save for one important new detail.

"I can't do this alone," Kellen said. "Misha was as crucial to the plan as me."

"Are you saying we shouldn't go through with it?" a woman asked.

"No. I'm asking for a volunteer. Misha and I were the logical choices because we have no families. Either we pick someone else, or we end it right here."

Everyone shifted uncomfortably.

"I'll do it," a woman finally said.

Her name was Arri G-Kove. She was a tall, light skinned woman with long blonde hair. Her husband, Penn G-Kove reacted instantly.

"No!" he exclaimed. "I need you here."

Arri turned to him. Her eyes offered sympathy, but her voice was pure steel.

"What we need is to give our son the chance of a better life," she said. "And protect him."

Penn opened his mouth to argue but didn't.

"Does anyone have a problem with Arri taking Misha's place?" Kellen asked the group.

From the tortured looks it was clear that many were conflicted, but no one spoke up.

"Arri," Kellen said. "Can you really do this?"

Arri looked to the others as if searching for help, or an answer.

"I don't know," she said. "We've had our differences, but the one thing we've all agreed on is that if the takeover failed, this had to be done. All I can promise is that I'll do my best."

Kellen nodded thoughtfully and said, "We can't ask for anything more." He looked to the group and added, "Any arguments?"

Nobody said a word.

"All right then," Kellen said. "Let's get started."

The women, including Arri, left the garage. Kellen and the men walked to the far end of the large, underground space where there was a closed garage door. In front of the door was a table that had a clean, blue cloth draped over it.

Standing next to it was the sixth man. He stood on a wooden box which raised him to the height of the others. He was a dwarf who stood just under four feet tall.

"You're on, Doctor Tenzig," Kellen said to him.

The doctor pulled back the blue cloth to reveal six, large, hypodermic syringes. The barrels were silver steel; the long needles encased in protective plastic.

"I loaded them this morning," Tenzig said in a deep, confident voice. "Didn't think we'd actually need them."

The women returned, each carrying a bundle that they held close to their chests as if they were precious and fragile, because they were. They were infant babies. The women looked tortured. A few quietly sobbed. They snuggled the babies, speaking softly to them. They gathered near the table, standing close together, trying to draw strength from the group.

"I can only imagine how difficult this is," Kellen said to them. "Take heart that you're doing this to give them a better life. After today, you will all be square in the sites of Regenesis, which means they will be too. You're giving them a chance. You're giving us *all* a chance. Our hopes go with these precious babies. These scions."

Kellen nodded to the doctor.

Tenzig said: "Saree One."

A woman brought her baby to the doctor. She hesitated, but Tenzig's sympathetic gaze told her that her child was in good hands.

"It's only a slight pinch," Tenzig assured her, saying it loud enough for the others to hear.

The woman nodded for him to continue. He swabbed the baby's leg with a numbing liquid, then picked up one of the syringes and uncapped the needle. With a practiced hand, he injected the baby in the fatty part of her thigh. The little girl barely whimpered.

The mother, crying, kissed her child and returned to the others.

Tenzig picked up the second syringe and said, "Karter Two."

Arri G-Kove came forward with her son, Karter. The doctor went through the same procedure. It was as simple and painless as the last. He then repeated the process with the remaining babies: Rendy Three; Pasha Four; and Teever Five. After injecting Teever Five, he leaned down and gave the baby a kiss on the forehead. Teever was his son. He then gave his wife, who wasn't a dwarf, a reassuring hug.

He injected each baby with the same gentle care. None cried. None complained. He then picked up the last syringe and looked to the final mother.

"Donovan Six," he said.

Donovan's mother brought him forward, held her son tight, and closed her eyes.

When the needle entered Donovan's thigh, he let out a squawk. He didn't like it. Not one bit. He gave Tenzig a deadly look.

"Sorry," the doctor said and rubbed Donovan's thigh.

Donovan kicked his hand away.

"Done," Tenzig said. "They all now carry a clone of Misha's Chrysalis chip. The only ones in existence."

Kellen said, "Regenesis will make us pay. But these babies have a chance. They'll grow up on different worlds where nobody will know who they are. Least of all Regenesis. They could live long, full lives without ever knowing their history. Or they may grow up to realize the power they carry and use it to succeed where we failed. We can only hope. For them, and for the future."

A sudden explosion rocked the basement, shaking the floor and sending a cloud of dust down onto the group.

"They found us," Arri cried.

"Let's go!" Kellen commanded.

He hit a wall switch, and the garage door rose on a room that held the large round sphere that was a Jump Ship.

Another explosion shook the foundation.

"Hurry!" Tenzig exclaimed.

The hatch was open. The ship was waiting. Kellen hurried inside, followed by the six women carrying their babies.

Inside the Jump Ship were two seats. Behind them were six basinets, lined up in a row. They were clear pods with bedding and small straps to secure the babies. The mothers fought back tears as they each secured their own baby into its pod.

Kellen took the pilot's seat and powered up the ship. The lights of the control panel flashed as the faint whine of the engines began to build.

"I hate to say hurry, but hurry," Kellen said to the mothers.

For the women who were saying good-bye to their children, it was a frantic, gut-wrenching moment. They each gave their babies one final kiss, then closed the clear pod-covers and sealed their children inside their cocoons.

They all gave Arri a quick hug that carried the silent plea: "Take care of our children."

One woman looked to Kellen and said, "You're responsible for them."

"Yes I am," Kellen said.

The five women backed out of the ship and Kellen activated the hatch door. He glanced back to catch the look on their forlorn faces. It lasted only a moment before the door slid shut, but it was a sight that would haunt him for years.

"Strap in," he commanded Arri.

Arri jumped into the seat next to him and buckled the straps.

"I hope you know what you're doing," Arri said.

"Getting us out of here? No problem," Kellen replied. "What happens after that, well, like she said, they're our responsibility. No pressure, right?"

"I'm sorry about Misha," she said.

Kellen swallowed hard. "Yeah well I'll be damned if I'll let her death be for nothing. These kids carry her legacy."

"Then let's get them out of here," Arri said.

Kellen entered the launch sequence, shot a quick look back to his precious cargo, and throttled the engine.

The silver sphere lifted off of its base and shot through the ceiling, ripping a hole so large it nearly made the entire building implode.

What was left of the leaders of the Tyrian League stood beneath the building's wound, staring up at the silver dot that was bound for the heavens.

Misha's Chrysalis no longer existed on Tyria. Clones would be scattered across the universe so as not to fall into the hands of Regenesis. They would be safe...

...until the day they would be needed once again.

CHAPTER 12

Kellen knocked back another shot. He was getting drunker by the second as he told his incredible story, which also happened to be *my* incredible story. I was afraid he'd pass out before finishing, but the guy was a pro. At drinking, that is.

"Damn," Bodie said with dismay.

He kept giving me strange looks once Kellen had revealed why everyone was calling me "Six." It was annoying, but I let it go. I had more important things to worry about.

"What happened to the other five babies?" I asked Kellen.

"Arri and I took them to different planets," he said, his voice slurring. "We wanted them to grow up without the threat of being hunted down by Regenesis. It worked, too. Until now."

"Yeah, lucky me."

"We've been watching out for you since you were a baby," Issa said.

"Who's *we*?" I asked.

"The Tyrian League didn't die that day," Issa said. "Though most of the scion parents were tracked down by the Regenesis Watch."

"Were they killed?" Bodie asked.

"Hard to say," Issa replied. "Most were probably sent off to remote places and are either in prison or doing hard labor."

Kellen let out a rumbling burp and put his head down on the bar. Passed out. Maybe he wasn't such a pro after all.

"What happened to him?" Bodie asked. "No way that's the same guy who did all the stuff we just heard about."

"That day changed him," Issa said. "I would like to have known him before, but…"

She let the thought trail.

"So the Tyrian League is still around?" Bodie asked.

"Yes. We've kept up hope because of the scions. That's one of the reasons we've been watching over them."

"You mean watching over the Chrysalis chips that were stuck in our legs," I said.

"That too," Issa said. "The scions each hold the power to bring Regenesis down."

I rubbed my thigh. Was it possible? Had I been carrying around an alien computer chip my whole life like a dog with a microchip I.D.?

"But it's like, old technology," Bodie said. "It can't still work."

"But it can. That's the beauty of what Misha T-Soo created. It adapts. It won't matter how much the Regenesis grid has evolved over the years, the Chrysalis will learn and compensate. It'll be as destructive today as it was fifteen years ago."

"Would people do it again?" Bodie asked. "I mean, try to overthrow Regenesis?"

"In a heartbeat," Issa said without hesitation. "Eighty percent of the people work like slaves for the other twenty percent. If given the slightest bit of hope that Regenesis can be taken down, they'll rise again. They're ready and waiting."

It was an incredible story, and I was one of the stars. Let's not forget that.

"What are you thinking, Donovan?" Issa asked.

"I'm thinking about that night on the football field. With Kralovenic's car."

"Yeah, I was following you."

I guess there are worse things than having a pretty girl following you around. But knowing somebody was watching every move I made is fairly creepy.

I looked around the bar, taking in the peeling paint, the dusty floor and the windows that were so thick with grime you could barely see out. It was pretty much like the rest of Essen-Tet. Dirty, poor, pathetic. Is this what Regenesis had done to the city? To Tyria? To other worlds?

Getting even with the janitor who stole my watch seemed like a very long time ago.

"What was Essen-Tet like before Regenesis?" I asked.

"I hear it was beautiful," Issa said. "People came from all different cultures. There was art and music and lots of green space. There were poor people, sure, and rich people, but mostly a whole lot of people who were just living their lives. Regenesis went after the people who struggled. The easy targets. They gave them false hope and took their money to build their empire. They started businesses that were so successful, other businesses couldn't compete. Manufacturing, shipping, energy, transportation, banking, farming, communications, you name it. Regenesis became more powerful than governments and armies."

"What about that church on Earth?" Bodie said. "In Stony Brook."

"Earth is their next target," Issa said. "They start small, build a following, take their money and their talent, then use it against the very people who made them. All in the name of this fake-God called the Regent. Ten years from now, Earth might look very different than it does today. I know it seems far-fetched, but it isn't. Essen Tet is proof of that."

She looked me straight in the eye and added, "If you help stop Regenesis here, you'll be saving Earth as well."

I'd heard enough.

"No!" I said.

"No what?" Issa asked.

"You don't need my help. You need the chip that's stuck in my leg. You say our parents did the noble thing to send us away? I think they used us to smuggle out the Chrysalis chips."

"That's not entirely true," Issa argued. "Your parents didn't want you to be victims."

"So they should have gone with us!" I snapped back. "They all should have."

"They wanted you to be beyond Regenesis' reach. For that you had to disappear. It would have been much easier to track down families than single babies."

"Turns out that's not true, is it?" I said.

"They did what they thought was right," Issa said, gently.

"Yeah and sentenced us to miserable lives." I pointed at Kellen and added, "What about him? He wasn't killed. Or sent to a slave factory. If Regenesis was so hot on shutting down the Tyrian League, how come they didn't get the big boss?"

"Because I left," Kellen growled.

I was so surprised that he spoke that I jumped. He lifted his head off the bar, but his eyes stayed closed.

"They looked for me, sure," he said, though his words were so slurred I couldn't be certain. "They're still looking. But I'm like smoke. You can see it, but if you try to grab it, it's gone."

"Yeah, and it stinks," Bodie said.

"That's just mean," Kellen said.

"What about my parents?" I asked.

"Your mother was one of the lucky ones," Kellen said. "Regenesis never identified her."

"And my father?"

Kellen ran his hand through his greasy hair and stared at the bar.

"The Regenesis Watch is ruthless," he said. "They forced people to give them information about us. I don't blame anyone for talking. I don't know what I'd do myself in that situation. But somebody gave them your father's name and pffft! Gone."

"But not my mother?"

Kellen sighed and said, "Your parents weren't married. They didn't want their union to be made official in a world controlled by Regenesis, so they planned to be married after the church was thrown from power."

"And that didn't happen," I said.

"No, it didn't," Kellen said softly.

Issa added, "Because they weren't married, Regenesis didn't make the connection. Whoever gave them your father's name, kept hers secret."

Kellen rested his head back down onto the bar, as if sitting upright was too much effort.

"Meet your mother, Donovan," Issa said. "It might help you to understand."

"Or make me hate her even more."

"You know what I think?" Bodie said.

"I don't care what you think," I snapped.

"Tell us, Bodie," Issa said.

Guys like Bodie always think people care what they have to say, so he kept talking.

"I don't know if your parents were right or wrong, but they probably thought it was right at the time."

"Doesn't matter," I said.

"Or maybe it does. You should hear her side. You may not like what she has to say, but at least you'll know what they were thinking back then."

"Stop talking," I said to him, then looked to Issa. "Can somebody take this Chrysalis thing out of my leg?"

"Yes," she said.

"Good. Do it. Then you won't need me anymore."

"But we do need you. Your being here is like a miracle. It's inspirational. You've seen how people react when they see you. You could help rally the league."

My emotions were all over the map. I was angry, sure. But I was also sad. As screwed up as this place was, my mother was here. I'd spent years wondering who my parents were. Never thought they'd turn out to be rebel fighters from another galaxy. Didn't see that one coming. So I was curious too. And though I hate to admit it, I was a little scared.

Maybe Bodie was right. Maybe I needed to know. But I was not about to be the face of a revolution.

Kellen sat up again, looking as if it took every ounce of strength to do it.

"So what's the verdict, kid?" he asked.

I jabbed my finger at the drunk who dumped me on Earth so long ago and said, "I'll meet her, then I want this chip out of me. After that, I want a ride home."

"Got it," Kellen said.

He stood up, leaned over the bar, and puked.

CHAPTER 13

Issa led Bodie and me through the filthy back alleys of Essen-Tet. We made sure to keep an eye out for any Regenesis Watch goons who might be wandering around, looking for trouble.

Or looking for me, which was the same thing.

The sun was going down, and I expected the city to come alive with lights. It didn't. There were no street lamps and not a whole lot of lights in windows. Those that had light didn't seem like they were bright enough to even read by. The city had a dull, depressing glow.

Except, that is, for the few "Prestige Manors" we passed. Those were lit up and alive like it was Christmas. It was a constant reminder to those who didn't live in one that if they obeyed and were good little members of the church, Regenesis might reward them. If it were me, seeing those places would just piss me off that I didn't live there.

"This is it," Issa declared as she led us into a crummy, three-story apartment building.

We passed an elevator that was out of order and stopped at a door marked: #104.

My palms were sweating.

"Bodie and I will wait out here," Issa said.

"Whoa, you're not coming with me?" I asked.

"This isn't about us," she replied.

As much as Bodie wasn't the kind of guy I'd trust to have my back, he was better than nothing. I didn't want to do this alone.

"Maybe I should go with him," he said to Issa.

"No," she said with finality. "Donovan will be fine."

I don't know why she was so certain about that because I sure wasn't.

She gave the door a quick knock, then opened it and motioned for me to go inside.

"This is a good thing, Donovan," she said, trying to sound reassuring.

"Yeah, we'll see," I said, and stepped inside.

I found myself in a small, dingy apartment that was lit by a few weak table lamps that gave the room an eerie, shadowy feel. Sitting on a well-worn couch in the center of the small room was a woman with graying hair to her shoulders. She wore a dark green dress and sat with her hands folded in her lap. She was waiting for us. For me.

She smiled and said, "Hello Donovan. Welcome home."

She seemed like a sweet old lady, but I felt absolutely nothing.

"I'm here to see my mother," I said, though my mouth was so dry I wasn't sure if my words sounded like words.

"I know," the woman said. "I'd like to hear your story. I know where it began, and what brought you back, but I'd love to hear about the in-between."

"The in-between?" I asked.

"What was your life like on Earth?"

Her casual question flicked a switch for me. Suddenly all the tension about meeting her disappeared and was replaced by something else. Call it rage. Yeah, rage is a good word. It had been building up for a very long time.

"That's what you think of my life? The in-between? Like it was a blip of time that didn't matter?"

"Not at all," the woman said, but she sounded unsure as if it that was *exactly* what she thought.

"Don't pretend like you care," I spat at her. "What difference does it make what my life was like? All that matters to you is that I'm back with that computer chip you stuck in me. So do me a favor. Take it back and leave me alone. Nice to meet you."

I turned for the door.

"Please don't go," the woman called out. "You have to understand what your life would have been like if you stayed."

I wanted to scream, that's how angry I was.

"Really? You think it was better to abandon me? I bounced around between foster homes and orphanages and treated like a

pain wherever I went. Nobody cared about me any more than the fee they got from the government said they had to. That was the in-between you're asking about. So what's worse? Living a lousy life with people who care about you? Or growing up alone?"

I never let anybody see me like that. Never. The emotions I'd been pushing back on my whole life suddenly kicked in. Now that I knew it could have been different, I was pissed. The women let me rant. The only way I knew she was even listening was that tears welled up in her eyes. I didn't care.

"Whatever, I'm outta here," I said and strode for the door.

"Donovan!" another woman called out.

I froze. Somebody else was in the room, standing in the shadows. She was much younger than the lady on the couch. Her hair was dark and cut short, with streaks of gray. She wore light pants and a short black jacket. When she stepped forward into the light, I knew.

"My name is Tessa," she said, with confidence.

I must have heard that voice when I was a baby. She probably told me bedtime stories or sang rhymes or told me warm stories about how she was going to get rid of me by shooting me into outer space. Maybe they were imagined memories, but the sound of her voice made my heart ache. I didn't know if I should scream at her for sentencing me to a horrible life or hug her for saving me from an even worse one. I spoke slowly so I wouldn't reveal the battle of raging emotions.

She stood with her hands in her pockets and both feet planted firmly on the floor. Though it was a tense situation, she looked confident, as if she didn't take grief from anybody.

In other words, she was like me.

"Can we sit and talk?" she asked tentatively. "Please."

I wasn't so sure I wanted to. I looked back to the room to see we were now alone. I hadn't noticed that the older lady had taken off. Tessa sat down on one end of the couch. I sat awkwardly on the other.

"Who was that lady?" I asked.

"A friend. She was here to support me in case…"

She didn't finish the sentence.

"In case what? In case I was a lunatic?"

"No! Well…yes."

We both chuckled at that. Maybe we had the same twisted sense of humor.

"It was silly," she said. "I told her there was no way my son would hurt me."

"Your son," I said. "You mean the guy you sent to the other side of the universe."

I saw tears in her eyes. Maybe she wasn't such a hard case after all.

"I could tell you it was the hardest thing I'd ever done; that I re-live the moment I strapped you into that Jump Ship every day. I could tell you about the Tyrian League and how we failed and sending out the Chrysalis chips was our last, desperate shot at ridding this world of Regenesis. I could tell you how much I've missed you and hate that I couldn't watch you grow. All that is true but hearing it won't change anything. The one thing you have to know is the reason we did it, the only reason that truly mattered was that we wanted to save you. I've heard about your life on Earth and my heart breaks over the trouble you've had. But nothing you've been through could be worse than what would have happened to you here."

"Except that I'd be with parents who cared about me," I said. "Or did they?"

She winced but didn't back down.

"When the revolt failed, things went from bad to unbearable. The Regenesis Watch hunted down anyone they thought was a conspirator. People disappeared. Babies were separated from parents. Older children were forced to join the Regenesis Watch. Some of them are standing guard over the Regenesis Compound right now."

"But you're still here," I said.

She bit her lower lip and said, "I am. Your father wasn't as lucky."

"Why didn't the parents go with the babies?"

"There was only one Jump Ship. And we feared it would be easier for Regenesis to track down the scions if we were together. You were babies. You could disappear into new lives. That was the idea, anyway. I still believe it was the right choice. I hope you can find it in your heart to forgive us. But I don't think you can unless you truly believe we did it because we loved you. We still love you."

"You don't even know me."

"Let's change that," she said with conviction. She sat up straight and held her hand out to shake. "Hello, Donovan," she said formally. "My name is Tessa T-Shay. I'm your mother."

I looked at her hand for a long second but couldn't bring myself to take it.

"No," I said. "My life has nothing to do with what's happening here."

"It will take time to adjust," she said.

"There's no reason to adjust," I said, and stood up. "As soon as they get this chip out of me, I'm going back to Earth."

"But—"

"I don't belong here."

She took a deep breath and said, "But you do. You just didn't know it."

"I know more than I want to know," I said and started for the door.

"You look like him, you know," she said. "Like your father. His name is Donovan."

That hit me in the gut. I wasn't expecting that. It would be great to say I ran back and gave her a hug, but that wasn't about to happen. I was hurting. She was too. But it wasn't my problem.

"I hope he's alive, and you find him," were my final words.

I fought hard not to look back and left the apartment. Issa and Bodie were waiting for me outside and perked up when they saw me.

"How'd it go?" Bodie asked.

"I did what you asked," I said to Issa. "I met her. I heard her side. Nothing changes. I want this chip out of me, and I want to be on the next Jump Ship out of here." I looked to Bodie and added, "That good with you?"

"Absolutely," he replied with enthusiasm.

"All right then," Issa said with resignation. "I won't argue anymore. Let's end this."

~ 129 ~

CHAPTER 14

I don't remember the last time I'd slept. This had to be the longest day in history, and it happened on two different planets.

As much as I wanted to end the nightmare as soon as possible, I was dead tired. Bodie was too. I could tell because he wasn't talking or trying to run the show. He just followed along like a zombie. We both needed rest.

Issa brought us to an apartment that looked like the one where I'd met my mother, but with less furniture. There were a couple of beds and chairs and that was about it.

"Homey," I said sarcastically.

"Useful," Issa said. "It's a safe place kept by the Tyrian League. I crash here when I'm home. So do other Tyros."

"Tyros?" Bodie asked.

"Children of the original leaders of the Tyrian League," Issa answered. "I guess you could call us the next generation of rebels."

"Can Tyros cook?" Bodie asked. "I'm freaking starving."

Rude, but I didn't call him out because I was hungry too.

Issa went to a closet to find a large cardboard box that was waiting for us.

"They take care of us," she said. "And since I'm here with a scion, I'm guessing this'll be pretty good."

She dropped the box on the plain kitchen table and opened it to reveal it was loaded with all kinds of goodies. There was bread and cheese and lots of fruit. There were jars filled with fresh vegetables that I wouldn't have touched on Earth, but when you're starving, anything tastes good. There were even a couple of cannisters filled with a cold, sweet, fruit juice. I could have downed eight of them.

Issa stood looking at the treasure but didn't dig in.

"What's the matter?" I asked.

"People gave up their food for us," she said. "For you. It may not look like much, but this could feed a family for a couple of weeks."

I should have felt guilty, but I was too hungry to be noble.

"They did it because they wanted to," Bodie said.

"Yeah they did," Issa replied. "Let's not waste it."

We sat down at the table and went for it. It had to keep myself from gorging. We ate in silence for a while, until Bodie felt better. I could tell because he started talking again.

"What's your deal?" he asked Issa. "We don't know anything about you except you're supposedly Donovan's guardian angel. And you're some kind of ninja."

Issa tensed up. I don't think that was a question she was used to answering.

"What?" Bodie asked, clueless. "Did I say something wrong?"

"It's okay," Issa said, but her mood turned dark. "I don't talk about it much. Or at all."

"Then ignore him," I said.

"No, I should tell you," she said. "I want to tell you."

Bodie gave me a smug look. Issa took a deep breath, as if bracing herself.

"When you're a little kid," she began. "Whatever life you have, good or bad, it's all you know so you don't question it. When I was young, I mean toddler young, I had no clue that our life was so wrong. There was Mom and Dad and my new baby sister. I remember being happy. I didn't know that my parents struggled to feed us. It was all fine, until it wasn't.

One day, without any warning, my baby sister was gone. My parents said she was visiting friends, but they were upset all the time. And she didn't come home. They kept telling me that everything was okay, and I believed them. Until the day they didn't come home either."

Issa's voice was quivering. These were tough memories.

"Imagine that. A two-year old all alone. And confused. And scared. I spent the night in bed with the covers over my head. I kept listening for sounds, hoping the door would open and they'd come rushing in to tell me everything was okay. I stayed in bed for three days. I only got out to scrounge food in the kitchen or go to the bathroom. After a while I began to fear every little sound. What if somebody came in and it wasn't my parents? Every time I heard footsteps outside our apartment I'd hide under the bed. Then the food ran out. I needed help, so I got dressed in about four layers of clothes like somehow that would protect me, and left."

She took another deep breath. Re-visiting these memories was tough.

"I went to a few neighbor's apartments on our floor, but when they opened their doors and saw me, they got this expression of absolute horror, like I was diseased. They slammed the door in my face. Every last one of them. Can you imagine doing that to a lost little girl? The only thing I could think to do was go to the place where Mom brought me to play during the day when they worked. It was a happy place. So I left our building to try and find it. I'd never been outside alone. It was like I was seeing the city for the first time. Everything was so big. And loud. People didn't give me a second look. I walked. Wandered, really. I don't know for how long. I didn't panic until the moment I realized that if I didn't find the play place, I wouldn't know how to get back home. That was the worst moment."

Tears ran down her cheeks. I almost told her to stop, but I wanted to hear the rest.

"Then I saw it," she said with a smile. "Probably because the front door was bright blue. I ran across the street, nearly getting hit by an aerobike, and ran inside. I can't tell you how happy I was to see the kids I played with every day, and the lady. Her name was "C-Lowe" or something like that. At first she looked as surprised to see me as the neighbors who slammed their doors. But she let me run into her arms and gave me a long, warm hug. I remember crying while telling her what happened. She kept saying "Poor baby" while stroking my hair. I couldn't have felt safer. But when I asked her where my parents were, she cried. I wasn't used to seeing grown-ups cry."

"Did you find out what happened to them?" I asked.

"No," Issa said, wiping her tears.

"Oh, Jeez," Bodie said.

"C-Lowe brought me to a group that took care of kids in the same situation. Turned out my story wasn't unique. People went missing all the time, leaving their kids behind. From then on, I was shuffled between homes to live with people who were nice enough but didn't keep me around for very long."

I knew the feeling but didn't say so. This was Issa's story.

"Eventually I learned the truth. We were all the kids of people who in some way had crossed Regenesis. The Tyrian League moved us around for fear the Watchers would take us to get revenge on our parents."

"Do you think your parents are still alive?" I asked.

"Maybe. I don't know. They could have been sent to work for a Regenesis company on the other side of Tyria. Or on another planet. Or they could be dead."

"How did you meet Kellen?" Bodie asked.

"After the failed rebellion, the Tyrian League stayed together, preparing for the day they'd get another chance. Part of that was working with the kids of lost parents. The Tyros. We were brought up on stories of hope and rebellion. I met Kellen when I was ten. He became a mentor, eventually teaching me to fly. Others taught me how to fight. But it was Kellen who made me who I am. And I kept him from drinking himself to death."

"Why did he pick you?" I asked.

"He felt a responsibility, but I didn't know that until a few years ago when I asked him about my parents. I wanted to know why Regenesis took them. He didn't want to tell me."

Issa wiped more tears and sat up straight.

"I kept at him until he finally told me. My parents were part of the original twelve. The ones who gave up their babies."

"Seriously?" I said with surprise. "Wait, that means your baby sister was a—"

"A scion. Yes. Saree-One. They shot a Chrysalis into her leg and sent her on her way."

I looked to Bodie. He looked as stunned as I felt.

"For that, Regenesis took my parents and left me alone. Some parents got lucky, like your mother. Most weren't. You could easily have ended up like me, Donovan. I know you had it rough on Earth, but it could have been worse. I'm proof of that. You want to know what my deal is? I'm going to find out what happened to my parents and I'm going to stop Regenesis from hurting anyone else."

Bodie was stunned speechless, for a change.

"Well this really sucks," I said.

"Why is that?" Issa asked.

"Now I can't complain about my own life anymore. Thanks a LOT!"

She gave me a confused look as if she wasn't sure if I was being serious or not. It took a second, but she finally let out a smile.

"You're kind of a jerk, you know that?" she said.

"I've been told."

It was good to see Issa smile after that horrible trip through bad-memory-land. She was tough. Tougher than me. Hearing her story made me see her differently. It wasn't that I felt sorry for her. It was more about respect. She was even more of a badass than I thought.

"You two should sleep," Issa said, back to business. "I'll clean up. First thing in the morning we'll see Doctor Tenzig."

"Who's that?" I asked.

"The guy who shot the Chrysalis into your leg. And the guy who's going to take it out."

CHAPTER 15

THE REGENESIS CORE

The six members of the Regenesis Ministry sat at a long conference table, having been summoned from their homes and their beds in the middle of the night. The room was on the ground floor of The Core and used solely for Ministry business.

None looked happy to be there. But when a summons came from Vail Kobain, you went no matter what you were doing or what the time of day.

The door slid open, and Kobain strode in, looking as fresh as if it were noon. Her black suit was razor sharp and her long red hair lay perfectly on her shoulders. Walking behind her was the short and round August C-Bonn, looking like the rumpled bed he just crawled out of.

The ministers jumped to their feet and bowed their heads with a collective, "Glory to the Regent."

Kobain walked purposefully to the head of the long table and motioned for everyone to sit.

"A loyal member of our flock spotted the scion, here in Essen-Tet," she announced. "As I feared."

Kobain nodded to August who spoke into his wrist communicator.

"We are ready," he said.

A large monitor behind Kobain came to life, showing a view of a dilapidated three-story stone building that was sandwiched between two others. It was building where Donovan had met his mother.

"He was seen entering this building," August said. "We've dispatched a team to abduct him."

On the monitor, two large hover-vehicles floated up to the building's entrance. As soon as they stopped, the doors flew open and a dozen brown-uniformed Watchers wearing black riot-helmets flooded out with stun weapons up and ready to fire. Without hesitation they charged into the building.

Kobain said, "I assembled the Ministry so that you may witness the scion's arrest and appreciate the importance I've placed on hunting down this individual."

"I don't understand," one minister said. "The Covian Solution is nearly ready to be deployed. You stated that the scion is no longer a threat. Why this show of force?"

Kobain focused her dark eyes on the man. It was the same minister who questioned Kobain when she ordered Magda T-Fair to kill her own child. The man sank into his seat, withering under her gaze.

"You were not in the Ministry fifteen years ago when those miscreants nearly crippled the Regenesis grid. If not for August here, the church as we know it today might not exist."

August stood up straight, filled with pride. He no longer cared about being pulled from his bed in the dead of night.

"So if you don't mind," Kobain went on. "I will take no chances when it comes to protecting Regenesis."

The other ministers looked down at the table. No one wanted to make eye contact with the Bishop.

"Forgive me Your Eminence," the minister said weakly. "You are quite wise to do so."

"Your approval means so much to me," Kobain said sarcastically.

"They're coming out!" August announced.

The Watchers appeared at the building's entrance, each pushing out someone they had rousted from their apartments. From their beds. The people looked dazed and frightened as they were shoved outside, all wearing the clothes they'd been sleeping in. Within minutes, several dozen people stood in the street outside the building, huddled together in fear. The Watchers man-handled them one at a time toward the camera that was recording the scene so that Kobain could see each person clearly.

Donovan was not among them. Nor were Issa or Bodie. Or Tessa.

August put a finger to his ear, listening to the communication coming from the street.

"You are certain that the entire building is clear?" he asked. He nodded in understanding, then looked to Kobain and said, "They've swept every apartment. This is everyone. The building is empty"

Kobain's jaw muscles clenched. It was the only sign of her anger.

"Finish it," she said through gritted teeth.

August lifted his communicator and said, "Complete the mission."

The hover trucks floated away from the entrance as two Watchers approached the building. Each had a long, heavy, rifle-sized weapon. They stood in the center of the street, took a knee, and aimed their weapons at the building.

"Commence," Kobain said.

"You have approval," August said into his radio.

The two Watchers fired their weapons, shooting invisible bolts of energy at the ground floor of the building. They continued firing, pummeling the walls as bits of stone and mortar spewed everywhere.

It was an eerie experience for the ministers because no audio was being transmitted. They could only imagine the violent sounds that were filling the streets. The people who had been pulled from their beds backed off in horror as they watched their home being destroyed. They were screaming and crying, but that sound couldn't be heard either. The relentless pounding from the powerful weapons dug deeper and deeper into the building until a third Watcher approached the shooters from behind and placed a hand on each of their shoulders. In response, the shooters stopped firing, stood up, and backed away.

Dust filled the air, but not enough to mask what then happened. The entire building collapsed onto itself. The upper two floors came crashing down into the shattered remains of the first floor. A huge plume of dust blew out and obliterated the view of the camera.

The screen went dark. The show was over.

Kobain turned to the ministers who looked white with shock. Their mouths hung open as they stared at the blank screen in astonishment.

"We need to relocate those residents," Kobain said to August. "See to it that they have a place to sleep."

August bowed to her and said, "It will be done, Your Eminence."

August hurried out, leaving Kobain alone with the Ministers.

"Questions?" Kobain asked.

"Forgive me," one woman said. "What was your thinking in destroying the building?"

"It is a warning," Kobain replied. "To anyone who considers harboring the scion."

"What if the scion was hiding somewhere in the building and the Watchers missed him?" another woman said.

"In that case," Kobain said with an uncharacteristic smile. "We have nothing more to be concerned about."

CHAPTER 16

odie and I sat in a crummy little apartment, just like the other crummy little apartments we'd been to, waiting to begin the chip-sucking procedure that would end this nightmare.

"I don't think he's a real doctor," I said, while looking around at the sad place.

"Who knows what's real anymore?" was Bodie's reply.

After a long night of dreamless sleep, and a breakfast of leftovers from the night before, Issa had brought us to this falling down building. But not before we saw a dramatic and disturbing demonstration.

Only a few minutes before, as we hurried through the city streets, the sky came alive with an image that was projected high above. It was like watching a movie in the clouds. A disaster movie.

"Is that the place--?" I asked.

"It is," Issa said, soberly.

It was the apartment building where I met my mother the night before. Two Watchers had serious-looking weapons that they fired at the ground floor until the whole place collapsed.

People who lived there were gathered outside and cried in anguish as they watched their home being destroyed. It only took about twenty seconds to go from building to rubble. Dust from the destruction created a white out, then the video repeated. And repeated again. It was on a loop for all the people of Essen-Tet to see.

For me to see.

"Was she killed?" I asked, shakily.

"No," Issa said, but she sounded about as shaky as I felt. "Your mother doesn't live there."

"Then why?" I asked.

"They must have found out you were there," Issa said. "Many people are loyal to the church. Someone must have reported seeing you."

"So Kobain wants to kill me?" I asked.

"Maybe. Or maybe she wants to scare you and anybody who might try to help you. That's why they're showing this to the whole city."

"Mission accomplished," I said. "I want this chip out of me more than ever."

We made it to the building where we now sat, but the whole way I kept looking over my shoulder in case some rat was watching us. Issa led us along a filthy hallway that smelled like fried donkey and up to a grimy door. Not exactly the sort of place you'd want somebody digging around inside your body.

"I was kind of hoping for a hospital," I said. "You know, with doctors and sterile equipment and no plague."

She ignored me and knocked twice. I heard someone scuffling inside followed by a scraping sound, as if something were being dragged across the floor.

"What?" came a raspy, man's voice from inside.

Issa positioned herself in front of the peephole so that whoever was inside could see her.

"He's here," she said.

There were more scraping sounds. Then multiple locks were opened. I tensed up. Issa reached for the knob and pushed the door open.

Nobody was there. That didn't seem to bother Issa as she boldly walked in. Bodie and I followed. I looked behind the door to see who had opened it, but nobody was there.

"Move," came a gruff voice.

I looked down to see that somebody *was* there.

It was a little person. A dwarf, I guess. He couldn't have been much more than three feet tall, which explained the scraping noise. He needed a step ladder to look out of the peep hole. I stepped out of the way so he could close the door.

The guy had long, black hair that was tied back. He wore dark pants and a black smock-shirt that went down below his knees. He looked pretty much like a full-sized person, except he wasn't.

"This is Donovan," Issa said to the man. "Donovan, this is Tenzig. He'll do the procedure."

"I'm Bodie," Bodie said.

Tenzig ignored him. He was focused on me.

He looked like a serious guy. It was a little weird that he was so small, but even if he were a handsome, six-foot-two guy who looked straight out of a Doctor TV show I'd still be nervous about him sticking a needle in me to fish out a computer chip that had been stuck there since I was a baby.

"Tenzig," I said. "That a first name or a last name?"

He looked me up and down (from his angle it was mostly up) and said, "Right. You were the annoying one."

"You knew me?" I asked.

"Not much to know about a baby," Tenzig said. "But I remember a lot of fussing and kicking. Donovan Six. I figured you'd be the last one to make it back here."

"Good to see you too," I said sarcastically.

I wasn't so sure I was going to like this Tenzig character.

"Tenzig collaborated with Misha to develop the Chrysalis," Issa said.

"Does he know what he's doing?" I asked.

Tenzig gave me a sideways look that meant he thought I was still annoying.

"Wait here," Tenzig said. "I'll show you what I know. Issa, come with me."

The guy turned and walked quickly toward a back room. Issa gave me a little smile and a shrug, then followed.

Once they were gone, Bodie said, "Well this is just odd."

We could either sit on a worn couch that was probably home to a flea colony, or a wooden chair that was missing one leg. We looked to each other, and both bolted for the chair.

Bodie got there first. I was stuck with the couch and sat down.

"I don't think he's a real doctor," I said, then jumped back to my feet and paced nervously. I was too amped to sit still.

Bodie watched me, looking as though he wanted to say something.

"What?" I blurted out.

"This place sucks."

"Gee, you think?"

"I mean the church and the rebels and the scions. It's crazy."

"Orphans," I said quickly. "Don't make it sound like it's something special. I was abandoned. Let's not forget that."

"Yeah but which is worse? Abandoned on Earth, or growing up here?"

"You have no idea what it was like for me growing up," I said with disdain. "My life isn't like yours."

"You don't know what my life is like."

"You can't be serious," I said with a laugh.

"We've all got stuff to deal with," Bodie said with a shrug.

"Yeah, well I'll take your stuff any day."

What was he thinking? Did he want me to feel sorry for him? The rich kid who had everything handed to him? No chance.

He added, "I'm just saying that whatever our deal is at home, it's nothing compared to here. Regenesis just destroyed an entire building looking for you. I mean, seriously? This is messed up."

"Not my problem."

"But maybe you can help these people."

I stopped pacing and faced him.

"One, mind your own business. Two, I don't know these people and I don't owe them a thing. Three, if anything I should be pissed at them for messing up my life. And four, mind your own business."

"Ready!" Issa announced.

I wanted to run out of there, but I also wanted this to be over. So, I sucked it up and went into the next room. I expected to find another crummy bedroom. What I saw instead was both incredible and a little bit scary. The room was definitely crummy. It was mostly empty, except for a ratty bed and a table next to it that was covered with a white cloth. What mattered were the walls. Every last inch of space was covered with complex mathematical equations. It was all written in black charcoal, with spots that had been erased and written over many times.

Tenzig was either a genius, or a mad genius.

"Misha K-Soo and I were partners," Tenzig said. "I may be brilliant but compared to her I'm an imbecile."

A brilliant imbecile. Great. And he was about to dig into my body. He walked around the room, gazing at the slew of numbers and symbols like they were his beloved children.

"I've tried to duplicate the Chrysalis here, to re-create it. But I'm not Misha. I have her notes, but it's like working with a recipe that doesn't show all the ingredients. She was very careful not to have a complete record of it in case Regenesis got hold of it. Bottom line is it's good that you're back."

"Whatever. Can you get it out of me?"

"I put it there, I can get it out," he said with absolute confidence.

"Then do it," I said.

"Lie down," Tenzig commanded.

I took a look at the bed that had a stained mattress and a ratty blanket.

"There?" I exclaimed. "Shouldn't we be in a hospital or something?"

"Too risky," Issa said. "Secrecy is important."

"So is infection," I said. "I don't want alien germs getting into me."

Tenzig went to a table and pulled off the white cloth to reveal a modern silver box that looked totally out of place in this grim room. He flipped open a latch and I saw that instead of a right hand, Tenzig had a two-pronged silver hook.

"What happened to your hand?" I asked.

"I don't know," he replied. "You'd have to ask the Watcher who cut it off."

"No. I mean how come…wait, a Watcher cut it off?"

"Gross!" Bodie exclaimed.

Issa shot him a "shut up" look.

"I wouldn't give them any useful information about the Tyrian League, so they made an example of me. No matter. I'm left-handed."

He held up his left hand and wiggled his fingers.

I truly wanted to be back on Earth, or anywhere but there.

Tenzig opened the silver case and took out a bottle filled with blue liquid; a white ping-pong paddle looking thing, another bottle filled with clear liquid, and a silver syringe that had a huge hypodermic needle attached. At least he was using tools that seemed clean and professional. Then again, the needle looked like something you'd use on a cow.

"I'll first do an ultrasonic scan to locate the chip," Tenzig explained. "Then I'll numb the area with anesthetic. I'll insert the needle and extract the chip. Done."

"Fine, do it," I said with finality.

"There's a part of this you won't like," Tenzig said.

"I don't like *any* of it!"

He pulled the filthy blanket off the bed to reveal leather straps tied to the metal headboard and base board.

My stomach fell.

"No way!"

"It's a precaution," he said. "The Chrysalis has been part of your system for most of your life. There could be involuntary physical reactions when I remove it."

"You mean I might punch myself?"

"Or worse. It's not likely, but this is unexplored territory. You're the first scion to return."

I glanced at Issa. She looked pained. Probably not as pained as me but pained just the same. Bodie just stood there, wide eyed. He didn't know what to say, for a change.

"I just want this out of me," I said.

"Then please," Tenzig said. "Let's do it safely."

The idea of being cut in to, while being strapped to a filthy bed was like something out of a horror movie. Then again, having a computer chip from an alien world living inside me wasn't much better. So I laid down.

"Wait," Tenzig said. "The chip is in your right thigh."

It took me a second to realize what he meant.

"Oh," I said. "Right."

I had to take my pants off. I threw a sheepish look to Issa, who rolled her eyes.

"Really?" she said. "You're being modest?"

I took that as a challenge, stood up and dropped my pants. At least my shirt was long enough to cover my parts.

The bed was even less comfortable than it looked. A couple of sharp mattress springs stuck out. If I started thrashing around, I'd lose blood. Tenzig and Issa fixed the leather straps around my wrists and ankles. For somebody who needs to be in control, this was the worst feeling in the world. Any world.

Issa put a calming hand on my shoulder.

"Keep looking at me," she said gently. "I'm your guardian angel, remember?"

That helped. I liked Issa. And she was pretty cute, let's not forget that. But at that moment, her cuteness wasn't as important as her being somebody who I believe cared about me. I didn't run across many people like that.

"You wait outside," Tenzig said to Bodie.

Bodie took a step back.

"No," I said quickly. "I want witnesses."

Bodie looked back and forth between Tenzig and me, not sure of what to do. He then straightened up and said, "I'm staying."

In that moment I almost liked Bodie. Almost.

"Fine. Let's begin," Tenzig said.

Tenzig dumped some liquid onto a clean cloth and swabbed my right thigh. He then took the paddle and waved it slowly over the spot. It beeped.

"There it is," he announced. "Right where I put it. Though you were a might smaller back then."

He touched the paddle down and I felt a slight tickle. When he lifted it, there was a glowing red dot on my leg.

"X marks the spot," Bodie said.

He looked around, expecting people to chuckle at his clever comment.

Nobody did.

Tenzig swabbed some of the blue liquid on my leg. The area went numb instantly.

"The numbness won't last long," he assured me. "Just long enough for me to extract the Chrysalis."

He picked up the needle and syringe. My stomach twisted. He took the cap off the needle and my stomach twisted further. The needle had to be four inches long. And it was thick.

"I promise you won't feel a thing," Tenzig said.

"Just do it!" I exclaimed.

I closed my eyes.

Issa put her hand on my forehead.

I opened my eyes, and she gave me a sweet smile.

"Try to relax," Tenzig said, soothingly. "Don't flex your muscles."

Easier said than done.

I made two fists and focused on Issa, waiting to get stabbed.

"It's almost over," Issa said, with more than a touch of sadness. "After this we'll take you home and you can forget all about us, if that's what you want."

"I'm in," Tenzig said.

I hadn't felt a thing. Whatever that numb-stuff was, it was great.

"You okay?" Issa asked.

"Yeah," I said, almost laughing. "I don't feel a--"

Suddenly, the world turned upside down. It was as though the room had disappeared, and I'd been transported to another place. A horrifying place. There were flashing lights. Words floated past that I couldn't read. I heard the voice of a woman, but I couldn't make out what she was saying. Numbers blew by me forming strange equations. There were tones and clicks and chimes. Everything jumbled together like a horrifying nightmare.

A nightmare.

Like the ones I'd been having my whole life. But this was worse than anything I'd ever had because I wasn't asleep.
This was real.

CHAPTER 17

I had this wild dream many times before, though this one was far more intense and way more crazy. I now understood why, sort of. It was the chip. The Chrysalis. The alien device that was planted in my leg was the cause of my recurring nightmare. I wasn't crazy after all. I wish I could say it was a relief, but given the truth, maybe being crazy would be better.

I think I screamed. It's hard to say because there was so much chaotic noise happening that I wouldn't have heard it. I don't know how long it went on. It could have been seconds or days. The first sense of reality I had was a lone voice that cut through the din.

"It's over," Issa whispered. "Come back, Donovan."

I hung on to those words like a lifeline as I tried to pull myself out of the frenzy.

"Issa?" I said with a gasp.

"I'm right here," she replied reassuringly. "Take some deep breaths."

I did, the images dissolved, and the reality of the apartment returned. The first thing I saw was Issa standing over me, looking like an angel. A sad angel. It felt like there was a heavy weight on my chest. It took a second for me to understand what it was.

Bodie.

He was sitting on me and holding my right hand down onto the bed. His eyes were wide with panic.

"What're you doing?" I managed to whisper.

"I...I...you were flopping around," Bodie exclaimed. "You yanked your hand so hard you broke the strap."

I looked to see that my right hand was free, and Bodie was holding it down.

"I thought you were gonna hurt yourself," he said, his voice quivering.

"So you sat on me?" I asked, incredulous.

Bodie nodded quickly and said, "It's all I could think of."

My wrists hurt. I must have really been struggling against the straps.

"I'm okay now," I said to Bodie. "You can get off."

"Oh, right," he said, embarrassed that he was straddling me. He quickly jumped off.

"Dude," he said. "That was intense. You screamed a couple of times."

"I'm sorry," Issa said. "We didn't know that would happen."

"Un-tie me," I said.

They freed me from the other straps, and I rubbed my wrists to get feeling back.

"What happened?" Bodie asked.

I was still dizzy, so it took a while for me to find the words.

"Whatever it was," I said. "It's happened before."

"What!" Issa exclaimed.

"I've had this recurring nightmare for as long as I can remember. It's a jumble of images, numbers, and lights. But this was different. This was like going out of my mind."

"Wait," Bodie said. "You've had nightmares about seeing numbers and symbols—?"

Before I could answer the door opened and Tenzig walked in, followed by a new visitor. Kellen. Was he there the whole time? Didn't matter. Neither looked happy. Kellen gave me a dark look I didn't like.

"This wasn't supposed to happen," he said to himself, out loud.

Any leftover dizziness was wiped away by a surge of adrenaline.

"What wasn't supposed to happen?" I demanded.

Kellen leaned against the door frame, looking sick, and I don't think it was about being drunk.

"What's wrong, Kellen?" Issa asked.

"The Chrysalis," he said. "It's been too long."

"What happened to it?" Issa asked with a touch of panic.

Tenzig was focused on a device he held that looked like an iPad.

"The chip is dead," he announced soberly. "It's useless."

"How can it be dead?" Issa exclaimed. "Was it erased?"

"Not erased," Tenzig said gravely. "Dumped."

"What does that mean?" I demanded.

Tenzig put down the pad and approached me. He was holding four white circular pads the size of quarters.

"Whoa," I exclaimed and threw my hand up. "I'm done."

"You're going to have to trust me, Donovan," Tenzig said.

"You are not going back inside my leg," I said and leaned away.

"I'm not. I need to put these receptors on your head. It's nothing to be alarmed about. There will be no pain, I assure you."

"Forget it," I said and jumped up.

My head spun for a second, but it passed.

"Tell me what you experienced," Tenzig said.

"I saw numbers, and words, and heard voices, everywhere. I'd been having that same nightmare my whole life."

Tenzig and Kellen exchanged grave looks. This was news they hadn't expected. Bodie didn't look any better. He stared at his shoes, looking like he might puke or something. I don't know why he was so bothered by what happened. I was the one who was out of my mind.

"They weren't nightmares, were they?" I asked. "It was the Chrysalis."

"Yes. These sensors will help me to stop you from ever having that nightmare again."

That sounded good to me.

"It won't hurt?" I asked.

"No," he said, and I believed him. What other choice did I have?

I sat back down on the bed. The sensors were sticky on one side. He stuck two to my forehead and the other two to the back of my neck.

"Sit back," Tenzig said. "This could make you a little dizzy.

I tried to think happy thoughts.

"Let me know when you're going to start," I said.

"I've already started."

No sooner did he say that, then I felt like I was falling. I knew I wasn't actually falling, but my heart thumped anyway. It was like I was floating. The weird thing was that I was totally awake and aware.

"Can you hear me Donovan Six?" Tenzig asked.

"Just Donovan," I said.

"I'll take that as a yes."

Other than the weird floaty feeling, everything was cool. I didn't get those strange hallucinations; there were no odd sounds; and I could talk. I was beginning to think that I was worried for nothing.

That's when it began.

The numbers reappeared. But it wasn't as crazy as when he pulled the Chrysalis out. This was more like in my dream. The numbers, letters, and symbols were mostly white, which made them stand out in the dark room. It was as if the equations floated off the walls and were drifted around the room. It was my nightmare, only I wasn't asleep.

"I'm seeing the numbers!" I exclaimed.

"So am I," Tenzig said with glee. "Hello Misha."

"You see them all around the room?" I asked.

"No," Tenzig said. "On the tech pad. I'm in your head."

Kellen hurried over to him and looked at the screen.

"Damn," he said, stunned. "Is that it?"

"It is," Tenzig said, barely able to control his excitement. "Look how well ordered the code is. This is only a fraction of it. Look at the dark data. Those are packets, like files. We're looking at a three-dimensional view of Misha's Chrysalis. It's beautiful."

"Hi darlin'," Kellen said.

"Why am I seeing this?" I asked.

"The Chrysalis is quite remarkable," Tenzig said. "It's like a living being that bonded with your nervous system."

"The chip dumped this into my brain?" I asked nervously.

"That's why the physical chip is dead," Tenzig said. "The program uploaded itself into you."

Bodie and Issa hurried to look at the tech pad over Tenzig's shoulder.

"Oh man," Bodie said with a gasp. "This is the Chrysalis thing?"

Issa laughed giddily. Everybody thought this was cool, except for me.

"Stop playing," I exclaimed. "Take it out of me!"

"Right," Tenzig said.

He input something on the pad and frowned. He did it again. His frown deepened.

"What's the matter?" Kellen asked.

"Stand up Donovan," Tenzig commanded. "Slowly. We don't want you passing out."

He was suddenly all business. The joy of seeing the Chrysalis come to life was gone.

I stood up carefully and felt a little loopy, but it passed.

"What are you seeing?" I asked.

"I believe I'm seeing exactly what you are," Tenzig replied. "Do you see the string of numerals to your left? They're bolder than the digits around it and dark green."

"Yeah. Yeah I do."

"Good, go to it."

I walked toward it, slowly. There were thousands of numbers and strings of data floating all around me. I put my hand out, thinking I would pass right through it. Instead, when I touched a number, an entire line of data drifted away like a helium balloon, then gently floated back into position. Just like in my dreams.

"You saw that, right?" I asked.

"I did," Tenzig replied. "It means you can interact with the data."

"But I'm not really touching anything," I said.

"Not physically," Tenzig explained. "But the Chrysalis senses your intent."

"Like a VR game," Bodie offered.

Nobody I knew had ever played with a VR game, but Bodie was rich so, of course, he had.

"Do you see the words MISHA K-SOO?" Tenzig asked.

I looked around and sure enough saw MISHA K-SOO floating to my left.

"I do," I said.

"Go to it," Tenzig ordered.

I walked slowly through the sea of code until I stood in front of the name of the woman who had created this craziness. It hovered in front of me at eye level.

"Now what?" I asked.

"That's a link to a sub-string of code," Tenzig said. "Open it."

"How?"

"Touch it. And pray that I'm right."

I didn't like that ominous warning. What was going to happen? Would I pass out again? Would my head explode?"

"Do it, Six," Kellen barked.

I held my breath, reached up, and touched the word with my finger.

All the data went blurry. It quivered for a heartbeat, then went out of focus and disappeared.

"Uh…" I said dumbly.

A second later an entirely different array of data appeared. It was such a sudden barrage of images that it made me take a step backward.

Bodie ran to me and grabbed my shoulders.

"I got you," he said calmly.

"What just happened?" I asked.

"You opened the launch file," Tenzig exclaimed with excitement. "You have control."

Tenzig hit a few keys on his pad and the floating data disappeared. It jolted my brain, and I had trouble keeping my balance.

While making sure I didn't fall over, Bodie directed me back to the bed where I plunked down and closed my eyes.

"How do you feel, Donovan?" Tenzig asked.

"Like somebody spun me around three times and kicked me in the head. But I'll live."

"Good."

"Yeah, I think so too."

"C'mon, Tenzig," Kellen implored. "Did you get it?"

Tenzig waddled to a table, grabbed a bottle of green liquid and held it out toward Kellen.

"Join me?" he asked.

He splashed some of the green drink into a dirty glass.

"You have no idea how tough it is to say this, but no," Kellen said. "Unless it's a celebration drink."

"It isn't," Tenzig said, and downed the liquor in one gulp.

"What's the problem?" I asked. "I thought it was good that I had control."

"It is," Tenzig said. "Very good. It means there's still hope."

"So did you get it out of me?" I exclaimed.

"I'm sorry, Donovan," Tenzig said. "No."

"Why not?" Kellen asked through clenched teeth.

Tenzig poured themselves another drink.

"The good news is that Donovan was able to access the program and control it. Bad news is that I couldn't extract it."

"Why not?" I asked.

"Because you, Donovan Six, you have become the Chrysalis."

I wanted to cry. It was a feeling of total, crushing, hopelessness.

"But you said he can access it, and control it," Kellen said to Tenzig with a hint of desperation. "There must be something we can do."

Tenzig shot the second glass of liquor. "There is. It's why I wanted to see if Donovan had control. I believe we can still make this work."

"Uh…how?" I asked.

Tenzig gently removed the receptors from my head.

"Is the Tyrian League prepared to act?" Tenzig asked Kellen.

"Now more than ever," he replied. "News that a scion returned lit the fuse. Groups have been gathering from all over Sandoor. We're ready. But that's not the problem, is it?"

"No it isn't," Tenzig said. "It wouldn't matter how many of us stormed The Core. As long as the Regenesis power grid is functioning, we'd be turned back by the technology that powers their weapons."

"Yeah I know the plan," Kellen said. "But if we can't get the Chrysalis out of Donovan and into a drive, there's no way to input it into the grid."

"Unless Donovan becomes the drive," Tenzig said as he popped off the last receptor.

"What's that supposed to mean?" I asked.

"The Chrysalis has only one purpose, to infect and disable the Regenesis grid," Tenzig said. "It's why I can't download it. It will only migrate into the grid."

"And my brain," I said.

"So what do we do?" Issa asked.

"Get Donovan into The Core," Tenzig said with authority. "I'll sync him into the grid the same way I accessed the Chrysalis here. Donovan will activate the Chrysalis, and it will infect their network the same as if there was a direct, physical input."

"Whoa, wait," I exclaimed. "You want me to go into the center of Regenesis-world so you can jack me into their system like some kind of human thumb drive?"

Tenzig gave me a sheepish look and said, "I wouldn't exactly put it that way."

"How exactly would you put it?"

"Well, I guess, all right maybe that is how I'd put it."

"Forget it!" I exclaimed. "I did what you asked and now I'm done. Take me home."

I jumped up. Big mistake. The room swam, my head spun, and the lights went out.

CHAPTER 18
FACTORY B

The assembly-line workers on the factory floor tried not to look up to the catwalk that ran above their stations. Being distracted from their work was not tolerated and they would surely be punished for doing so. But the temptation to look was hard to resist because they had visitors.

Walking above them was Vail Kobain, the Bishop of Regenesis. Her bright blue scarf and flaming red hair stood out boldly against the drab gray of the factory. Seeing her in this dreary factory was like seeing an angel float through a dark attic.

Walking close behind Kobain was August C-Bonn, her Chief Counselor. The rotund little man in the perfectly tailored suit held a tech pad that he continually referred to.

"We've completed twelve Covian Cubes," he said with pride.

He looked to Kobain for a reaction, maybe even a little praise. He got nothing.

On the factory floor, a gray-haired man stopped working and fixed his gaze on Kobain. He didn't seem to mind that he'd be accused of slacking off. He watched the woman as she passed by from above, like an ominous shadow.

His eyes were filled with tears.

August said, "At this pace of production, we'll be turning out five complete units a day. Each will be earmarked for a different province of Tyria, starting here in Essen-Tet then on to the Outer Banks of the Sandoor Federation."

Kobain stopped to gaze over the busy factory.

"Is this not to your satisfaction, Your Eminence?" August asked with concern.

Kobain said, "You have described the execution of a plan that has been well conceived and implemented. I expected nothing less, therefore I see no reason to offer praise."

"Oh," August said, disappointed. "I see your point, I suppose."

The gray-haired man on the floor was trembling. He reached beneath his workstation to a wooden box filled with tools and took one that was wrapped in an oil-stained red cloth. Clutching the tool, he left the station and walked toward the stairs that led up to the catwalk.

Those around him saw what he was doing and whispered warnings.

"What are you doing?"

"Get back to your station."

"Don't!"

He ignored them and continued walking, zombie like, with his eyes locked on Kobain.

August was also looking to the Bishop, but with concern.

"Is something on your mind, Your Eminence?" he asked. "You seem troubled."

"Why has the scion not been located?" she asked coldly.

That was the last question August wanted to answer because he didn't have one. He had hoped that good news about the completion of several Covian Cubes would make the Bishop forget about the Earth-boy named Donovan.

"I assure you," August said, while wiping nervous sweat from the back of his neck. "He will be found."

"That does not answer my question," Kobain said through clenched teeth.

"Right, it...it does not," August said, stumbling over his words. "From what I've been told, the scanner isn't helping. On Earth it detected Tyrian genetics, which is how we finally found him. But on Tyria, well, we all have Tyrian genetics so...."

Kobain's disdainful glare made him want to shrink into his suit.

"You do realize his companion is from Earth," Kobain said. "Shouldn't the scanners sense Earth creature genetics?"

"Yes, of course they should! But we've never had to do that. The scanners aren't programmed to detect them. But I promise we're working feverishly to adapt. It's only a matter of time."

The gray-haired worker reached the bottom of the stairs and began the slow climb up.

The workers surrounding him didn't know what to do. Should they stop him? Should they call out a warning? Or perhaps they should let destiny take its course. Whatever their opinions were, nobody made a move.

Kobain's focus was squarely on August.

"You do understand the danger he presents," she said.

"Of course, I do," August said, wiping more sweat from his chin. "He will be neutralized before he has any chance to—"

"Magda T-Fair!" the gray-haired man called out.

That got Kobain's attention. She looked down to see the man standing on a landing that was halfway up the stairs to the catwalk. If she was alarmed, she didn't show it.

"Oh no," August whimpered.

"You took my wife," the man called out, his voice trembling with emotion. "Magda T-Fair. And my son Dorrian. I want them released."

The workers on the floor drifted away from their workstations, drawn to the drama that was playing out on the stairs above them.

"Come with us, sir!" August called out to the man. "We'll bring you to them."

"I don't want to go to them," the man growled. "I want them home!"

"Well, I'm sure we can—"

Kobain raised her hand, silencing August.

"I'm afraid that isn't possible," she said to the man. "They are in the service of the Regent now."

The man was so overcome with emotion, he was physically shaking.

"You mean you killed them!" he shouted.

He dropped the red cloth from the tool he was carrying to reveal a stun-pistol. It was a three-inch silver disk attached to a pistol grip.

Several of the workers gasped. Some shouted, "No!" but did nothing, letting the drama unfold.

August stepped forward, putting himself between Kobain and the assassin. It was a position he clearly did not want to be in but had no choice. He was quivering with fear, but he stood his ground, protecting the Bishop.

"Please sir, take a breath and consider what you are doing," August said, trying to sound calm and reasonable. He failed at both.

The man continued to climb higher.

Kobain didn't show a hint of concern.

"I know exactly what I'm doing," the man said through his rage. "It should have been done a long time ago."

"Stop right there!" bellowed a man from the floor.

A lone Regenesis Watcher came running from the far corner of the factory while pulling his own pistol from his hip holster.

Without hesitation, the gray-haired man spun and fired at the Watcher. An invisible bolt of energy flew across the factory and hit the charging Watcher, knocking him off his feet and sending him crashing into a wall.

August stared down at him in shock as their best hope of rescue had just been knocked unconscious.

The assassin re-aimed his pistol at Kobain and August.

"Please don't," August begged.

Kobain put a hand on August's shoulder, pulled him aside and took a bold step toward the assassin.

"You should pray that the Regent will forgive you," Kobain said.

The man shook his head as if he couldn't believe what he'd just heard.

"Forgive me?" he said with dismay. "I'll be remembered as a hero."

"You will be remembered," Kobain said. "But not as a hero."

The man steeled himself and raised his pistol

Another bolt of energy flew across the catwalk.

Not from his gun.

A flying drone had quietly settled in behind him and fired an energy bolt directly at his back. The man stiffened. He dropped his pistol and fell backward, tumbling down the stairs like a rag doll, hitting each stair with a sickening thud, finally coming to rest on the landing. If the drone-shot didn't kill him, the fall certainly did.

Those on the floor stared up at him in stunned wonder.

"Shall we continue?" Kobain said to August, unfazed by what had just occurred.

She turned and strode purposefully back along the catwalk. August looked at the dead man on the landing, sick to his stomach over how close he had come to his own end. He then looked out over the sea of workers who were staring up at him. He opened his mouth to say something, but no words came. He turned and hurried after the Bishop.

Several Regenesis Watchers had finally arrived, running in with their pistols drawn.

The workers returned to their stations as if nothing had happened. They turned their focus back to the job at hand.

They were assembling the Covian Cubes.

CHAPTER 19

I woke up in a bed. It wasn't the same disgusting flea-hotel that I was strapped to for the chip-suck. This room was more civilized, and the sheets were clean. I think. Opening one eye, I looked around to see this was probably a lady's bedroom. The walls were light-green and there were a couple of flowered pillows lying around. It wasn't fancy, but at least somebody was trying. It was the nicest place I'd been in since landing on Tyria. For a second I thought I might be back on Earth.

"You all right?" Bodie asked.

I twisted around to see that he was sitting on a chair next to the bed. So much for being on Earth. I sat up, but my vision went blurry again, so I fell back and closed my eyes.

"They sent me to wake you up," he said. "How do you feel?"

"Worse than when we woke up in that church. How long was I out?"

"Most of the day."

"Were you sitting there the whole time?"

"Nah. That little doctor dude kept checking on you. I hung with Issa."

I felt a little sting of jealousy. Issa was supposed to be my guardian angel. What was she doing with Junior instead of watching over me?

"Really?" I said. "Wow."

"Is that a problem?"

"No," I said quickly. "Where are we?"

"In your mother's apartment."

I sat up again. My head pounded again.

"I don't want to be here," I exclaimed.

I got to my feet, but the room spun. Bodie grabbed me before I fell over and lowered me back onto the bed.

"Take it slow," he said. "Tenzig says you'll be okay once you start walking around."

We were silent for a few minutes as I tried to straighten my head out.

"I'm sorry, Donovan," Bodie said, awkwardly.

"For what?"

"For being kind of a tool."

That was weird. I looked to him to see if he was kidding, but he was dead serious.

"It's cool," I said cautiously. "I'm used to it."

"It's not cool. It's a bad habit."

"Being a tool?"

"Always taking charge like I have all the answers." I can't help it. It's something my parents drilled into me."

"I guess that's why you're the QB," I said.

"And I'm not even that good. I know that. But don't tell my parents. They're always pushing me. So I keep trying. But I'm tired of failing."

This stunned me. Bodie was the golden-boy who had it all going on. Or so I thought.

"Nobody's perfect," I said.

"True. I'm just the loudest. Not like you."

"You don't want to be like me," I said.

"Except you're dealing with this a lot better than I would. I don't know what I'd do if I was in your shoes."

Did I hear right? Was that an actual compliment from Bodie Willard Junior?

"Then it's a good thing you aren't in my shoes," I said.

Bodie looked really troubled. The whole idea of the Chrysalis taking over my brain seemed to bother him as much as it did me.

"Just know I'm on your side," he said. "We're the only friends we've got here."

I never thought of Bodie as a friend. Okay, I kind of hated the guy. But he was right, we were all we had. The conversation was making me uncomfortable.

"Why am I here?" I asked.

"You mean philosophically?"

"Give me a break. I mean why am I in this room?"

"Issa said it was safe." He paused, then continued, "And it's where your mother lives."

"That means less than nothing to me."

"She's the only mother you've got."

"I don't care!" I shouted. "I don't care about her; I don't care about that drunk Kellen, and I don't care about any of these people. I want to go home."

"You mean you want to go back to the place you blame your mother for sending you to?"

"Why are you defending her? Is this you trying to take charge again?"

Bodie opened his mouth to argue but instead he backed off and said, "Sorry."

My head was pounding. I didn't know if it was because of the Chrysalis or because I wasn't used to thinking so much.

"Tenzig wants you to move around and clear your head," Bodie said calmly. "But slowly."

"Clear my head?" I said with a scoffing laugh. "If I could do that I wouldn't be here."

Bodie chuckled too and said, "True. But can we give it a shot?"

I went along, mostly because I didn't want to be there. I stood up slowly. This time my head didn't go wonky. Bodie led me toward the door, but I stopped.

"Wait, is my mother here?"

"No."

I can't say if I was relieved or disappointed.

Bodie led me out of the bedroom and through the living room of the tidy apartment. I wondered if this was where my parents lived when I was born. Where I lived. I looked around to see if any of it looked familiar. It didn't. We left the apartment and entered a long hallway.

"We're on the fourth floor," Bodie said. "There's an elevator."

He led me to the end of the hallway to a small elevator that could barely hold two people. Bodie hit the lowest button, and we started down.

"There's something else I'm about to be sorry for," he said. "This wasn't my idea."

I went on alert. "What wasn't your idea?"

"You're a pretty big deal for these people."

"Yeah and?"

The elevator came to a stop, the door slid open, and I was faced with a large basement-room full of people, all staring at me with big smiles.

"Surprise!" they screamed.

It was a party.

"Don't hate me," Bodie said.

"Too late."

I wanted to hit the elevator button and get out of there. I also wanted to hit Bodie, but an old lady reached in, took my hand and gently pulled me out before I could do either.

"I can't tell you how happy we are to see you," the woman said with a sweet, broad smile. "My name is Renna. Remember me?"

It was the same lady who asked me about my "in between" life on Earth. As she led me through the crowd, men smiled at me and women wiped away happy tears. Everyone had on more colorful clothing than what they wore in the factory, like they were dressing up. This was a special occasion for them. For me, not so much.

A band was in the corner playing odd guitars with short necks, while somebody beat on a drum, and another played a flute-thing. It was like happy Irish music.

People's voices blended into a jumble of well-wishes. I was on display, and I didn't like it. I caught sight of my mother, Tessa T-Shay. She stood off to the side, talking to a woman, but her eyes were on me. She was wearing a pretty dress with a colorful flower pattern that for some reason made me sad. It was like she was really trying. We made eye contact, but that was it. Neither of us acknowledged the other.

"We have parties like this every so often," Renna said. "But your being here makes it that much more special."

I didn't know what to say to that:

"Thanks"?

"Aw shucks"?

"Don't get used to it because I'm outta here"?

Nothing seemed right so I just nodded.

She led me to a row of empty chairs and gently pushed me down into one.

"You must be starving," she said. "I'll get something for you."

She gave me a pat on the cheek then disappeared into the crowd. I sat there, feeling more than a little awkward. People wandered by and gave me a wave and a smile. It was weird. Everybody wanted to get a look at me, but most didn't say anything. I guess they didn't want to overwhelm me, but it was like being behind an invisible wall in a zoo, and I was the weird new exhibit.

As I sat there, not knowing what to do with my hands, the band kicked in with a jig-like song that got a rise out of the crowd. I guess it was a fan favorite because there were lots of whoops and happy shouts. Several people cleared the floor while others formed three lines, held hands, and did a line-dance. There were people of all ages from gray-hairs to little kids, and they all knew the steps. They clicked their heels, stomped, spun around, shuffled left, right and forward…all in unison to the upbeat jig. It was the first fun I'd seen since landing on Tyria. It almost made me want to get up and join in.

Almost.

I stayed planted, but I did tap my toe a little.

Seeing these people having so much fun made me realize that they hadn't given up. The Tyrian League may have been about fighting for their freedom, but it was really about something much simpler. They wanted their lives to be about something more than just survival.

As the dance went on, I saw something that knocked me back. Bodie was in the middle of it all. He had no idea what he was doing, but that didn't stop him. He hit every fourth step and kept bumping into people, but they all laughed as if his clueless dancing just made it more fun. I couldn't take my eyes off of him, until I spotted something even more shocking.

Dancing next to him was Issa. She wore a bright red dress and let her hair hang loose. She actually looked, dare I say it, kind of girly. I knew she wasn't a typical kid. But in that moment, she looked like a normal girl having fun, laughing, and dancing with friends.

With Bodie.

When the song ended, everyone clapped and left the dance floor.

I made eye contact with Issa. It seemed like she was embarrassed that I had seen her dancing with Bodie. Or maybe I was imagining things.

"Donovan?"

I turned around to see my mother standing there. I think I gasped in surprise.

"This was supposed to be a welcome home party," she said. "I think maybe it wasn't such a good idea."

"It wasn't. This isn't my home."

"Can I sit down?" she asked.

I couldn't say no. That would have been a jerk move. I nodded to the chair next to me. She smiled and sat.

"I feel like I'm on display," I said.

"I don't blame you. Nobody knows what to say."

We sat there quietly for a painfully long time. I guess neither of us knew what to say either. But something needed to be said, so I gave it a shot.

"Whether it was or not, I believe you did what you thought was right. I'm trying not to be angry."

"Thank you for that," she said.

"But it doesn't matter because I'm leaving. We'll never see each other again."

She winced as if my words stung her. Maybe she was thinking I'd forgive her and come to the rescue of Essen-Tet and that the Tyrian League would topple Regenesis, and we'd all live happily ever after. She'd be wrong.

"Just so you know," she said. "I haven't given up on your father. I'm going to find him, and when I do, the people who took him will regret it."

"That's bold," I said.

"Maybe so, but there's one thing about me: I don't get mad. I get even."

I caught my breath. Did she actually say that? She had an intense look in her eyes that made me believe she did, and she meant it. This was my mother, no doubt about it. It hit me with a rush of mixed emotions that I didn't know what to do with.

"I gotta go," I said and stood to leave.

"Donovan!" she said.

I turned back to her. It seemed as though she wanted to say something but couldn't find the right words. After a few awkward moments she said, "Good night. Good bye."

My throat burned like I was about to cry.

"Good bye," I said and hurried off through the crowd.

"What's going on?" Bodie said as I charged past him.

I ignored him.

Issa appeared behind me and said, "Keep moving."

I had no idea where I was going so I let her push me along. We ended up in the elevator.

"Let's go someplace quiet," she said and hit the top button.

We rode up in silence. I had nothing to say, and I didn't want her to try and convince me to stay on Tyria. The elevator came to a stop and the door opened onto the roof. Issa got out first and walked straight for the front of the four-story building. She stood near the edge and gazed out at the filthy city of stone buildings that was Essen-Tet. There were hardly any lights in windows. There were no streetlights or signs or anything else that made normal cities look alive. Because the light was so dim, the stars lit up the sky.

"Looks like you were having fun down there," I said.

"I was. We still have to live."

"Yeah, line dancing must really make life worth living," I said with a sarcastic chuckle.

I instantly regretted it. Issa gave me an angry look. I was torn between thinking she was about to kick my ass, and the fact that she was probably the prettiest girl I'd ever known.

"Maybe it does," she said coldly. "Regenesis controls our lives. The last thing we want to do is tell somebody how they should live theirs."

She was pissed.

"I'm sorry, that wasn't cool."

"Let's go back down," she said and turned to leave.

I grabbed her arm to stop her.

"Wait. What about the other five kids?" I asked. "The scions. Maybe the Chrysalis didn't creep into their brains and Tenzig can fish it out. You should bring them back."

"We can't," she said.

"Why not?"

"Because we lost track of them."

"What!" I exclaimed. "How? I thought you were watching over them all?"

"We were. At first. Earth was the most primitive planet Kellen sent a scion to. It's the only one that doesn't have interplanetary travel. The other five scions got swallowed up into the various societies on other worlds. We tracked them for a while, then lost them. For all we know they might not even be on the same planets anymore."

"And you didn't lose me because I couldn't leave Earth?"

"Yes."

"So I'm the only one who can--?"

"Do you smell that?" Issa said.

I took a whiff.

"Something's burning," I said.

We looked over the side of the building. Orange light flickered out from several of the windows directly below us.

"Fire!" Issa exclaimed.

She took off running back the way we'd come. She went straight to a door near the elevator, pulled it open, and we were hit with a brutal wave of smoke and heat. Issa slammed the door shut and we staggered away, coughing.

"A fire doesn't spread that fast," I exclaimed.

"Unless it was meant to," she replied.

"How do we get down?" I asked. "Is there a fire escape?"

We ran back to the front of the building and looked down to the street where people were stumbling out, coughing and rubbing their eyes. I hoped to see Bodie. And my mother.

I didn't.

And there was no fire escape. We were trapped on the roof of a building that was burning beneath our feet.

~ 173 ~

CHAPTER 20

People were streaming out of the building four stories below us, coughing and staggering around, dizzy from breathing in smoke. I wished we were with them.

"Look!" I said and pointed down the street where an odd vehicle was slowly making its way toward the building. It looked like a floating platform. Resting on it was a tripod that stood maybe twenty feet high. At the top of it was a heavy, silver, two-pronged fork. Hovering between the tongs of the fork was a black metal cube about eighteen inches square. It reminded me of a parade float. A really strange parade float.

"Is that a fire truck? I asked.

Issa looked as though she was about to be sick.

"No," Issa said. "We've got to get down."

"You get no argument from me."

We took off running to the far side of the roof where I was relieved to see a metal fire escape ladder. Issa climbed over and started down. I was right after her. Heat blasted from the windows we passed. I hoped the people who lived there were all at the party.

Once on the ground, we hurried through an alley that led to the front of the building. As we ran, I saw something odd on the far side of the street. Beams of colored lights danced across the buildings. It looked like a carnival light show, but with no music. Maybe it was a parade float after all.

Issa reached the mouth of the alley, peered out, and quickly pulled back.

"Don't look!" she shouted and pushed me back.

She looked terrified, and Issa didn't scare easily.

"What is it?"

"We heard stories," she said, breathless. "We didn't think it was possible."

"Tell me!" I demanded.

"This is what they've been building in Factory B. See for yourself, but do *not* look at the black cube. Not even for a second."

Normally when somebody tells me not to do something, it's the first thing I do. But Issa was genuinely scared, and I wasn't going to question her. I took a peek around the corner, fighting the urge to look straight at the weird device that was spitting out light.

What I saw scared me too.

Standing in front of the building were the people from the party, and they were no longer in the mood for dancing. It was an eerie sight. They stood together, all staring at the flashing cube. Nobody moved. Nobody spoke. They stood with their arms straight at their sides, staring at the cube as it flashed colorful beams of light that swept over them.

My mother was there. She had the same, blank expression as everyone else. Bodie stood next to her, looking just as dazed.

"They look like they're under a spell or something," I said.

"We heard that Regenesis was developing technology capable of mass hypnosis, but it was just a rumor. Until now."

"What's the point? Don't they already control everybody?"

"No, because we can still think. They want to take that away from us too."

"No way," I said and started toward the crowd.

"Donovan, no!"

She grabbed at me, but I pulled away and kept going. I stayed focused on Bodie and my mother to keep from accidently looking at the lights shooting from the cube.

"Hey!" I shouted at the crowd. "Wake up!"

Nobody reacted. This thing had total control of them. I walked backward toward the cube. I wasn't sure what I would do once I hit it, but I had to do something. And I was good at breaking things.

My weak plan went out the window when I heard an amplified voice coming from the device.

"Good evening, Donovan. So good to see you again."

I froze. I knew the voice. It was Vail Kobain. I had just done something incredibly stupid by revealing myself.

"Where are you?" I called out.

"Sitting comfortably in my office," she said. "But I can see you. And your violent girlfriend. Bodie too. Tell me, is your mother there as well?"

I looked to Issa, who had followed me. She gave me a slight shake of the head as if to say: *don't tell her.*

"I called out, "If you know so much, you tell me if she's here."

"Touché'" Kobain said with a chuckle.

Issa nudged me and motioned to the building next door. Three Watchers stood in the shadows created by the fire. They were laying back, waiting.

"What's your deal?" I asked. "Did you have your goons burn the building just to get everybody outside so you could use your mind-control gizmo on them?"

"Bravo!" Kobain exclaimed. "This "gizmo" is a Covian Cube. Its purpose is to protect the faithful from the treachery of non-believers."

Issa said, "You mean it's a way to control people who don't agree with you."

"Isn't that a bit dramatic?" Kobain said with a chuckle. "Call it insurance against malcontents like you and your little band from undermining the good work of our church."

"Keep telling yourself that," Issa said, snidely.

"One more time," Kobain said. "Please point out your mother."

Kobain didn't know that Tessa was standing a few feet away, and I wasn't about to tell her.

"Understand something," Kobain said. "I'm giving you the chance to save her."

"From what?" I shouted.

"Bodie," Kobain called out. "Go back into the building, please. "

Without hesitation, Bodie turned and started walking back toward the front door that led into the building that had quickly become a furnace.

"Bodie!" I screamed. "Stop!"

He didn't.

I couldn't give up my mother to this creep, but if Bodie went inside, he'd die.

"Stop him!" I shouted to Kobain.

"That would be up to you," Kobain said, calmly.

I didn't know what to do. But Issa did. She sprinted after Bodie and tackled him.

"That won't stop him," Kobain said with a laugh.

Bodie struggled to get away from Issa. This machine let Kobain put the idea into Bodie's head that he had to walk into a fire, and nothing was going to stop him. Issa dug in her heels and tried to drag him back, but it was no use. She couldn't hold him forever.

I ran to help, moving past the crowd of people who were staring up at the Covian Cube as if nothing else was going on around them. I threw myself on Bodie, pinning him to the ground.

"Bodie," Kobain called out. "Come back to the group."

Bodie instantly relaxed.

"You okay?" I asked him.

He didn't hear me. He was focused on Kobain's voice. I let him go and he got up to walk obediently back to the group.

I looked around for Issa and said, "We've got to shut this thing down before—"

She was standing up straight, staring at the cube. This thing had her. I jumped up and got right in her face. She had a vacant look in her eyes that said her body was there, but her mind wasn't. I grabbed her shoulders and shook her.

"Wake up!" I shouted.

She didn't.

"Issa," Kobain called out. "Join the group please."

Issa obeyed and walked past me. I couldn't even turn around to see where she was going for fear I might accidently look at the lights.

"What's the point!" I shouted over my shoulder. "You're in control. If you think my mother is here, tell her to show herself."

"I could," Kobain replied. "But I'd like it to come from you."

There was anger in her voice. I'd heard plenty of people use that tone with me. It meant I'd gotten under her skin, and she wanted me to suffer for it. She wanted the satisfaction of having me throw my mother under the bus.

"You're out of luck," I said.

"Is that what you think?" Kobain replied, smug.

I didn't like the sound of that. What was I missing?

"Attention everyone," Kobain called out. "Forgive me for disturbing your evening. Please, you may all go back inside."

The entire group of people, including my mother, Bodie and Issa turned around and started back toward the building.

"No!" I shouted in total panic.

They all moved past me like obedient robots, headed toward their doom.

"Stop it!" I shouted at Kobain. "What kind of church does this?"

"One that cares for its loyal congregation, and serves the Regent," Kobain said.

I ran to the front of the group, holding out my arms in a useless attempt to stop them.

"Fight it!" I screamed at them. "You'll die if you go in there!"

I might as well have been yelling at a wall. The people moved, zombie like, growing closer to the inferno. There was only one thing I could do to stop them.

"All right!" I shouted out to Kobain. "You win!"

"Everyone please stop," Kobain announced.

They all stopped instantly and stood in place. My relief didn't stop the sick feeling that I was about to betray my mother. What was Kobain going to do with her? Send her off to whatever nightmare my father was in? Or make her walk into the burning building as punishment for what she'd done years ago?

After all this time, Regenesis was about to find her, and Kobain wanted me to be the one to give her up. It wasn't just about finding her. She could have done that on her own. She wanted me to suffer. She wanted revenge."

"Please, enlighten me," Kobain called out. "Which of these women is your mother?"

A loud whining sound cut through the crackle of the fire. From the corner of my eye I caught a shadow moving impossibly fast, headed directly for the Covian Cube. The shadow lifted into the air and slammed square into the tripod, knocking the cube out of its yoke. The flashing lights died instantly as the metal box fell and bounced onto the pavement.

"Kellen!" I shouted.

Kellen A-Quiss was aboard a flying aerobike. He spun into a tight turn and flew back toward the group.

Whatever spell the cube had cast, was broken. The people looked around, disoriented, as if they'd just woken up and didn't understand why they were outside of the building.

The three Watchers who were standing in the shadows came running, drawing their pistol-weapons.

Kellen reached behind his seat to pull out Issa's pack. He tossed it to her as he flew by.

"Here they come," he announced.

That's all Issa needed. She had her wits back and clicked into battle-mode. She clutched the strap of her backpack and lurched away from the group, ready to meet the charging Watchers head-on.

I went for Bodie and grabbed his arm.

"We gotta get outta here," I said.

Bodie looked at me with confusion, then nodded. I was about to run when I saw my mother standing there looking dazed. Should I go for her? Or would that reveal her to Kobain?

The Watchers opened fire on Kellen as he flew past them. Shots of energy crackled through the air, raising the hair on the back of my neck. Kellen maneuvered his bike expertly, zig-zagging his way along, making a difficult target. In that one moment, I saw the guy I imagined Kellen had been so many years ago. He was quick, fearless, and dangerous. He had one hand on the handlebars and a pistol in the other. While still moving he took aim at a Watcher, fired, and knocked the guy off his feet.

The people around us scattered or dove to the ground to avoid getting hit.

Issa dropped to one knee and flung her pack at the second Watcher. Like a cowboy's lariat, the line unspooled and wrapped around his ankles. Issa pulled it tight, and he went down hard, firing his pistol aimlessly. Issa quickly leapt at him while he was still stunned. She grabbed his pistol, spun, and shot a bolt of energy at the third Watcher who was coming up from behind her. The guy took the shot and landed flat on his back, unconscious.

With Bodie in tow, I went for my mother.

"C'mon," I said. "We don't want to be here."

Her look of confusion turned to one of relief when she realized who I was. The three of us ran across the street, away from the mayhem. From the safety of a doorway, we huddled together to watch the last of the battle.

Two more Watchers appeared, firing at Kellen. Kellen flew to Issa, reached out, and pulled her up on to the back of his bike.

"Go!" she commanded.

Kellen made another tight turn, and they flew directly at the final two Watchers.

There was an explosion inside the doomed building. Several floors collapsed, blasting out a massive bloom of smoke, sparks and heat from the windows and doors.

The two Watchers threw up their hands to protect themselves. It was all that Kellen and Issa needed. They fired their weapons, one shooting right and the other shooting left. Both Watchers were hit and knocked unconscious.

The attack was over.

Kellen landed his aerobike near the unconscious bodies of the Watchers.

I left our hiding place to join them.

"Are you guys okay?" I asked.

"Sure," Kellen said. "Sorry I crashed your party."

"They must have set the fire," I said, pointing to the Watchers. "To get everybody outside."

The distant sound of a siren cut through the crackling roar of flames.

"Firefighters," Issa said. "A little late."

"Or more Watchers coming to finish the job," Kellen said.

Bodie walked up, carrying the dented and destroyed Covian cube.

"There was a flash of light, and then I lost it," he said. "I knew what was going on, but I couldn't fight it."

He dropped it to the ground and kicked it angrily.

"They're making loads of those things," Issa said. "If they deploy them, it's game over. We'll never stop Regenesis."

The siren grew louder as the heat from the fire made it hard to stay there. The people who lived in the doomed building gathered together, dazed, looking for comfort, and answers.

"We've got to find places for these people to stay," Issa said.

"What about us?" Bodie asked.

"Stay with Issa," Kellen said. "We'll take off for Earth at dawn."

I looked across the street to see my mother walking our way. Unlike the rest of the people who seemed lost, she was walking with purpose. She looked angry.

"Thank you," she said to me.

"Are you okay?"

"No, I'm not," she said. "This can't go on."

I looked to Kellen and said, "How many?"

"How many what?" he asked.

"How many people do you have ready to attack?"

Issa threw a surprised look to Kellen.

Kellen focused on me, trying to read my mind.

"Doesn't matter," Kellen said. "We can't do anything without the Chrysalis."

"Who's in charge?" I asked. "Is that still you? A drunk who blew it the first time?"

Kellen's solid stare didn't waver from me. I wasn't sure if he was going to explode with anger or burst out in tears.

"You suddenly got a lot of questions, kid," he said.

"One more. How are you going to get me into The Core? And if you do, are you sure it'll work?"

Issa smiled broadly.

"That's two questions," Kellen said, with a sly smile. "We'll get you in, and it'll work."

I felt a gentle hand on my shoulder and jumped with surprise. It was my mother. She didn't say a word. She didn't have to.

I looked to Bodie and said, "Go home. This isn't your fight."

"Then who'll have your back? You need me, Mutt." He smiled and added, "Mutt and Junior, sounds like a cartoon."

It was the first time I actually liked Bodie. Kind of.

"All right," I said to Kellen. "Tell me what I have to do."

CHAPTER 21
FACTORY B

It began as a normal workday. The assembly-line workers arrived at their stations to continue building the complicated devices they had been assembling for weeks. The Covian Cubes. They lifted their tools and went to work. There was nothing unusual about any of it.

Except now they knew what they were building.

The word had spread fast. Kellen A-Quiss made sure of that. They were now fully aware that they were assembling mind-control devices that would lead to their own subjugation.

A drone floated silently overhead. Its electronic eye scanned the workers to make sure everyone was in their place and working efficiently. The drone would make its pass and return a half-hour later to do it again. The half-hour between passes was all the workers would need. As soon as the drone completed its route, a silent act of rebellion would begin. The plan was simple and bold.

The workers would sabotage the Covian Cubes.

The changes would be undetectable: a damaged motherboard; incomplete circuits; missing chips; defective batteries. At worst, the sabotage would slow down production. At best, the cubes would be shipped to wherever Regenesis planned to deploy them.

But the cubes wouldn't work. The hope was that sabotaging the devices would give the Tyrian League time to gather once more to try and topple Regenesis. It was a hope that sprang from the fact that a scion had returned.

Everyone knew. The time to act was now. It could very well be their last chance.

The silent eye-in-the-sky drifted slowly over the multiple workstations, occasionally shining a spotlight down on a worker to get a more detailed view.

The risks of the plan were huge. If they were discovered, they would be arrested. Their hope was that by the time the truth came out, the Tyrian League would have overthrown Regenesis. They were willing to take that risk. That's how desperate their lives had become.

They were the front line of the new revolution.

The drone completed its pass, flew to the ceiling and shot through an opening. It would be back in thirty minutes. The worker at the last station looked down at the assembly line and gave a small nod. Those further along the line repeated the signal. Within moments, every worker knew it was time.

The rebellion was about to begin.

"Attention," came a booming, amplified voice.

The workers froze. This was not an ordinary event.

"Step back from your workstations," a man's voice added.

The worker's exchanged nervous looks. What was going on? What should they do? Was the plan still on? As they backed off from their workstations, Watchers appeared on the catwalk above them. They marched in from either side, filling up the narrow walkway that stretched the length of the factory floor.

The workers looked up in nervous wonder. Whatever was happening, it wasn't good.

Leading one line of Watchers, was August C-Bonn. The chubby church official strode to the center of the catwalk where he met the oncoming line of Watchers. He stopped there and gazed down at the workers.

A visit by August C-Bonn and the Watchers was bad enough, but the workers saw something much worse. Standing with C-Bonn were a man and a woman. They were workers who should have been on the factory floor. A sense of panic gripped the crowd. These workers knew about the sabotage plan. The fact that they stood with a top official of Regenesis did not bode well.

Had these two betrayed them?

"Good morning!" August C-Bonn's amplified voice filled the cavernous room. "So good to see you here today, ready to honor the Regent with a hard day's work!"

The chubby C-Bonn's jovial manner didn't put anyone at ease. Nervous glances were exchanged. The only thing that kept them from fleeing was that they'd be caught by the Watchers before they could reach the doors.

"Before you begin, please focus your attention overhead," C-Bonn declared with glee, as if ready to present them with a wonderful gift.

All eyes went straight up to the ceiling where four mechanical devices were being lowered. They had been hidden in the shadows and shielded by dark drapes. Now, they slowly dropped into the light where the workers could clearly see them.

There were gasps all around because they immediate knew that all hope was gone.

Looming above them were four Covian Cubes.

C-Bonn, the two workers, and the Watchers put on dark goggles. The hypnotic effect of the lights would not reach them.

The mechanisms locked into position. The cubes started to spin and spit out light.

"Take a good look," C-Bonn announced with a sly smile.

He needn't have bothered. Every last worker was already mesmerized by the flashing, hypnotic lights. They stood still, staring up at the devices they themselves had assembled.

"Now," came the amplified voice of Vail Kobain. "You have work to do. Properly, with no flaws. Once your work is complete and evaluated, you will be escorted to a transport vehicle. I hope you said good-bye to your families this morning for you will not be seeing them again."

Nobody reacted. They were under the spell of the Covian Cubes.

"Now please, continue your work," Kobain commanded.

The workers obediently returned to their stations and went to work.

The two workers who stood with August C-Bonn would be rewarded for having revealed the plan for sabotage. They would receive promotions, pay raises, and allowed to live in Privilege Manors.

The workers they betrayed would have little or no memory of what happened. They would be taken away from Essen-Tet and sent to a work colony. A day that began with great hope would end in despair.

The revolution would not begin in Factory B.

CHAPTER 22

We were preparing for what would be the most important event of my life, other than being born and shot into space, that is.

"One more time," Tenzig commanded.

We were practicing for the moment when my brain would be jacked into the power grid of the church of Regenesis…all words that meant nothing to me a few days ago.

We were in Tenzig's odd bedroom, with the confusing equations scrawled all over the walls. I held a small radio-drive that would power the brain-to-grid operation and make the connections.

"I find an unoccupied workstation with a docking module," I said, trying not to sound bored because I'd already gone through it a dozen times. I held out the four white disks that Tenzig had used to tap into my brain. "I stick two of these transmitter-things on my forehead and two at the base of my neck."

I stuck them on, just as Tenzig had done to me earlier.

"Then I put the radio-drive into the docking station."

I sat at a computer that Tenzig had set up on a table next to his grimy bed. It was playing the part of the workstation we'd use to tap into the Regenesis grid. I inserted a radio drive into the docking port. This would first send power to the transmitters.

"Done," I declared.

Tenzig had his tech-pad on his lap. Kellen stood over his shoulder, watching closely.

"Now I make the connection," Tenzig said.

On the computer screen was an image of a waterfall that meant nothing, other than it was a pretty waterfall. A moment later, the waterfall image appeared on Tenzig's pad.

"Done," Tenzig said, all business. "Activating the Chrysalis."

I sat back, closed my eyes and said, "Now the fun begins."

After a few seconds, the floating feeling returned. When I opened my eyes, the Chrysalis code once again filled the room. It didn't surprise me anymore.

"You seeing this?" I asked.

"I am," Tenzig replied.

The waterfall on the computer screen had disappeared, replaced by the sea of code that was the Chrysalis. Tenzig saw the same images on his pad that floated around me. The link-up was complete, from my brain to Tenzig's pad and back to the computer on the table.

"Find the launch link," Tenzig said.

I looked to my left, through the sea of figures, until I saw the words: MISHA K-SOO floating where it always was.

"You'd think she would have come up with something less obvious," I said.

"Just do it," Kellen snapped. He wasn't in a joking mood. It didn't matter how many times we ran through this; he was still nervous. He didn't want to mess up twice.

I stepped up to the words that floated at eye level, touched the air where they were and closed my eyes because I knew what came next. The Chrysalis data disappeared, which always made me dizzy.

"There it is," Tenzig said.

I opened my eyes to see the word ENGAGE floating in front of me.

"Here comes the really hard part," I said sarcastically. I touched the word, and it instantly flipped to the word: UPLOADING.

"Phew! Good thing I got that right."

"Done," Tenzig said and quickly closed out of everything.

I asked, "If the Chrysalis shuts down the power grid, won't that also shut down the Chrysalis?"

"Oh no!" Kellen exclaimed with mock surprise. "I can't believe Misha never thought of that!"

"Don't try to out-sarcasm me," I said.

"That's one of the beauties of Misha's virus," Tenzig said. "It functions using only a trickle of residual power."

I popped off the transmitters and handed them back to him. "Can we practice a hundred more times?"

"Let's both skip the sarcasm," Kellen said.

"We're just making sure it works," Tenzig said. He wasn't interested in sarcasm.

"It works," I said. "I'm more worried about getting into The Core. Then getting out. Let's not forget that."

"We're working on that," Kellen said.

"Work harder," I shot back. "Are you positive we can't do this from a distance? I mean, it's all wireless."

"The connection wouldn't be strong enough," Tenzig said. "If you aren't close, it could take hours for the upload and by then Regenesis will detect a breach and block it. And arrest you."

"Right, that," I said, glum.

"You have to be in there, Donovan," Tenzig added.

I knew that was going to be the answer, but I had to ask.

Kellen and I left Tenzig's apartment and walked to the garage where he had hidden his aerobike. Kellen was surprisingly silent. I figured he was probably thinking about the details of the plan. The weird thing was that he wasn't drunk. At least I didn't think he was. He was pretty clear-eyed. And he wasn't belching. Much. That alone made it easier to be with him.

"If we pull this off, what happens after?" I asked.

"The legit elected government is back in power, the Regenesis Watch is disbanded, the city police take responsibility for security and Vail Kobain and the other church leaders go to prison."

"That's here. What about other planets?"

"What we do here will inspire others to fight back."

"And what if we don't pull it off?"

He didn't answer right away. It couldn't have been a happy thought.

"We'll never stop fighting," he said.

"Speak for yourself."

We hopped on Kellen's aerobike and flew toward the Tyrian League apartment where we'd slept the night before. Issa, Bodie and my mother would be there waiting for us.

As we flew along the streets of Essen-Tet, I couldn't shake the image of those people walking in a trance toward the burning building. I didn't really understand how a church could control entire worlds or convince people that they were doing it for their own good, even if they did let some of them live in fancy buildings. But one thing was clear: they were evil. It helped me to understand why the scion parents chose to send their babies away. If Vail Kobain was willing to push people into a horrible, mass suicide, what would she have done to the babies of her enemies?

My mother said it best, "This can't go on."

I didn't ask for this responsibility. But if I had the chance to help these people stop Regenesis and didn't at least try, I wouldn't be able to live with myself. I must be getting soft.

The plan was in place, Kellen was sober I think, the Tyrian League was ready to go. Maybe I was kidding myself, but I was starting to feel confident.

We rounded the corner near the apartment building to see black smoke billowing from the window of the apartment where the others were waiting for us.

So much for confidence.

Kellen hit the throttle and the aerobike launched forward. He flew us to the front entrance where we leapt off and ran into the building. People were staggering through the lobby toward the door, coughing from the smoke that billowed down the stairs. None of them were Issa or Bodie, or my mother.

We took the stairs up, two at a time. The smoke was so thick it burned my eyes and made it hard to breath, but we didn't stop. When we reached the second floor we sprinted to the far end of the hall. Kellen kicked the apartment door to break it down. He didn't need to. It swung open easily. Somebody had already busted the lock. We hurried inside and found the fire. It was burning in the back bedroom.

"Issa!" Kellen yelled.

I ran to the back room, but the heat turned me away. I was near panic, fearing the worst. That's when I heard a cough.

Somebody was there, and alive.

We both spun to see someone lying on the floor on the far side of the front room. It was Issa. Alive. Dazed, but alive. Kellen scooped her up and went for the front door.

"Wait!" I yelled.

Kellen stopped. I reached for Issa and held her face, trying to get her to focus.

"My mother and Bodie. Are they back there?"

Issa was barely conscious. She fought to focus and said, "No. Gone."

Best news I'd heard all day.

"Go!" I shouted to Kellen.

We carried Issa out of the apartment, down the stairs and out into fresh air.

"There's water under the seat of my bike," Kellen said.

While he carried Issa to safety across the street, I went to his aerobike to grab a water canister. I ran to join them as Kellen was gently resting Issa down to the pavement. He took the canister, popped the cap and brought it to Issa's lips.

"Try to drink," he said gently.

Issa responded and took a few sips but coughed it back up.

"Slow, slow," Kellen said.

He gave her a few more sips that she kept down.

Kellen was in tears. I didn't know if it was from the smoke, or fear for Issa. These two were partners. She was probably the only family he had.

"There you go," he said. "You'll be fine."

"What about Tessa and Bodie?" I asked Issa.

"They came," Issa said, her voice raspy and raw.

"Who?" I asked. "The Watchers?"

Issa nodded. She opened her eyes wider and focused on me. Her frightened look told me that whatever she had to say, it wouldn't be good.

"I'm sorry, Donovan," she said, tears running down her cheeks. "I fought, but there were too many. They torched the bedroom and left me. I'm so sorry."

"They must feel threatened," Kellen said. "Or they wouldn't be so aggressive. They fear us."

Either Kellen was kidding himself, or he was an idiot. The Watchers didn't fear us. This was a message. To me. They kidnapped my mother and my friend. I didn't think they'd kill them. If they wanted to do that, they would have left them in the burning building. No, they wanted to get my attention.

Mission accomplished.

But they didn't know me. To them I was just a nuisance kid with information that might hurt them. But they made a serious miscalculation. They got my attention all right. I fought my whole life to stay in control. Over the past few days, I'd lost it. But I was about to take it back.

And I don't get mad, I get even.

CHAPTER 23
THE CORE

Few things are more frightening than the unknown. Bodie Willard and Tessa T-Shay were being led into the unknown.

The Watchers had battered down the door without warning. They swept in quickly and grabbed Tessa and Bodie. Issa fought them, but she was no match for the crew of professionals, and they knocked her out cold.

The Watchers put sacks over their heads, dragged them from the apartment, turned their torches on the back room, and left Issa to die. It had taken less than two minutes from the time the Watchers arrived in a hover-truck, to when the prisoners were in the back of that same truck and flying away.

"Where are you taking us?" Tessa asked calmly.

She got no answer.

"Issa?" Bodie called out. "Are you here?"

Again, no answer.

"We'll be okay," Tessa said to him, reassuringly.

Bodie didn't believe her. He heard a loud hum right next to his ear and ducked away.

"What is that?" he exclaimed.

"Relax," a man said firmly. "It's a medical scan."

"What does that mean?" Bodie asked fearfully. "Why are you doing that?"

He didn't get an answer.

There was no way to know where they were going, or why. It wasn't long before the change in sound told them they had entered a building. They were pulled roughly out of the truck and pushed along until they stepped into the quiet of a small room. The room jolted. It was an elevator, and they were going up. When the door opened, sound rushed in. Surprising sound. It was soft, soothing music with no melody or lyrics. They were pulled out of the elevator and the plastic ties that bound their hands were cut.

A Watcher said exactly one word to them, "Wait."

Tessa and Bodie stood there, not sure of what to do.

"Hello?" Tessa finally called out.

"Tessa?" Bodie said tentatively. "It's you, right?"

"Yes," she replied. "I'm going to take this bag off my head."

"You sure we should? I don't want to piss these guys off and--"

His bag was abruptly pulled off by Tessa.

"I don't care," she said.

Both were surprised to see they were in a beautiful apartment. It was huge, with antique furniture, plush rugs and framed artwork.

"Uh. Wow," Bodie said.

He took it all in, trying to understand. His eyes stopped when they landed on a long table loaded with food.

"I am all over that," he said.

He started for the table like a predator moving on its prey.

"Don't!" Tessa admonished.

"I'm starving," he said. "If they're going to do something horrible to us, it's going to be on a full stomach.

The table was filled with trays of meat, fruit and bread. On one end was a stack of plates.

"See?" Bodie said. "It's a party."

He took a plate and quickly filled it with sliced ham, a dark bread roll, several chunks of a succulent red fruit that could have been watermelon, and a pile of something that looked like potato salad.

"I don't want their food," Tessa said with disdain.

"Why not?" Bodie asked. "We don't even know who they are."

"Of course you do," came a woman's voice from across the room.

Bodie nearly dropped his plate. He knew that voice.

On the far side of the room, Vail Kobain sat regally on a blazing-white couch.

"Glory to the Regent," she said. "The feast is for you. Enjoy."

Her black suit, royal blue scarf and long red hair created a dramatic contrast to the brilliant white furniture. She also wore a pair of large, black-framed eyeglasses.

Bodie lost his appetite and put the plate back on the table.

"I'll pass," he said.

Tessa stood defiantly, with her legs apart and her hands at her sides.

Kobain got up and walked toward them.

"Don't be silly," she said like a gracious host. "You're hungry. And I don't want to be accused of mistreating my guests."

"There's enough food here to feed three families for a month," Tessa said with disdain. "The people of Essen-Tet made this possible, yet they'll never enjoy such a feast."

"That's their choice," Kobain said as she plucked a succulent grape from a bunch.

She raised her hand, triggering an invisible control that opened the drapes that ringed the apartment. Sunlight streamed in through floor-to-ceiling windows that looked out over a view that was far different than anything Bodie had seen in Essen-Tet. Extravagant mansions were scattered throughout the lush, green, park-like setting.

"Where are we?" Bodie asked in wonder.

"The Regenesis Compound," Kobain replied. "This is my home. As you can see, the Regent provides for the faithful. Those who serve him are rewarded. Those who don't will never enjoy a feast such as this, as you pointed out."

She popped the grape into her mouth, savoring its flavor.

Bodie's stomach grumbled.

"The Regent is a hoax you created to justify your crimes," Tessa said boldly. "Even now you're doing it. You're tempting this poor boy, knowing he's starving. You're shameless."

"And I'm happy," Kobain said. "Can you say the same?"

"I have a clear conscience," Tessa said.

"And what has that clear conscience gotten you?" Kobain asked as she rounded the table, headed toward Tessa. "A miserable life, hiding in squalor, without your only child. Or your husband? But he wasn't your husband, was he?"

Tessa stiffened, as if the words were a punch in the gut.

"But now your son is home," Kobain said with a smile. "A long-lost scion has returned. That's what you call them, right? Scions?"

Kobain stood directly in front of Tessa and touched her glasses to adjust them.

"I can't imagine how that felt," Kobain said. "You haven't seen your son in fifteen years. He's grown up without you. What did you say to him when you were re-united?"

Tessa fought to control her anger.

"Why do you feel the need to torture me?" she asked.

"Forgive me," Kobain said. "I don't mean to upset you. I'd truly like to know."

Tessa stood up taller and said, "All I care about is that he knows I love him, I've missed him, and I think about him every day. But I don't imagine you'd understand feelings like that."

Kobain adjusted her glasses again and gave Tessa a small smile.

"Thank you," she said.

"For what?" Tessa asked.

Kobain took off her glasses and placed them on the table.

"And Bodie," she said warmly. "Such a pleasant surprise. I must admit; I had no idea."

"About what?" Bodie asked.

Kobain gave him a long, thoughtful look, as if she didn't understand his question. She locked eyes with him, making Bodie squirm.

"You don't know, do you?" Kobain asked.

"Don't know what?" Bodie asked.

Kobain laughed. "Wonderful. Glory to the Regent."

"Yeah, whatever," Bodie said. "I think maybe I will eat."

He grabbed a chunk of bread from the table and took a big bite.

Kobain went to one of the huge windows that looked out over the Regenesis Compound.

"Having you two here is a blessing," Kobain said. "Your presence will help me put an end to the treacherous plans of the non-believers."

"How do you figure that?" Bodie asked with a full mouth.

"Come," Kobain said and gestured out of the window. "Such a beautiful day."

Bodie and Tessa exchanged confused glances.

Kobain waved her hand and called out, "Please begin."

She turned to gaze out of the window as an image appeared in the sky. It was a huge projection that could be seen for miles, just as the video of the apartment building destruction was seen.

It was the face of Tessa T-Shay.

"All I care about is that he knows I love him," Tessa's image said, as if it was speaking from the heavens. "I've missed him, and I think about him every day."

It was a recording made moments before.

"That's what you just—" Bodie said, stunned.

He looked to Tessa, who had gone pale.

"That lovely moment will be seen and heard in every corner of Essen-Tet," Kobain said. "We'll continue to play it until it has reached the right eyes."

"Donovan," Tessa said, barely above a whisper.

"I'm sure he'll do whatever he can to protect his mother," Kobain said. "He proved that last night. Though I can't imagine why, seeing as you abandoned him as a baby. No matter. He'll be here soon enough."

The recording continued, repeating again and again.

Tessa stood still, staring out of the window. At her image. She started to shake. Pure, raw fury was bubbling up inside. She grabbed one of the plates from the table and smashed it down on Kobain's eyeglasses, destroying the device that recorded her heartfelt words.

"I don't know who's worse," Tessa said through clenched teeth. "Your phony God, or you."

"I am but a loyal servant to the Regent," Kobain said.

"You're the devil."

Kobain called out, "Please make our guests comfortable."

Two Watchers appeared from nowhere. They grabbed Tessa and Bodie and roughly pulled them toward the elevator.

"Take heart," Kobain called to them. "After that stirring performance I don't believe you'll have to wait another fifteen years to be reunited with your son."

In the sky over Essen-Tet, Tessa's message continued to play.

CHAPTER 24

Seeing that image of my mother in the sky was worse than the Chrysalis nightmare. Kobain was taunting me. Luring me to come out of hiding.

"It's making me crazy," I said to Issa. "When are we going to go?"

"Soon," Issa said. "We'll find out for sure tonight."

We were standing outside a huge warehouse. Work was done for the day, but hundreds of people were arriving quietly. They crept through the darkened city streets in ones and twos, avoiding the Watchers, to gather inside.

"We'll listen from the back," Issa said. "We don't want to disrupt things. You're kind of a celebrity."

"Yeah, I'm a regular superstar," I said sarcastically.

We entered through the back door and found a spot in the shadows where we wouldn't be noticed. Though the place was jammed, it was strangely quiet. People spoke softly, like it was a library. This was an illegal gathering. The last thing they wanted was to be raided by the Watchers.

The same thing was going on all over Essen-Tet. The meetings happened in warehouses, school auditoriums, basements, factories and even Regenesis churches. The leaders of the Tyrian League were gathering their forces. People came from all over the Sandoor Federation to get their final instructions.

These were the rebels who would storm the Regenesis Compound and take control of The Core. The heart of the church.

They handed out thin, metal batons. They weren't exactly dangerous weapons, especially against the Watchers who had those energy-firing guns. But once the Regenesis grid went down, the Watcher's weapons would go down with it and those armed with low-tech weapons would have the advantage.

For that to happen, I had to come through. No pressure.

Kellen entered and walked to the front of the group, stood up on a box, and raised his hand to get everyone's attention. The crowd went silent.

"Many of you know me, but most don't," he began with a clear voice. "My name is Kellen A-Quiss. I formed the Tyrian League sixteen years ago with several other brave souls who were intent on crawling out from under the thumb of Regenesis. You all know the story. We failed."

Kellen had everyone's attention. He sounded confident and in charge. What happened on that night fifteen years before may have changed him for the worse, but getting a second crack at Regenesis had given him new life. He was now a guy I believed could lead the Tyrian League.

"Since then, our lives have only gotten worse," Kellen said. "Our once beautiful city has become a prison. Our only job is to service this criminal church and its false God. Well, to those who were with us on that dark day so long ago, and to those who have joined us since, I'm here to say that the wait is over. Tomorrow, we take back our lives."

The people who had been stonily silent sprang to life. They let out a cheer of joy and defiance. I sure hoped there were no Watchers within earshot.

I motioned to Issa that I wanted to leave, and we snuck out the back door.

"Don't you want to hear the rest?" she asked.

"Why? We know the plan. I'd rather talk to you."

"About what?"

"You want revenge, I get that. And you want answers. But take your emotions out of it for a second. I need you to be honest with me."

"What do you want to know?"

"Do you really think we can do it? I mean, can we really bring Regenesis down? Or is it just some desperate long-shot at getting revenge?"

Issa didn't give me a quick answer. It was too important a question to throw out the easy, obvious answer.

"You may not want to hear this," she said. "But yeah, I think we can do it."

"Why wouldn't I want to hear that?" I asked.

"Because the whole show depends on getting the virus into the grid. If that doesn't happen, we don't stand a chance. But if we can do it then yes, we can take over The Core and start the recovery."

She was right. I didn't want to hear that because there was no getting around it.

This was all coming down to me.

CHAPTER 25
THE REGENESIS CORE

The six members of the Regenesis Ministry were gathered in the conference room, without Vail Kobain. They were in a deep, heated discussion.

"The Bishop is obsessed with this so-called scion," one man said. It was the same man who had questioned Kobain earlier. "We cannot let her jeopardize our plans by chasing ghosts from the past. The Covian Solution is ready to be deployed throughout The Sandoor Federation. Now. In a matter of days we will have complete control over every last citizen, whether they are loyal to the church or not. We can't allow progress to be slowed by a delusional fear."

"What you're saying is blasphemous," a woman argued. "She is the highest-ranking member of the entire church."

"And she has lost sight of our goals," the man shot back. "I believe we should begin the procedure of removing her."

"Is that what you believe?" said Vail Kobain.

Her amplified voice boomed through the room, making every last minister snap to attention. The large monitor at the head of the table sprang to life, showing a live image of Vail Kobain sitting at her desk.

The ministers were speechless.

"I have grown tired of your insolence," Kobain said to the male minister.

The door to the conference room slid open. August C-Bonn hurried in, followed by three Watchers.

The man who had been brazenly critical of her, panicked. "I am only looking out for the best interests of the church. We all answer to a higher power."

The Watchers surrounded him.

"Yes we do," Kobain said. "And you answer to me."

"You've lost your way!" the man screamed.

"Remove him," Kobain said.

The Watchers grabbed the minister and pulled him toward the exit. He struggled, but it was futile.

"This is not serving the Regent's vision!" he yelled.

"I say what serves the Regent and what doesn't," Kobain said calmly. "As of this moment, you do not."

The Watchers pulled him out of the room and the door slid shut.

"Now," Kobain said. "Does anyone else share the former minister's concerns?"

The remaining ministers exchanged looks but stayed quiet.

"C-Bonn!" Kobain shouted.

August instantly jumped, ran to the monitor and bowed his head.

"Your Eminence."

"Donovan?" she snarled.

C-Bonn dropped his eyes and said, "I'm afraid he has not surfaced as we had hoped."

This was not what Kobain wanted to hear. She was used to having her orders obeyed instantly, and with great success. Frustration wasn't familiar to her. But she was smart. She had to change tactics.

"They must be preventing him from trying to help his mother," she said, thinking out loud.

"Who?" C-Bonn asked.

"This so called Tyrian League. They may be saving him for something more important than the well-being of two individuals."

C-Bonn laughed and said, "But we destroyed that rebel group ages ago!"

Kobain gave him a steely look.

C-Bonn stopped laughing.

"We did, didn't we?" he asked, unsure.

Kobain focused on her desk-top computer. "Tell me the status of the Covian Cube shipments."

"Ahead of schedule!" C-Bonn announced proudly. "The initial units are on transport vehicles, ready for shipment. In two days, three at the most, they will be installed and operational. All you need to do is—"

"Unload them," Kobain said, without taking her eyes off her computer screen.

C-Bonn glanced back to the ministers, who all had looks of confusion and concern.

"Yes, of course," C-Bonn said. "They will be unloaded once they reach their destinations and—"

"Unload them here."

"I don't understand," C-Bonn said. "The Covian Solution is about all of Sandoor and then Tyria--"

"It is," Kobain said with growing impatience. "But until we determine how real the threat is from this rabble, the devices will be more useful here."

"Forgive me, Your Eminence." It was the woman who stood up for Kobain against the recently ousted minister. "But the pitiful outcasts from years ago are no threat to us. There's no need to slow down our plans—"

Kobain slammed her hand down on her desk, making everyone jump.

"It's not the rabble that concerns me, it's that technology."

"You're referring to the virus created by Misha K-Soo?" C-Bonn said, dismissively. "I guarantee our firewalls will protect the grid."

Kobain locked eyes with C-Bonn. Though it was from a monitor, August felt the heat of her gaze.

"Will you guarantee that with your life?" she asked. "Will all of you?"

C-Bonn looked at his shoes. Everyone else shuffled nervously and stayed quiet.

"I suppose there would be no harm in being cautious," August said.

"Unload the cubes," Kobain commanded. "Install one outside every gate of the compound. If any unauthorized person even dares to think about entering the compound, they will be neutralized."

The monitor winked out and went dark. There was a long moment of uneasy silence, then August turned to the Ministry, and smiled.

"Perhaps this is fitting," he said. "If there is a threat, the first full-scale demonstration of the Covian Solution will be to wipe out whatever might be left of this Tyrian League."

CHAPTER 26

Issa stared at me with an intensity that was making me uncomfortable. Clearly there was something on her mind that she was reluctant to share. I tried to ignore her, but finally couldn't take it anymore.

"What?" I blurted out, annoyed.

"Are you okay?"

That was it. She was worried that I wasn't up to the job. If I was being totally honest, I'd tell her that I was scared. Maybe for the first time in my life. It wasn't so much because we were about to do something incredibly dangerous. (Okay, maybe it was a little because of that) It was more because the hopes of thousands of people were riding on me. No, the hopes of an entire city. And country. And world. And why not throw in the entire universe? Let's not forget the universe. Not to mention trying to save my mother and Bodie. I'd never had anybody rely on me before. Not even one. Now, technically speaking, I had millions. Maybe billions. So was I okay? Hell no I wasn't okay.

"I'm fine," I replied.

We were in a subterranean room beneath a building that was a few blocks from the Regenesis Compound. I was wearing the kind of dark blue coveralls that the maintenance staff wore who worked in The Core. Issa had on a white smock and black pants that was the uniform of the kitchen staff.

The plan was stupid-simple. Kellen found two volunteers who looked like us, more or less, and worked inside the compound. They gave us their identity badges and their work clothes. When the shift changed, we'd go through security with a bunch of other people arriving for work. If the Watchers at the gate didn't look at the I.D.'s too closely, we'd be in.

"What about you?" I asked Issa.

"Scared," was her reply.

She was being more honest than I was.

She added, "You'd have to be stupid not to be."

That meant I was either stupid, or a liar.

"All right, fine," I said. "I'm a little nervous."

"What are you most afraid of?" she asked.

"You mean besides being captured and executed?"

"Yeah, besides that."

"Screwing up," I said with total sincerity.

"So that means you actually care about what happens to the Tyrians?"

"I'm beginning to think that Tyria is as much a part of me as Earth is."

"Really? So it's about revenge for you too?"

"Maybe. But it's more about making sure that no more kids will be abandoned."

We held eye contact, and I saw tears well up in Issa's eyes. She leaned over and gave me a kiss on the cheek.

"I'm glad it's you, Donovan Six," she said. "We're going to do this."

I believed her. I had to. After all, she was my guardian angel.

I didn't mind the kiss, either.

The door opened and in strode Kellen and Tenzig. Kellen had his game face on. I took a quick whiff and was relieved that he didn't have booze-breath.

"Take these," Tenzig said and handed me a pair of flesh-colored ear buds. "That's how we'll communicate. They fit deeply into your ears, so they won't be seen. The battery charge doesn't last long so only activate them when necessary."

"And we don't want a Watcher seeing you talking to yourself," Issa said.

"You have the ID cards?" Kellen asked.

We showed him the ID cards that were hanging around our necks on lanyards.

"What's your name?" he asked Issa.

"Kaylee P-Sedd."

"And you?" Kellen asked me.

"Pitter D-Faye."

I looked at the card, and the picture of the real Pitter D-Faye. He could have been my brother. He was older than me, but I had some bulk, so I looked older than my age.

"Who names their kid Pitter?" I said, sarcastically. "Where I grew up, you'd take a beating for that."

"Let's run through it one more time," Kellen said. "Take me step by step."

"We got it," I said, impatiently. I was tired of going over old ground.

"Humor me," Kellen snapped.

He had a look in his eye that told me there was no room for fooling around. This was his last shot at Regenesis, and the stakes were way higher than before. Once they turned on the Covian Cubes, there'd be no more Tyrian League; no more chance to fight back; no more freewill. If I was scared, he must have been terrified. I wouldn't have blamed him if he'd had a couple of drinks.

"What's first?" he asked.

"I get into the line of workers entering Gate B and Issa—"

"I go to Gate C," she said, finishing my sentence.

"Is the layout of the compound solid in your head?" Kellen asked.

"As good as it's going to be," I said.

"We'll get where we need to go," Issa said with confidence.

"I'm a maintenance worker," I said. "The guys who clean the toilets. I go right to the custodian area on Level C to get a cart that's filled with mops and cleaning stuff."

"And four receptors," Tenzig said. "Along with the radio drive that will allow me to sync you with the grid."

"Makes me feel like a robot," I said.

"In a way, you are," Tenzig said with an apologetic shrug.

Issa said, "They were smuggled in yesterday by the person whose place I'm taking. A cook. I report to the kitchen, log in, and tell them I'm going to the loading dock to receive a shipment of vegetables. But I don't go to the receiving dock, I go to Level D which is the tech floor."

"That's where I meet her with the cleaning cart," I said. "Do they really put kids to work in there? I mean, won't we stand out?"

"Everyone works for Regenesis," Kellen said. "Doesn't matter how old you are."

"Man, there's no end to their suckiness," I said.

"We find an unoccupied workstation and pretend to be cleaning it," Issa said.

Tenzig said, "Issa will place the four receptors on Donovan and insert the syncing device into the workstation. That's where I come in. Donovan, take a seat and clear your mind. I'll link to you and activate the Chrysalis, then link you to the grid. You'll activate it, and the Chrysalis will upload into the Regenesis grid. Then--"

"Then the Chrysalis destroys the grid," Issa said.

"And I give the command to strike," Kellen added.

"How do you do that if the power is out?" I asked.

Kellen showed me his small communicator. "Our network is self-contained and runs on battery power."

"We don't need the grid," Tenzig added.

"When the attack begins," Kellen said. "You two find a safe place to ride it out until the takeover is complete. We'll send in a team to find Tessa and Bodie."

"Good," I said.

I didn't mean it. I was not going to follow that part of the plan. I wasn't kidding myself. The chance of pulling this off without any problems was slim. Even if we were able to upload the Chrysalis and it did its job, it was going to be chaos. I knew how to deal with chaos. I was going to find my mother and Bodie on my own.

"That's the best-case scenario," I said. "Let's pretend something goes wrong."

"If we can't upload the Chrysalis, we have two choices," Issa said. "Hopefully nobody will know what we tried to do, and we simply walk out of the compound."

"But if we're discovered, we won't be walking out," I said. "Not without a fight."

"In that case we have back-up," Issa said. "One of our people in transportation will have a vehicle powered up and ready to go. If we can get to it, I'll fly us out of there."

"That's a very big if," I said.

"It won't come to that," Kellen said with confidence. "There are lots of friendlies inside. But there are also plenty of people who are loyal to Regenesis. Don't be surprised if you're offered help but be careful who you trust."

We all looked at one another, not sure of what else to say.

Issa went to Kellen and gave him a hug. Kellen looked awkward, as if he wasn't sure if he should hug back.

"This is Misha's day," she said.

At the mention of Misha's name, Kellen gave in and hugged Issa.

"I'm proud of you," he said sincerely. "We wouldn't be here without you. I wouldn't be here without you."

"Thank you for saying that," she said. "Remember your promise."

"You know I will," Kellen said.

Kellen gave her one last squeeze, kissed her forehead, then let her go.

"Good luck," he said to her, then looked to me and added, "To all of us."

Issa led us out of the room and through a long corridor that ran beneath one building and on to the next.

I leaned in close to her and whispered, "What did he promise you?"

"He's going to help me find my parents."

Issa had even more at stake then I imagined.

At the end of the corridor was a huge, basement room that was packed with hundreds of people standing silently. Waiting. They were the people of the rebellion.

The Tyrian League.

They didn't look much like an army. They were all ages and races, with as many women as men. Most carried the slim, metal batons they would use to battle the Watchers.

Seeing those, my stomach turned. If all went well, the Watcher's energy-spewing weapons would die, and Regenesis would be at the mercy of a swarm of vengeful people intent on running over them to seize The Core. The fight would be downright Medieval. If the Watchers put up a fight, it would be a bloodbath.

The people cleared a path. All eyes were on us as we walked by. Each and every person either nodded to us, or smiled, or waved. Silently. They didn't look scared, they looked ready. It gave me a feeling of pride, like an old-timey soldier marching through town on his way to war. Which, come to think of it, was pretty much what I was doing.

"This is only a fraction of our force," Kellen said. "We have many more in multiple buildings surrounding the compound. As soon as you're on your way, we'll send a few hundred to gather outside of Gate B. We've been staging protests every day, so the Watchers won't be suspicious. That group will be the first wave to attack when the power goes out. Then the others will join them. We'll put thousands of people into the compound within minutes."

"The Watchers will fight back, even without their guns," I said.

"They might," Kellen said. "But they'll be outnumbered ten to one." He winked at me and added "It won't be a fair fight."

We passed a group of people in uniforms I hadn't seen before.

"The Essen-Tet police," Kellen said, reading my mind. "For the first time in years they'll be allowed to do their job and keep the peace."

I got a few nods of acknowledgment from the police-people.

We arrived at wide stairs that led up to the ground floor. When we climbed halfway up, I turned and looked back over the sea of people who were jammed in below. It was an awe-inspiring sight and proved just how desperate, and dedicated these people were. Knowing that many more people were waiting in buildings all around the compound made my confidence soar. The Tyrian League may just pull this off.

As long as I did my job.

Oh. That.

An odd thing then happened. Every last person raised their hands, holding up five fingers on one hand and one on the other. Six fingers. It was like a silent salute.

I gave a questioning look to Issa, who smiled back and raised her hands to offer the same salute.

"Good luck, Six," she said.

I had to choke back tears. They all knew my story. At least the first part, anyway. They'd been waiting a long time for this moment. Their salute filled me with pride, and more than a little bit of terror.

I gave a quick wave back, then headed up the stairs to the lobby of what looked like it was once an office building. Looking out through the glass doors I could see the city street, and the massive silver-steel wall of the Regenesis Compound a few blocks away. Even from this distance I could see the break in the wall that was Gate B.

"It's time," Kellen said. "The shift is changing."

"I'll set up on the roof," Tenzig said. "It's best for reception."

"Go," Kellen commanded.

Tenzig gave Issa a quick hug, then looked to me and held out his hand to shake.

"Good luck, Donovan," he said.

I shook his hand and said, "See you inside…my head."

"Yes, you will," he said with a wink, and hurried off.

Turned out I kind of liked Tenzig.

Kellen kept his eyes on Gate B in the distance.

"You can go in any time," he said. "It's all right if you're a little early and--"

He abruptly stopped talking because he saw something that made his eyes go wide.

Issa saw his reaction. "What's the matter?" she asked.

"I don't believe it," Kellen muttered to himself.

"What?" I asked, more insistent than Issa.

He pushed open the door and hurried along the sidewalk, headed for the compound. Issa and I followed but held back so it didn't look as though we were with him.

"What's his problem?" I asked.

Issa looked ahead, and she saw it too.

"Oh God no," she exclaimed in horror.

I had no idea what they were looking at, until a few people moved out of the way, and I got a clear view.

Kellen and Issa weren't over-reacting. Moving into position in front of Gate B was a floating platform with a tripod on top.

"The Covian Cube," I said in awe.

We picked up the pace until we got to the intersection. Kellen leaned one arm against the building like he needed the support.

"We're out of time," he said, his voice shaking.

"It's okay," I said. "How much damage could one cube do?"

Kellen gave me a look that told me I had said something dumb.

He gestured for us to look down the street.

Issa and I stole a peek around the corner to get a view of the wide boulevard that ran parallel to the compound wall. What I saw made my knees buckle.

There wasn't just one Covian Cube. Stretching along the road to either side of us were several more, each positioned in front of a gate.

I took a few steps back, stunned. Issa now looked as bad as Kellen.

"If they activate all those cubes..." she said.

She didn't have to finish the thought.

"What do we do?" Issa asked, rattled.

Kellen didn't have a quick answer.

But I did.

"We go," I said. "Now. Once we kill the grid, those cubes will die along with it, right?"

"I...I have to think so," Kellen said, shaken.

Issa looked to me, and I saw panic in her eyes. But she was too tough to buckle.

"Right. See you inside," she said and hurried off toward Gate C."

Kellen looked sick. He clearly feared our chances of success were slipping away. Again.

"We got this," I said with confidence. "Be ready to roll."

Kellen nodded quickly, as if relieved that at least one of us still had faith.

I slapped him on the back, then made my way toward Gate B, walking by the Covian Cube that loomed above, ready to start shooting out its mind-bending beams of light.

Unless we shut it all down.

CHAPTER 27

I waited in line along with a bunch of workers who were headed into the Regenesis Compound. Nobody looked happy to be there, but does anybody look happy on their way to work at a sucky job? I tried to act all casual, but the harder you try to look casual, the less casual you look. The Watchers at the gate were armed with the disk-pistols in hip holsters, watching the crowd for signs of trouble. One was checking IDs. Two others ran a scanner that everyone had to pass through. Two more Watchers stood beyond the detector. They were the enforcers. If something went south, they'd be the ones to start shooting.

My biggest worry was the guy checking IDs. If I got past him, I'd be in. Everyone had to take off the ID that hung around their neck and hand it to the checker. That guy would put it through a scanner to make sure it was valid and matched the person. Gulp.

There were no problems with the people in front of me. They all got checked, scanned, and allowed into the compound. The Watchers looked bored. I didn't want to give them any reason to get more interested in their job.

When it was my turn I stepped up, pulled the lanyard from around my neck and handed it to the guard. He looked at the picture and then to my face. I smiled at him. Not that I wanted to be friendly, but the I.D. picture of Pitter D-Faye was all sorts of sour-looking, like he had diarrhea or something. I figured that by smiling it would change my look enough so it wouldn't seem strange that I didn't look exactly like the guy in the picture.

Maybe it was my imagination, but it seemed like this guard was giving my ID way more scrutiny than he gave to the people before me. But I kept smiling.

He passed it under the scanner and looked at his computer screen as information about Mr. D-Faye came up. The guard read it, then looked at me with suspicion.

"Little young to be working here," he said.

Think fast, Donovan, think fast.

I shrugged. "Gotta eat, you know?"

The guard gave another look to the card, then to the screen, then to me. He handed the ID back to me and nodded for me to enter.

I wanted to scream, "Yes!" and punch the air in victory, but that would have been stupid. So I took the card back as if I'd done it a thousand times before and looped the lanyard around my neck. Moving on, I stood behind a few people waiting to be scanned. I wasn't in yet, but the pressure was off. I had nothing suspicious on me. Issa had given me a small pack with a sandwich and a chunk of cheese to complete the illusion that I was there for a long shift. When it was my turn, I handed the pack to the guard, who dug through it and handed it back. It was only the first check. I still had to walk through the scanner.

I stepped up to the door-sized scanner frame and was motioned to walk through. I stepped through with confidence...

...and an alarm went off.

I think my heart stopped.

"Step back," the Watcher commanded.

I took a step back through the scanner and waited to be called through again. The Watcher on the far side checked a computer screen that I guess had information from the scan.

"Again," he said to me.

I walked through and alarms went off again. I fought the urge to run.

"Why is it doing that?" I asked, innocently.

The Watcher who had checked my bag joined the second guy and they both looked at the computer screen. They were definitely seeing something they didn't like. Behind them, the other two Watchers strolled over in case there was going to be trouble.

I didn't know what to do. What had they seen? Was there still a physical piece of the Chrysalis in me? Was there some kind of warning programmed into their system that would recognize me? Were there "WANTED – DEAD OR ALIVE" posters with my picture hanging around? All I could do was stand there and look innocent. I wasn't exactly sure of how to do that, especially since I was pretty guilty.

The Watcher who checked my bag said, "What do you have in your ears?"

His tone was harsh, as if he'd detected a weapon in my shoe. Or my ears.

"My ears?" I said and for a moment I truly didn't know what he meant.

Then it hit me. I had the communicators in my ears that would let me speak with Tenzig. Why hadn't Kellen smuggled those into the compound along with the receptors? This was about to go very wrong, very fast.

"Oh!" I said, pretending to realize what he was talking about. "You mean these?"

I took out both buds and held them out for the Watcher to see.

"I forget to take 'em out," I said. "Sorry."

The Watcher looked at them with curiosity.

"What are they?" he asked.

"Huh? I replied.

"What are they?" he asked again.

"Sorry, my hearing isn't so good. What did you say?"

The guy was losing his patience. He grabbed one of the devices away from me and held it up in front of my nose.

"What are these?" he said, raising his voice.

"Hearing aids," I said, a bit too loud. "I can't hear much without them."

The Watcher shoved the device back into my hand.

"Put them in," he commanded.

"Huh?"

"I said put them in your ears!" he screamed, pointing at his own ears.

"Oh! Okay," I said and inserted both devices into my ears. "That's better. Now what do you want to know?"

The frustrated Watcher gave up and said, "Nothing. Go to work."

He left me and headed back for his scanner.

"Okay," I said. "Thanks."

The two armed Watchers had already wandered away. I was annoying them. Something I was very good at.

"Enjoy your day," I said to the guy who waved me in. Though by letting me into the compound he had pretty much insured that he was going to have an incredibly rotten day.

I hoisted my pack onto my shoulder and walked off. A floating tram filled with sightseers rolled past me, just like Kellen had described.

"Welcome to the Regenesis Compound!" the tour guide announced cheerfully.

There were families and grandparents and little kids with ice cream cones. This was like a visit to Disneyland for them. Only there were no rides, and it was definitely not the happiest place on earth. But it did show me that in spite of their Covian Cube, Regenesis was still pumping out the propaganda that if you believed in the church and were totally loyal, you may one day live in a mansion inside the compound.

Dirt bags.

I glanced to my right to Gate C to try and spot Issa, but it was too far away and there were lots of people wandering around. I had to trust that she'd make it in. I had a half an hour to find the maintenance department, get my cleaning supplies from a Tyrian League sympathizer, and find my way to Level D. The pressure was on and wouldn't let up until Regenesis was brought to its knees.

Or I was killed.

My instructions were to board the monorail and take it to the stop called "Core." I found the station easily because that's where everybody was going. I stood on the platform with a handful of people and didn't make eye contact with anybody. I wondered how many knew what was about to happen. I only had to wait a few minutes before the sleek monorail train glided silently into the station. I boarded and took a seat by the window to be sure I wouldn't miss the sign for "Core." The doors slid closed, and the train accelerated smoothly.

The futuristic train sparkled as if was being constantly being polished. It was so clean you could lick it. Other than the spaceship I had flown in on, and the various flying vehicles on the city streets, this was the most modern thing I'd seen on Tyria. The rest of Essen-Tet was a depressing, dirty ghetto.

The Regenesis Compound was not.

Kellen had described it when he told me of the events that happened years before, but I didn't imagine it would be this, well, perfect. This place was like something out of millionaire-heaven. The homes were built between trees and running brooks and flowers that must have been cared for at least as much as the monorail was polished. The further we travelled into the compound, the bigger and fancier the homes became until it seemed as though every one of them was like a country club.

This was what Regenesis was truly about. Money. These people built big businesses and cushy lives using the money that poor people gave them. Was it like this across the rest of Tyria? And other worlds? Up until that moment I feared these fake religious people. Now I hated them.

As I gawked out of the window, I caught sight of the massive, castle-like building we were headed toward. There were turrets, spires, and balconies everywhere, all constructed from gleaming silver-steel. This was The Core. The center of Regenesis and the home of Vail Kobain. I can say one thing about my journey into the heart of darkness, everything I saw only gave me more confidence that these people had to be stopped.

I didn't get mad, but I was determined to get even.

The monorail pulled in to The Core station which was easy to see because it was the last stop. Duh. The train emptied and I melted into the flow of people headed for the building. As I got closer the structure seemed to grow before my eyes. It soared skyward, its silver skin gleaming in the sun against a bright blue sky. As I stepped out of the light and through the swinging doors, I had a brief moment of panic, wondering if I'd ever see daylight again.

I had to stop thinking so hard.

Inside was a huge atrium with a soaring glass ceiling. I had pretty much memorized the route to the maintenance area on level C from the maps I was shown. It was three floors down. Escalators connected the floors like a mall, and I went straight down. Level C looked way different than the ground floor. The ceiling was low. There were no fancy decorations. This was for the workers, not the residents.

I took the route I had memorized, walking down a long corridor with closed doors to either side until I came to a door marked: 311 – Custodial Staff. I went straight inside to find a surprisingly large space with aisles of floor-to-ceiling racks that held various janitor equipment. There were bottles of cleanser, rolls of toilet paper, stacks of mops, and most everything else a janitor would need to…janit. Several people pushed carts up and down the aisles, picking out whatever items they needed to do their job that day. It was like a janitor-superstore.

Directly inside the door was a guy sitting behind a counter, checking in workers as they reported for their shifts. I got in line behind a few women and waited. When my turn came, I wasn't exactly sure of what to do. It wasn't like I was going to step up and say: "Hi. I'm here to destroy Regenesis. Where's my gear?" I did the same thing that everyone did in front of me and showed him my ID card. Or rather Pitter D-Faye's card.

The guy glanced at it, then to me with a curious expression that told me something was wrong. Or maybe something was right. Either way, this guy knew I wasn't Pitter D-Faye.

"Come with me," he said, then called out, "Kiera, take over for a minute, would you?"

A woman came out from one of the aisles carrying an electronic clipboard.

"Sure," she said. "Happy to get off my feet."

The guy motioned for me to follow and walked down an aisle of shelves loaded with cleaning supplies. He moved quickly, and a few times he glanced over his shoulder to make sure I was following him. Or maybe he was worried about somebody following the both of us.

At the end of this long aisle in the center of janitor wonderland, the guy opened a door, glanced around again, then motioned for me to follow him inside. I didn't hesitate. If he was worried about somebody spotting us, then I was too.

The room beyond was a much smaller storage area that had stacks of cardboard boxes filled with…whatever. In the center of the room was a fully loaded janitor's cart. There were a couple of mops and brooms; bottles of cleaning fluid, small dust-brushes with dustpans; and a stack of yellow sponges. Hanging off of both sides were empty black plastic trash bags.

The guy went straight to the cart and grabbed one of the larger, white bottles.

"It came in early this morning," he said, his voice shaky with nervous tension. You'd think he was holding plutonium. "The sooner you get it out of here the better."

He unscrewed the cap and emptied the contents onto his open palm. There was no soap inside. What came out were the four receptors that would be attached to my head, along with the radio-drive.

"Do you know what they're for?" he asked.

"Yeah," I said. "Do you?"

"No, and I don't want to. If the Watchers show up and start asking questions, the less I know the better."

He dumped the hardware back into the bottle and screwed the cap on.

"If you get caught, they'll arrest my entire department," he said.

"If I get caught, you're gonna have a whole lot more to worry about than that."

"Yeah, I guess you're right," he said and placed the bottle back on the cart.

The guy stood up straight and said, "Thank you."

"Don't thank me yet," I replied. "I haven't done anything."

"Yeah you have, just by being here."

"Then I know how you can thank me. Tell me where my mother and my friend are."

The guy got a puzzled look as if I'd spoken a different language.

"Regenesis arrested them?" he asked. "Why?"

"To stop me from doing the thing you're going to thank me for after I do it," I said.

He frowned. "I can't say for sure. But if I were to guess, I'd say they were being held on the second floor of the west building. We've cleaned prison cells there."

"Thanks."

He went for the door, then turned back to me and said, "Act like you belong."

I grabbed the handle of the cart and wheeled it toward him.

"No problem," I said. "I'm an expert at pretending like I belong."

He opened the door, stole a quick glance outside to make sure there were no curious eyes around, then stepped out of the way.

"Good luck, Six," he whispered in case curious ears were listening.

"To you too," I said and wheeled past him.

I pushed the cart back to the entrance. Nobody gave me a second look. I must have looked like a real janitor. Kralovenic would be proud. The dirtbag.

My heart was beating like crazy. Everything had gone according to plan, but how long would that last? I couldn't take the escalator with the cart, so I went in search of an elevator. I'd only gone a few steps when I saw two Watchers headed my way. My hands started to shake. I had to act like everything was cool, but I had trouble controlling my breathing. The last thing I needed to do was hyperventilate and pass out in front of these two goons.

"Hey!" one of them shouted.

I froze. Did he recognize me?

"Yeah?" I asked.

One of the Watchers approached and stood on the opposite side of the cart from me.

"You always work this hard?" he asked.

I shrugged. "What do you mean?"

"You're sweating like you've been digging a ditch," he said.

He was right. My face was covered with nervous sweat. The guy tossed a paper cup into one of the trash bags hanging from my cart.

"Relax, you'll live longer," he said and the two walked on.

"I'll try," I said. "Thanks."

I wiped the sweat from my forehead, took a deep breath to calm myself, and continued to the service elevator. I hit the button to go down and the door opened right away to reveal another Watcher. I gasped, hoped he didn't notice my nervous reaction, and backed the cart away so he could get out. He walked past me without giving me a second look.

I pushed the cart onto the elevator and could finally breathe again. I had to get a grip. If I was going to panic whenever I saw a Watcher, this mission was doomed. I hit the button for Level D and the elevator descended. A few seconds later the door slid open to reveal an entirely different world than the one I'd just left.

Level D was the tech center of The Core. Ahead of me were glass doors that looked out onto a sea of workstations with people focused on their computer monitors doing whatever it was they did to keep the criminal empire running. This was where Kellen and Misha tried to upload the Chrysalis into the grid fifteen years before.

"Ready?" came a familiar voice.

I jumped like a nervous cat as Issa stepped from the shadows.

"Any problems?" she asked.

"Nope. Everything's here."

"Then let's do it," she said and strode for the glass doors.

The doors slid open. Issa turned back to me, smiled, and said, "Now it's our turn."

History was about to repeat itself, only this time there was going to be a better outcome. At least that's what I kept telling myself. This was the final leg of a journey that had begun when I was a baby. A journey I had no idea I was on. But here I was. Knowing there were thousands of desperate people waiting outside the walls of this compound, counting on me not to screw up, didn't make it any easier.

"This is going to work," I said.

"Yes, it is," Issa added.

I'm not sure if either of us truly believed that.

CHAPTER 28

There were hundreds of people at work stations, lined up in rows, focused on computer monitors. There was no way to know who was loyal to the church and who was going along because it was the only way they could get a job. Working in this clean, modern building was way better than slaving on some grimy assembly line. Though by the looks of things, this was just as much of an assembly line as Factory B. It just smelled better.

I pushed the cart along an aisle, passing shoulder-high cubicle walls that sectioned off each workstation. Issa walked next to me. I hoped nobody was going to question why a cook and a janitor were strolling through the tech nerve center of Regenesis, but everyone was totally locked on their computer screens and didn't even notice.

We walked to the far side of the room, searching for an empty station. Going this deep worried me because if we had to make a quick exit, it would have been nice to be near the exit. But the far side of the sprawling room seemed less busy so that's where we went.

"There," Issa said, pointing to an empty office.

Rather than a cubicle that was out in the open and easy for people to see us, this office was a room with a door. My palms started to sweat. Since we'd made it this far, I was getting less worried about uploading the Chrysalis into the grid and more concerned about what would happen afterward. But I couldn't look too far ahead. My job wasn't done yet.

"Wait here," Issa said. "I want to make sure there's an input port in there."

When she left to go scout, I glanced back at the sea of workers and tried not to imagine the mayhem that was about to descend on them. How many knew what was coming and how many were about to get the shock of their lives?

"We're good," Issa said as she stuck her head out of the door.

I grabbed a brush off the cart. If somebody asked us what we were doing, I wanted it to look like we were there cleaning, as lame as it might seem. Issa stayed at the door as a lookout, and I went inside. We exchanged silent looks. This was it.

I was suddenly grateful for the dozens of times we'd practiced this because I was on auto-pilot and didn't have to think. I went straight for the desk and sat down. In front of me was a computer monitor, a keyboard, and a black box with input ports.

I touched the earpiece in my right ear, activating it.

"We're in," I said.

Tenzig's voice came through loud and clear.

"Tell me where," he replied.

I let out a relieved breath because Tenzig was now with me. There was no excitement in his voice. He was calm and focused on business. I pictured him sitting on the roof of the building across from Gate B, alone, with his tech-pad.

"I'm at a workstation in an office on Level D," I said.

"I'm not reading the Chrysalis," he replied.

I looked to Issa, who was standing over me, holding the four receptors that would link my brain to Tenzig's computer.

"Oh, right," I said. "Stand by."

Issa placed two receptors on my forehead and the other two on the back of my neck.

"Install the drive," she said.

I took a nervous breath, lined up the radio-drive and clicked it into place. With that move we'd already gotten further than Kellen and Misha T-Soo had.

"Try now," I said to Tenzig.

After a few seconds, Tenzig said, "I've got you. Here we go."

The monitor in front of me came to life. I knew that's what was supposed to happen, but it made me jump with surprise anyway.

On the monitor was the rising-sun logo of Regenesis.

"You seeing this?" I asked.

"I am," Tenzig replied.

I had become a human modem, wirelessly connecting my brain and Tenzig's computer.

My hard-drive of a head.

"Sit back, I'll access the Chrysalis," Tenzig said.

"Wait."

Issa shot me a surprised look.

"What's the problem?" Tenzig asked.

"No problem," I replied. "You're in their system. Find my mother and Bodie."

Issa tensed up. This wasn't part of their plan.

Too bad. It was part of my plan.

"Donovan, we've got thousands of people ready to move," Tenzig said curtly. "We can't waste time."

There was definite tension in his voice.

"It's not wasting time," I said. "Once the Chrysalis is uploaded, you won't need me anymore. I'm going after them."

"We're sending in a team to get them," Issa said with rising concern.

"Good," I replied. "Do that. But I'm going after them too. Stop talking, Tenzig. Search the building. Start by looking on the second floor of the west building."

"Donovan, you're being unreasonable," Tenzig said.

I looked to Issa who was staring at me with such intensity that if looks could kill, well, this story would be over.

"I'm here to help you," I said calmly. "The least you can do is help me too."

The image on the monitor changed. The mad genius had already gone to work. He scrolled through several screens of data until he came upon a map that was the layout of The Core buildings.

"We're wasting time," Issa whispered through clenched teeth.

I ignored her.

She went back to the door to make sure nobody had spotted us.

Tenzig knew what he was doing. Several screens slid by as he scrolled through maps. It took maybe a minute, though it felt like an hour. The screen finally landed on a diagram that showed the cells on the second floor of the west building that the janitor-supervisor told me about.

"That's probably where they are," Tenzig said.

My heart leapt. I stared at the map, doing my best to relate it to the places I'd already been and to take a mental picture of the route.

"Got it," I said. "Thank you."

"May we continue?" Tenzig asked calmly, though I knew he wasn't.

"Go for it," I said.

I suddenly felt dizzy. Tenzig was digging into my brain. I had to close my eyes for fear I'd fall out of the chair.

"Talk to me," Tenzig said.

I opened my eyes and yet again, was startled by what I saw. The Chrysalis was back, filling up the room. It was so dense I could barely see Issa through the digits.

"And?" Issa asked with a strained whisper.

"He's in," I said. "I see the code."

"So strange," Issa said in awe. "I don't see a thing."

"Find MISHA K-SOO," Tenzig said.

I scanned the floating figures. It wasn't hard to pick out MISHA K-SOO, seeing as the bright green letters stood out against the sea of white figures. I stood up and walked through the data, pushing aside the digits that drifted about like dandelion seeds floating on a breeze. In seconds I was in front of the large words: MISHA K-SOO."

"Ready," I said.

"Touch it," Tenzig commanded.

I didn't close my eyes. Big mistake. When I touched the words, the data disappeared. It was so sudden and disorienting that I nearly fell over.

"You okay?" Issa asked.

"I'm fine."

What was left was the only word that mattered. It floated in front of my eyes, tempting me to touch it.

ENGAGE.

We'd done it. Not that I doubted we could but, okay, I doubted we could.

"Everybody ready?" I asked Tenzig.

I looked to Issa, who gave me a tentative smile and a nod. This was the final step. I was about to light a fuse that would set off the fireworks, and fulfill my destiny

"Do it, Donovan," Tenzig commanded with more than a hint of impatience.

I took a quick breath, reached up, and touched ENGAGE.

The word disappeared and was replaced by: UPLOAD 1%. The process of emptying my brain into the grid wasn't instantaneous. The percentage grew steadily, but slowly. 2%...3%...4%... It wasn't going to take long to get to one hundred, but every second felt like a lifetime. Tenzig was right. I needed to be there. If I'd been outside the wall, the process might have taken hours, if it worked at all.

"What's going on?" Issa asked.

"It's uploading but slowly," I said. "It'll take a couple of minutes before--"

Something flashed on the computer screen.

"Trouble," Tenzig said.

I ran back to the desk to see two words flashing on the screen: SYSTEM BREACH.

"What is that?" I asked.

"It means the grid detected the virus," Tenzig said, the strain in his voice was obvious.

"But it's still uploading," I said as the floating data now showed: UPOLOAD 20%. Does that mean they can't stop it?"

"Given time, maybe," Tenzig said. "They don't have that time."

"But can they trace it to us?" I asked.

Tenzig didn't reply which meant he didn't know, or he didn't want to tell us.

"What do we do?" I asked.

My answer came from Kellen. He must have joined Tenzig on the roof.

"Get out of there," Kellen commanded. "Take the radio-drive and get to the evacuation point."

"What is going on?" Issa demanded.

"They want us to take the radio-drive and get out," I said.

"But that'll stop the upload," Issa said.

The upload was at 35%. Still a long way to go and with no way of telling how long it would take to finish, or for the Watchers to show up.

"I'll stay," Issa said. "You get to the evacuation point."

"And do what?" I said. "You're the pilot, remember? And I've got to be near the radio-drive, or the upload will be even slower."

"Get out now!" Kellen commanded.

"I'm not leaving without Bodie and my mother."

"No!" Kellen exclaimed. "If the Watchers get you, you're done for good. We're all done. You've got to get out."

The upload progress was at 40%.

"I'm staying," I said to Issa. "It won't take much longer."

We heard a commotion coming from the far end of the tech center. The outside doors slid open, and Watchers came flooding in. If they knew exactly which office we were uploading from they'd be on us in seconds. But they were searching, which meant we still had time, but not a lot.

Issa grabbed the radio-drive out of the jack.

The sudden change made my head spin. The upload progress winked out at 42%. The computer screen went dark.

"We're out of here!" she exclaimed.

She grabbed my hand and yanked me toward the office door. I was still dazed from having my brain monkeyed with and didn't put up a fight. She pulled me out of the office, stopped at the janitor's cart, and reached down deep into one of the garbage bags. I watched with confusion, wondering why she would do that...until she pulled out her backpack.

This girl was badass. Let's not forget that.

We walked quickly to one side of the huge space, opposite from where the Watchers were making their way toward the office we'd just left. I pulled the receptors from my forehead and neck and stuck them in my pocket. We were suspicious looking enough. Having chunky looking antennas sticking out of my head would only make it worse. The workers had yet to figure out something was going on. If they were seeing the SYSTEM BREACH notice on their screens, they didn't realize it was happening right under their noses. They were more interested in the Watchers who were hurrying through, methodically searching every station.

We worked our way to the front of the vast room, moving along the opposite wall from the Watchers. The trick was to move quickly but not draw attention. And to be invisible, but it's not like that was an option. We made it to the exit at the same moment the Watchers hit the office we'd been in. They quickly tore apart the janitor's cart.

"Gotta go," Issa said and pulled me to the door.

It slid open and we were out of the tech center.

"We've got to get to the transpo center," Issa said.

I dug in my heels. "You go. I'm going after Tessa and Bodie."

"There isn't time," Issa exclaimed.

"I'm not leaving without them."

Issa grabbed me by the shoulders and shoved my back against the wall.

"One, you have zero chance of finding them before the Watchers find you. Two, even if you did you wouldn't make it out of the compound on foot. Three, the only chance we have of saving them is to bring down Regenesis. Four, without you we can't do that. Five...I can't think of a five but one through four are pretty good reasons."

"I can't abandon them," I said.

"You're not," Issa said, softening a bit. "You're setting up to take another run at Regenesis. This isn't over unless you get caught."

I hated to give in, but she was right.

"Is there a plan B?" I asked.

"There's always a plan B," Issa said.

"All right," I said. "Let's get out of here."

She led us up a flight of stairs to ground level, and the lobby of The Core. We went straight for the exit and left the building. I expected to see Watchers all over the place, scrambling to find the rebels who dared to infiltrate their grid. But all was calm. The word hadn't spread. Yet.

"We have friends here," Issa said, under her breath. "Lots of them. They've got a shuttle craft warmed up and ready to go."

"You know that for sure?" I asked.

"I know for sure that was the plan," Issa replied.

That didn't give me huge confidence.

"Is there a Plan C?" I asked.

"That is Plan C."

"What happened to Plan B?"

"You're Plan B."

"Oh, right."

I'd forgotten that this had been tried before.

We kept moving with our heads down. Whenever we passed a Watcher, we turned away so as not to be recognized. I couldn't help but worry that the longer it took for us to fly out of there, the better organized these bad guys would get. Sneaking in to upload the Chrysalis had one thing going for it: surprise. We lost that when the grid sounded the alarm. I couldn't begin to think how we were going to get another shot at it. But if we didn't get out of there, we wouldn't get the chance to figure one out.

The "transpo center" was a big, open parking lot filled with floating vehicles and aerobikes.

"Don't say anything," Issa warned me. "I'm not sure who our contact is."

"How are you going to find them?" I asked. "Some kind of secret code word?"

"Well…yes," she said flatly.

"Oh. Works for me," I said with a shrug.

We entered through a gate that opened up to a sea of vehicles. Issa went straight for them and for a second I thought we might just hijack one. But an aerobike flew up and cut us off. The woman aboard wore black coveralls and had grease on her hands.

"Need something?" the no-nonsense woman asked as she wiped her hands on a dirty rag.

"Yes," Issa replied. "We need a tandem jumper. Regenesis business in the seventh quad."

The woman eyed us suspiciously. She was taller than me, but I had a few pounds on her. If I had to, I could take her down.

"You have a level nine travel order?" she asked.

Uh oh. It was looking like I was going to start throwing punches.

"No," Issa said. "Travel orders only go up to level eight."

I tensed up, ready to rush the woman before she could make a move. Or sound an alarm.

She got off the hovering bike and said, "Follow me."

I threw a questioning look to Issa.

Issa shrugged and said, "I didn't say it was a complicated secret code."

We'd found our contact.

The woman led us to a long row of vehicles that looked like sleek, miniature jet-fighters. They had two seats, one behind the other, beneath a clear canopy. The wings were stubby, and the tail was short. It looked like the kind of toy you'd see outside a grocery store that cost a quarter for a little kid to shake around on for a minute. But there was no place to put a quarter.

The woman pushed a latch just above the wing and the clear canopy hinged open.

"Now hit me," she said to Issa.

"What?" Issa asked, surprised.

"If you could knock me out, that would be better," the woman added, deadly serious.

"Why?" Issa asked.

"The Watchers will ask me why I let you take off with a jumper. The truth wouldn't be good for me. So hit me."

Issa gave me a squeamish look and said, "This is more your department."

I hadn't punched anybody in at least a week. I was overdue, but I wasn't used to hitting anybody in cold blood, especially not a lady.

"Do it," the woman said to me.

"Where do you want it?" I asked.

She touched her cheek and said, "Don't hold back."

In another life I would have loved this.

"I'm sorry," I said. "Thank you for helping us."

"Don't give up, Six," she said.

I took a deep breath, hauled back and swung a haymaker that landed square on her jaw. The woman let out a small yelp, stumbled back and hit the ground. Hard. I hoped I hadn't broken her jaw, or my hand. She didn't move. Either I'd knocked her cold, or she was acting as if I had.

Issa looked at me with wide eyes. She may have been a fighter, but she'd never seen me in action.

"Did you enjoy that?" she asked.

"Give me a break, no," I said while shaking my hand to get feeling back in my fingers. "Maybe a little."

"Stop right there!" came a bold command.

A Watcher was on a dead run, headed our way.

"Get in back," Issa commanded as she climbed aboard in the front seat.

I got in and barely got my hands out of the way as the canopy closed over us. Issa powered up the engine as the little craft was hit with a blast of energy from the Watcher's pistol. The whole craft shook.

"It's okay," Issa said, though her voice was cracking with tension. "These fighters are built to take more than that."

"Can we go, please?" I shouted as I strapped in.

"On three," she said. "Three."

The craft shot straight up, pushing me into the seat with I don't know how many G-forces. I think my stomach stayed on the ground. But we were airborne. Within seconds I could see the wall that surrounded the compound. It was a few miles away, but we were high enough that I could see the filthy city of Essen-Tet beyond. It was a dramatic contrast with the green garden world that was inside the walls.

"Tenzig, do you hear me?" I said.

I got no response.

"I lost Tenzig," I said.

"They might be jamming frequencies," Issa said. "Nothing he can do anyway so—"

Our craft was hit with another bolt of energy that was way more powerful than what the Watcher had fired. We shook so hard I though my brain would come loose in my head.

"Whoa, what was that?" I asked.

"They're already after us."

I looked over my shoulder to see two similar vehicles flying our way.

"These things shoot?" I asked.

"They do. Do you get airsick?"

"I don't know."

"Don't puke down my neck."

Issa threw the joystick hard to the right and hit the throttle. The engine whined and we shot forward. I wasn't ready for that, and my head hit the canopy.

"Can we outrun them?" I asked.

"They'd just follow. We'd never be able to put down."

"So what do we do?"

"We shoot them out of the sky."

Whoa. I wasn't expecting a dog fight.

"Can you do that?" I asked, incredulous.

"I'm sure as hell gonna try," she said and pulled back on the joystick.

We shot higher and my head slammed into the seat back. The last thing we needed was for me to hurl so I closed my eyes. That only made it worse, so I tried to focus on the horizon. What I saw instead was one of the fighter-craft headed our way, directly in front of us.

"Incoming!" I declared.

"He's an amateur," Issa said with confidence.

"And you're not?"

"I learned from the best."

She thrust the joystick forward and we dropped fast. I heard the faint sound of the energy bolts that were fired from the other ship as they whizzed past us overhead.

Issa rolled us into a figure-eight. At least my stomach told me that's what it was because we made a couple of turns that made my head spin one way and my stomach the other. When we leveled off, we were behind the fighter that had fired at us.

"One down," she said.

"It's not down, it's right there," I said.

"Is it?" she said with glee.

She squeezed the trigger in the joystick, firing two bolts of energy at the clueless ship. The powerful charges hit the rear engine, dead on. The ship spun into a barrel-roll.

"He can't stabilize, he has to land," Issa said proudly.

"Damn!" I shouted, totally impressed. "That was awesome!"

"I told you, I learned from the best."

"Kellen?"

"Who else?

Our jumper shuddered. It wasn't as violent as the first hit, but a wheezing sound told me were losing power.

"He torched our main engine," Issa said, oddly matter-of-fact calm. "We lost forward thrust. That's a problem."

"You think? Are we gonna crash?"

"Not if I can control the descent."

Issa let go of the joystick which had become useless. She put both hands on the control panel and a series of toggle switches.

"I can manually ignite the stabilizers to control our fall," she said.

Issa alternated throwing the toggles. With each new switch, I heard different, smaller engines whine to life, shut down, or fire up again. I don't know how many engines this thing had to give us lift, but Issa knew how to alternate between them to keep us stable and not plummet nose first. I didn't say a word. I didn't want to ruin her concentration.

Kellen really had taught her well.

"We're going down too fast," she said.

I looked down to see we were headed for a stand of tall trees.

"Maybe the trees can cushion us," I said.

"Or tear us apart," she replied. "But it's the best chance we have."

The ship bucked like an angry bronco while Issa desperately tried to keep us stable.

"Don't give up, Donovan," Issa said. "We're not done yet."

Then we hit the trees.

THE CORE

Vail Kobain stood at the massive window of her apartment, looking out over the expanse of the Regenesis Compound. *Her* compound.

In the years since the Tyrian League's failed coup, Regenesis had grown far more powerful. Under her watch and thanks to the donations from gullible followers looking for a better life, it had built itself up from humble beginnings into a juggernaut that had complete control over the economies of multiple worlds, and their people.

But there was a flaw. The church relied on its technology. If the grid went dark, Regenesis would be blind and helpless. The idea of it all being torn down seemed impossible, until the traitorous genius Misha K-Soo created a program that could throttle it. She was killed, but her insidious virus didn't die along with her. When the rebellion was crushed, the virus was sent off in multiple human carriers...the babies they called scions. These hosts quickly disappeared throughout the universe.

Regenesis learned of the entire plot after arresting and torturing many of the rebels to get the information. It was a chilling realization for Kobain to learn just how close they had come to being overthrown.

The Watchers had been hunting the scions ever since but after so many years with no sign of them, Kobain was beginning to think the children were all lost, or dead, or had no idea of the power they held. Kobain allowed herself to breathe easily.

Until they found Donovan. It was a fluke. While preparing to expand the church to this primitive planet called Earth, a routine medical scan of the population detected Tyrian genetics. Pinpointing him took time, but they eventually found him.

It meant the danger had not passed.

And now, "Donovan Six" was back on Tyria, presumably carrying Misha K-Soo's virus. For the first time in her life, Kobain was worried. She needed to protect the grid, The Core, and ultimately the entire church.

The elevator door to the apartment opened to reveal Tessa and Bodie. They were pushed out of the elevator by a Watcher and had to squint when hit by the bright sunlight that poured through the huge windows of the luxurious apartment.

"Good afternoon," Vail Kobain said flatly.

She was no longer cordial toward them. This was business. She motioned to some chairs.

Bodie looked to Tessa, letting her decide if they should accept the invitation.

"I'll stand," Tessa said.

"Yeah," Bodie said quickly. "Me too."

Kobain reacted with a shrug.

"I brought you here because I would like your help."

"You're dreaming," Bodie said defiantly.

"I have an offer," Kobain said. "Many people work in the Regenesis Compound. While most are loyal to the Regent, I understand there are a few non-believers who have chosen to be part of your misguided venture."

Bodie threw Tessa a look. Tessa didn't blink.

"These heathens may try to act against Regenesis, or aid those who try to damage the church. In the spirit of peace and unity, we can't allow such a thing."

"Why are you telling me this?" Tessa asked.

"For their own safety it would be best if they were relieved of their duties before they did anything foolish that might put them in danger."

"You mean you want to arrest them before they cause trouble," Bodie said.

"It would be best for everyone," Kobain said.

Tessa said, "So you want me to tell you who isn't loyal to the church so you can save them from themselves? Is that it?"

Kobain smiled, which didn't happen often. "That's precisely what I'm asking."

"And what makes you think I know any of these people?" Tessa asked.

"Don't be coy," Kobain said. "I know all about Donovan's father. Why do you think he was transferred out of Essen-Tet?"

Tessa stiffened. "Transferred?" she asked, hopefully.

Kobain strolled directly in front of Tessa and looked her square in the eye.

"Yes, he's alive," she said. "Give me the names of those who are plotting against Regenesis, and I'll bring him back to you."

Tessa fought to keep up the image of calm defiance.

"I...I don't know any of the people you're talking about," she said, her voice quivering with emotion."

"Yet your son is one of those people," Kobain said. "We both know that. When we catch him, he won't be given the same mercy that we showed his father. But if you cooperate, then maybe—"

"You call yourself a woman of the church?" Tessa asked with disgust. "Your power comes from fear, and I am not afraid of you."

"No?" Kobain said. "Let me show you something."

She walked to a far wall where a large video monitor hung. She touched the screen, and an image appeared. It was a live video feed from the street outside of Gate B. Hundreds of protesters were grouped together in defiance of Regenesis.

"Another fruitless protest from non-believers," Kobain said.

Tessa knew the truth. These people weren't there to protest. They were the first wave of invaders that would attack once the Regenesis grid went dead. It gave Tessa hope. If the people were gathering, it must mean the plan was in motion.

"Why are you asking me for names?" Tessa said. "You can see the people you think are your enemies right there."

"But we don't know who is working inside the compound," Kobain said.

She touched the screen. The camera panned right, settling on something that made Tessa catch her breath.

"Oh man," Bodie said.

The Covian Cube loomed over the group, ready to be activated.

"You know what this is and what it does," Kobain said. "On my command these heathens will obey my every instruction. I could ask them to disperse, or to turn on each other and fight to the death."

Kobain touched the screen again. The image divided into four frames, each showing a different gate that had a Covian Cube planted in front. Several technicians swarmed around the devices, feverishly making final adjustments.

"It doesn't matter if these people fear me," Kobain said. "They can choose to accept the church or be commanded to. It will be much easier for those who make the right choice. I sincerely hope you make the right choice."

Tessa's knees went weak. She'd experienced the power of the Covian Cube. Once they were activated and their mind controlling power unleashed, there would be no more resistance.

"I told you," Tessa said in a small voice. "I don't know any names. And if I did, I wouldn't tell you. I've made my choice."

Kobain sighed and waved to the Watchers who had been keeping an eye on them from the elevator.

"I see," she said. "I was hoping to avoid this."

Two more Watchers appeared from the next room. Following them was a woman wearing a white lab coat carrying a silver tray of medical instruments. The two Watchers grabbed Bodie and pulled him toward the dining table that had once held a feast.

"Whoa, hey, what's this?" Bodie yelled.

"I was hoping you would willingly offer the truth, but there is another way," Kobain said.

Bodie fought but the Watchers lifted him up onto the table, forced him onto his back and held him down.

"This is crazy!" he shouted. "I don't know anything!"

"He's telling the truth," Tessa shouted. "He doesn't know a thing!"

She rushed to help Bodie, but a Watcher grabbed her and threw her to the floor. He stood over her with his boot on her arm, pinning her down.

The woman in the lab coat placed the tray down on the table and took out a silver scalpel.

"What are you gonna do?" Bodie shouted as he fought to get away. "Torture me?"

"Nothing quite so pedestrian," Kobain said with a sly smile. "We're going to put an end to the Tyrian League,"

The woman approached Bodie, who struggled desperately.

On the video monitor, a buzzer sounded.

Kobain shot a look to the screen where the words: SYSTEM BREACH flashed.

Tessa knew what that meant, and she smiled.

"I wouldn't bet on that," she said with a triumphant laugh.

A look of panic momentarily flashed across Kobain's face, but it was quickly replaced by one of total focus.

"Bring them back to the cells," she commanded the Watchers.

Bodie was dragged off of the table and Tessa pulled to her feet.

"What does system breach mean?" Bodie asked Tessa.

Tessa kept her eyes focused on Kobain and said, "It means things are about to get exciting."

The two were pushed into the elevator and the doors closed.

Kobain hurried to the monitor, touched it and the image of August C-Bonn appeared on screen. The chubby Chief Counselor looked wild-eyed and panicked.

"Talk to me," Kobain said.

"There was a grid breach moments ago," C-Bonn reported. "It was traced to an office in the tech sector."

"Are there any problems with the grid?"

"No. It's stable."

"Was it Donovan?"

"We don't know yet. I've locked down the compound and dispatched a security team to intercept the culprits."

"The Covian Cubes," Kobain barked. "Are they operative?"

C-Bonn was visibly shaking because the answer wasn't a good one.

"I've been told they will be fully functioning very soon."

"Define soon!" Kobain yelled, her anger growing.

C-Bonn wasn't used to seeing Kobain lose her temper. She was always in complete control, even when upset. It was unnerving for him to experience, especially since her anger was directed at him.

"Perhaps twenty minutes," C-Bonn said, and braced for a storm.

"We don't have twenty minutes!" Kobain screamed. "We may not have twenty seconds. I want those cubes active now!"

"Understood," C-Bonn said. "I'll relay that to our teams. Now if we can--"

Kobain swiped her hand across the monitor and C-Bonn disappeared. Still on screen were the images of the four Covian Cubes, all with technicians working furiously to bring them on-line and direct them at the hundreds of people that were gathering near the gates.

CHAPTER 30

I have never been in an airplane crash and can't say I'd want to be in another one. Issa did her best to control the fighter craft, but we were still going down.

"Brace yourself," Issa commanded.

She fired one last burst from a stabilizer-engine to try and hit the trees belly down. I hoped the thick branches would gently cradle us to the ground.

They didn't.

When we hit the branch it didn't break and instead flipped us over. Now we were falling, crashing through branches, heads-down with the ground coming up fast. Issa couldn't even fire the stabilizers to slow us because we were upside down.

"Protect your head!" Issa screamed.

She let go of the controls and wrapped her arms around her head. I did the same, as we smashed through the branches while being thrown, twisted and spun. Each time we hit a branch the craft was sent spiraling in a different direction. I sat there, helpless, squeezing my arms around my head, for whatever good that might do. We hit what was probably a thick fork in the tree that flipped us into a somersault, and we found ourselves falling belly-down again.

Issa reacted instantly. She grabbed the joystick and fired two stabilizers.

If that did anything to slow us down, I couldn't tell, because the ground was still coming up fast. We were seconds away from breaking through the last layer of branches, beyond which was a clear path to the ground, and disaster.

"One last shot," Issa announced.

She fired two of the rear-stabilizers. The tail bucked up and that sent us forward, directly toward a huge tangle of bushes. My last thought was that I hoped the landing spot was softer than the branches of this tree we'd just torn through. I closed my eyes and squeezed my head as we ripped through the last tangle. Seconds later we hit the ground with teeth rattling force. The fighter rolled, sending us head-over-butt once, twice, until we finally came to rest, upright. The only sound was the whine of dying engines.

I dropped my arms and did a quick check to see if I was still in one piece. Though I was totally dizzy, nothing hurt, which meant unless I was in shock, I was okay. I couldn't say the same for the canopy. The glass was a spider-web of cracks.

"Donovan?" Issa called out.

"I think I'm okay," I said. "What about you?"

"Nothing's broken," she said.

She reached for the controls and the ruined canopy lifted up.

"We gotta keep it together," she said.

I think she was talking about our emotions and not the ruined vehicle because that was totaled. I unbuckled and pulled myself out to see that we had come to rest on a grassy field, just past the damaged mess of bushes and trees we had torn through. It looked like a remote, wooded area of the Regenesis Compound. Both wings of the fighter had been snapped off and the tail was crushed, but the sturdy plane had done its job of protecting us.

Issa climbed out but her legs were wobbly, and I had to catch her as she collapsed.

"We made it," I said with joy.

The fighter jet that shot us down screamed by overhead.

"Or not," I added, with less joy.

"They're reporting where we crashed," she said. "We gotta move."

"Can you walk?" I asked.

I helped her to her feet. She did a quick hop to test her legs and nodded. She was good to go.

"Don't move!" came a shouted commanded.

Floating a few yards from us on an aerobike was a Watcher with his disk-pistol out and ready to fire.

Issa whipped off her pack, spun, and flung it at him. The straps extended, but the Watcher was ready. He dove off his bike, hit the ground and did a somersault as the pack flew by him. He kept on rolling and got right back up on one knee, with his pistol aimed directly at us.

There was a frozen moment where I wasn't sure which one of us he'd shoot first.

"Do you have level nine travel orders?" the guy asked.

Did I hear right? I looked to Issa, who seemed as unsure as I was.

"No," she said, tentatively. "Travel orders only go up to level eight."

The Watcher relaxed, stood up, and lowered his pistol.

"That was some crash," he said. "But you can walk away from it so, nice job."

Neither of us relaxed. I didn't dare to believe that a Watcher could be a friendly.

The guy must have sensed that because he said, "I can help you."

"Who are you?" Issa asked, skeptically.

"I'm a Tyro."

A Tyro! A son of the Tyrian League.

"You expect us to believe that?" Issa asked.

"Do you have a better option right now?"

I didn't know what to think and judging by the way Issa was standing there looking stunned, neither did she.

"What's your name?" I asked.

"Beck D-Farrow," the guy said.

Up until that moment, the Watchers had all seemed like nameless drones. Hearing that one actually had a name made him seem almost human. This guy didn't look much older than me. He was tall, with buzz-cut black hair and dark skin.

"My sister is a scion," he said. "Pasha Four. My parents were captured soon after the failed rebellion. They took me and stuck me in a Regenesis Watch training camp."

"Put the gun away, Beck," I said.

The guy hesitated, as if debating whether or not to give up his advantage.

"If you want us to believe you, you'll do what he says," Issa said.

The guy stood up and put his gun back in his hip holster. He held out his hands as if to show that he was now harmless.

"I did what I had to do to survive," he said. "But I've stayed in contact with the Tyrian League, just waiting."

"For what?" I asked.

"For today. Good to see you, Six. I've been following you since you took off in the fighter. Nice try, by the way. You almost made it."

"They got lucky," Issa said.

"So did you. I'm part of the escape plan in case things went sideways."

"They went about as sideways as possible," I said.

Issa let out a relieved breath but stayed on alert.

"Can you get us out of here?" she asked.

"I can try. We'll have to connect with some others."

"More Watchers?" Issa asked.

"Some, but mostly civilians who work here. We have an entire network waiting for the chance to take our lives back. Are we going to get that chance today?"

"Let's start with getting us out of here," Issa said.

"We have to get my mother and my friend out too," I said.

Beck gave me a dark look and said, "Seriously? There's no guarantee I can even get you two out."

"What's the plan?" Issa asked.

"The sanitation sector," Beck said. "We've had luck smuggling things in and out using sanitation vehicles."

"We're going to drive out of here in a garbage truck?" I asked.

"No. You're going to ride. In the back. In the trash."

Issa and I exchanged squeamish looks.

"Whatever," she said. "Let's just go."

He strode back toward his aerobike and said, "We've got to go fast. No doubt the pilot of that jumper reported the crash and—"

A surge of power hit his bike. It glanced off the metal surface and knocked him backward. He stumbled and fell while groping to get his pistol out of its holster.

My first reaction was to protect Issa. I tackled her and we fell to the grass not far from Beck.

"What was that?" I yelled.

"We're too late," Beck said.

He pointed to the meadow where three Watchers on aerobikes were speeding toward us. They were about a hundred yards out and closing fast. One had a pistol out and aimed our way.

"Find cover," Beck commanded. "Use the wreck."

He crawled to his aerobike and used it for protection as he fired back at the incoming Watchers. If anything, this proved he really was on our side.

The flying Watchers scattered to make it harder for Beck to hit any one of them. But they kept coming.

"C'mon," Issa commanded and pulled me toward the wreck. Her wobbly legs had lost all wobble.

I heard the sharp, electric sounds of power shots as they whizzed by all around us. These Watchers were *not* trying to capture us alive. Clumps of dirt kicked up everywhere; tree branches were hit and severed.

Issa and I used the wreck for protection while Beck fired from behind his aerobike. He took aim, fired once and hit the flying Watcher to the center, knocking him off his bike. The Watcher hit the ground as his vehicle landed, gouging out a long trench through the grass. It looked to be in one piece.

"We can get that," I said.

I made a move to run for the abandoned bike, but Issa held me back.

"No," she said.

"It's okay. They're shooting at Beck so I can—"

BOOM!

The downed aerobike exploded.

Issa and I ducked to avoid getting hit with flying shrapnel.

"Oh," I said. "Maybe not."

"The power cores of the aerobikes are fragile," she said.

The two other Watchers flew past us while Beck continued shooting at them. They didn't dare land, or they'd be easy targets. So they sped by and broke off in different directions.

"What are they doing?" I asked.

"They're going to make a run at us from different angles. Beck can't get them both."

We had to do something other than sit and wait. Our wrecked jumper had weapons. Though it would never fly again, I thought maybe we could use its guns against the Watchers. So I cautiously raised up and peeked into the open cockpit, trying to see if I could get to the trigger.

"Get down!" Issa warned.

"If I can get to the guns we can…whoa."

I saw something that might be better than any weapon. I stared at it for a second, not quite believing what I was seeing.

"The grid controls everything, right?" I asked. "I mean, all the technology that Regenesis uses is powered by the grid?"

"Yes," Issa said. "Get down!"

The two Watchers were making a wide circle around us, opposite from one another. If they made a run at us, Beck would be lucky if he shot one. Two would be impossible and we'd be done.

"That means this fighter vehicle is tied into the grid, right?" I asked.

"So?"

"That means it's got a computer on board that connects to the grid."

Issa's eyes lit up. We were now thinking the same thing. She raised up and looked into the cockpit.

The two Watchers came to a stop fifty yards apart and hovered in place. They would begin their attack run at any second.

"You see that?" I asked, pointing at the control panel.

"Yes I do."

There was an input port.

Without another word, she hoisted herself up and crawled into the cockpit as the two Watchers began their attack run.

CHAPTER 31

THE REGENESIS COMPOUND – GATE B

The "protesters" were growing restless. Those who had been there on that fateful day fifteen years before were getting an unsettling feeling of déjà vu. The timeline was broken once again. If all had gone according to plan, Donovan Six would have uploaded the Chrysalis and Regenesis would be crippled. But there was still power, and the technicians scrambling around the looming Covian Cubes were still hard at work.

Unlike the failure fifteen years before when they dreamt of fighting another day, if the Covian Cubes went active, any hope they'd have of destroying Regenesis would be crushed for good.

Some whispered that they shouldn't wait and attack the workers before the Covian Cubes were activated. It would be a suicide mission, but at least they'd have one moment of glory, knowing that they had fought back. The alternative would be a lifetime of mindless slavery that was far worse than anything they'd experienced.

Others urged patience, especially those who hadn't been there before. They held out hope that the scion would succeed. But how long should they wait?

In the basement rooms that surrounded the compound, an air of anxiety was growing among those who were primed for the attack. Each of the Tyrian League captains in charge of their groups were focused on their communicators, anxiously waiting for the long overdue command from Kellen to "strike".

On the roof of the building across from Gate B, Kellen stood over Tenzig who was futilely pounding on the keys of his tech-pad as if something miraculous might happen that would give them access to the Regenesis grid.

"Donovan," Tenzig said into the microphone for the hundredth time.

For the hundredth time, he got no response.

"We have to face it," Tenzig said. "The chances of them getting out are slim."

Kellen ran his hand through his graying hair as he fought back frustration.

"We have two choices," Tenzig said. "Retreat. That would save lives, but as soon as the Covian Cubes go active, we'd be done. For good this time."

"And the second choice?" Kellen asked.

"We attack before the cubes are activated. But we have no chance against their weapons. Hundreds will die. Perhaps thousands. And we'll still have lost all hope of toppling Regenesis."

"We could try again. Donovan and Issa still might get out, and there are other scions. Misha's Chrysalis would disable the Covian Cubes, right?"

"Yes, but with the kind of mind control that monstrous technology gives them, I don't see how we'd get another chance to use it."

Kellen let out a sigh of resignation and said, "So we can either die, or die nobly."

Tenzig didn't respond to that. He didn't need to.

"I'm not sure I can give the attack order," Kellen said, sounding tired. Defeated. "Not as long as there's some hope."

"I understand, but know that the people down there, the ones who have been preparing for this fight for years, might want you to give that order no matter what. Or they might not wait for it."

"I don't want to have their fate in my hands," Kellen said.

"You don't," Tenzig replied. "We're here because of Regenesis, not you. All you've done is give us hope. You and Misha. You've kept their spirit alive for years. For that, I thank you. Every last person down there will say the same, no matter what happens next."

Kellen looked over the edge of the building to the ground, and gasped.

"The technicians are moving back from the cubes," he said with rising panic. "Does that mean they're--?"

The cube in front of Gate B came to life. Beams of colorful light flashed from every surface, painting the crowd of protesters.

Kellen glanced up the street one way, and then the other to see that all the cubes had come to life. He lunged for Tenzig and grabbed the microphone they'd been using to stay in contact with all the captains.

"Pull back, pull back!" he shouted. "The Covian Cubes are—"

His words stopped coming. The insidious light had reached him and took control of his thoughts. Kellen A-Quiss was under the spell of the Covian Cubes.

The same was happening to the protestors on the street. The tension that had been building was gone as the multitudes stood quietly in place, awaiting a command.

Tenzig quickly turned around and crouched down, hiding behind an exhaust vent. He kept his back to the Covian Cubes, shielding his screen out of fear the light might hit it and reflect into his eyes.

The two options were gone.

They couldn't attack.

They couldn't retreat.

The only thing left was to hope for a miracle. For that, he had to stay on his tech pad.

CHAPTER 32

Like jousting knights, the two Watchers flew at us from opposite ends of the meadow.

Issa fell into the cockpit and quickly dug into her pocket for the radio drive.

"Put on the receptors," she commanded.

There wasn't time to think. Or question. I grabbed the four receptors out of my own pocket and stuck them on my forehead and the back of my neck. This would all be for nothing if I wasn't jacked into the grid. Or the computer was damaged in the crash.

Beck was the only thing keeping the Watchers from flying right up to us and blasting us out of existence. He kept firing at them, first one, then spinning and firing at the other. But he couldn't keep that up. Eventually one of the two would get to us.

Issa inserted the radio drive into the computer jack with a surprisingly steady hand.

"Tenzig better still be on-line," she said.

"He is," I replied.

"How do you know? Can you hear him?"

"No. I'm seeing the Chrysalis."

Sure enough, the Chrysalis code was back, floating in the air all around me. Tenzig hadn't given up on us. I knew what I had to do. Several yards away from the wrecked fighter, I saw the words MISHA K-SOO floating among the digits. I got down on all fours and crawled toward it.

"Be careful!" Issa shouted.

I wasn't exactly sure of how to be careful, but I appreciated her concern. I reached the floating words but had to stand up to reach them. I got to my feet and--

"Look out!" Beck shouted.

I looked up to see a Watcher flying right at me. I dropped to the ground as he flew past the spot where my head had been.

Beck shot at the guy, hit him, and knocked him off of the bike. The bike crashed and erupted in a massive fireball.

I couldn't take my eyes off of it as intense heat from the flames washed over me.

"Donovan!" Issa shouted from the cockpit. "Do it!"

She jolted me back into the moment. I jumped up and touched MISHA K-SOO.

As before, all the data disappeared and was replaced by the single word: ENGAGE. I jumped up again and hit it. The word UPLOAD replaced it, and I was relieved to see that the process didn't start over again. We were at 52% and climbing.

I felt dizzy from my brain was being tapped. I crawled quickly back toward the wrecked fighter, but the world was spinning. Having my brain invaded was getting to be scary. I felt nauseous and almost fell over a few times, like I had motion sickness. But I made it to the wreck and crawled inside with Issa.

"Is it uploading?" she asked.

I peered over the side to see; UPLOAD 65% floating in space.

"Sixty five percent," I said.

The small monitor in the cockpit flashed: SYSTEM BREACH.

"Here we go again," I said.

"Doesn't matter," Issa said. "They already know where we are."

"All we need is time," I said.

That was up to Beck. He had to keep the last flying Watcher from getting to us, and stopping the upload.

The Watcher circled around and began an attack run.

Beck stood and took aim at him. With only one flying Watcher to worry about, he was certain to knock him out of the air, unless the Watcher shot him first. But the Watcher stopped shooting and broke off, flying to the far side of the meadow.

"I got this," Beck called to us.

But he didn't.

The first Watcher who had crashed wasn't done. He jumped Beck, knocking the pistol out of his hand. Both scrambled to get it. They ended up wrestling and throwing punches in a tangle of arms and fists.

UPLOAD 78%.

"I'll get the gun," I said and was about to leap out of the fighter, but Issa held me back.

"No," she said. "I'll get it."

Before I could argue, she leapt out of the cockpit and ran for the gun.

UPLOAD 82%.

I felt helpless, but Issa was right. My brain was wi-fied into the grid. If anything happened to me, the Chrysalis wouldn't complete the upload. All I could do was sit and stare at the floating number, willing it to rise faster.

UPLOAD 85%.

I wanted to help Beck and take a shot at the Watcher he was fighting. It took every bit of willpower for me not to leap out of the wreck and start wailing on the guy.

The Watcher who was still flying made a wide circle and started another run at us.

Issa made it to the gun, picked it up, stood with her legs firmly apart and took aim at the incoming Watcher. She pulled the trigger…and nothing happened. She fired again. Nothing. It must have been damaged in the crash.

The Watcher drew closer. Issa kept trying to shoot, but it was no use. She threw the gun down in frustration and ran back to me.

"Ninety percent," I said.

The upload wasn't happening fast enough. The Watcher was flying closer and this time there was nothing stopping him.

Beck finally reared back with his fist and knocked the guy he was fighting into next week.

The flying Watcher had one hand on the handlebars of his aerobike. In other he held a pistol. He had us.

Beck got to his feet, staggered our way, and stood between us and the incoming Watcher, using his body to shield us.

"I'm sorry," he said.

"Don't be," Issa said. "Today is the day."

"I wish that was true," Beck said.

Issa smiled and said, "But it is."

The Watcher was almost on us. He took aim with his pistol.

I held Issa's hand.

Issa was surprisingly calm and said, "Whatever happens, this day will be remembered."

100%

The Watcher dropped out of the air. It was as if his aerobike had run out of gas. The look of surprise on his face was comical. The bike crashed, throwing the Watcher off and sending him tumbling. This aerobike didn't explode like the others.

But the Watcher wasn't done. He rolled and got back to his feet, still with the gun in his hand. He stalked toward us with the pistol up and ready to fire.

"Traitor," he shouted angrily. "You betrayed the Watch. You betrayed the church."

"Anybody who works for that church betrayed all our people," Beck said. "I couldn't live with that."

"You won't have to," the Watcher said.

He raised the pistol, aimed at Beck, and fired.

No energy bolt flew out.

The Watcher looked at the gun with surprise, as if he might see something that explained why it wouldn't fire. He shot again. Again, it didn't fire.

"Look," I said and pointed to the monitor.

It was dead. Every last light on the console was dark.

"I don't see the upload indicator," I said.

"Because it's complete," Issa said with satisfaction. "There's no power. The Chrysalis is in. It worked. The grid is fried."

"We did it," I said, more stunned than triumphant.

"Now the real fight begins," Issa said.

CHAPTER 33

THE REGENESIS COMPOUND – GATE B

Kellen felt as though he was waking up from a deep sleep. As his head cleared, bits and pieces of reality slowly returned. He realized that he was standing up, which meant he wasn't in bed. Or on the floor, which wouldn't be unusual. He didn't have a headache, which meant he hadn't passed out from drinking. Probably. He registered the sky, which meant he was outside. He blinked to clear his vision and looked out toward what he recognized as the wall that surrounded the Regenesis Compound. His gaze travelled down to see hundreds of people in the street, all facing the compound wall. They stood silently, looking as dazed as Kellen felt. Between the crowd and the wall, was a Covian Cube.

A dead Covian Cube.

"Kellen?" Tenzig said.

Kellen looked down to see his friend sitting with his back to the low wall that surrounded the rooftop. He'd yet to remember why they were there.

Tenzig smiled. Tenzig rarely smiled, which made the situation that much stranger for Kellen. Tenzig turned his tech pad so Kellen could see the screen.

It was blank.

Kellen felt as though a mental dam had suddenly broken loose as reality flooded in.

"Is it dead?" he asked.

"The pad is fine," Tenzig said. "Can't say the same for the Regenesis grid."

The surge of adrenalin washed away any last effects the Covian Cube had on Kellen.

"Are you sure?" he asked.

Tenzig stood up, looked toward the compound and said, "See for yourself."

Moments before the Covian Cube had been shooting out light that infected the minds of the people down on the street. Now, the cube was dark and the people in the street were waking up and growing restless.

"They did it," Tenzig said with a touch of awe. "They actually did it."

"I believe you can finally give the word," Tenzig said.

Kellen's heart raced. In those few seconds, the last seventeen years of his life flashed through his memory. His mind travelled back to meeting Misha K-Soo, the damaged genius who had lost her parents to Regenesis. It was the memory of her parents that drove her to create the engine intended to bring the church down. Kellen fell in love with her and embraced her quest. It cost Misha her life. Losing her cost Kellen his own. He went through the motions of doing what he could to protect the scions and keep the rebellion alive, but there was a hole in his heart that he could never repair. He had become a ghost who floated through life feeling angry, depressed and useless.

But now, as he stood overlooking the wall that separated the monsters from their victims, it began to sink in that his beloved Misha's quest was about to be completed. He hadn't allowed himself to believe that it was truly possible. Now that they were on the verge of success, the realization filled him with a positive energy he hadn't felt in a very long time.

"Kellen?" Tenzig said. "There are a lot of people waiting."

Kellen gave Tenzig a warm squeeze on the shoulder, then touched the communicator in his ear and cleared his throat.

"This is Kellen A-Quiss," he said with confidence. "We have our assignments. We know what needs to be done."

He looked down to Tenzig, who gave him a wink and a nod.

"Say it," Tenzig said.

Kellen hit the communicator again and announced, "Strike! Strike! Strike!"

A cheer went up from the crowd.

At Gate B, frantic Regenesis Watchers scrambled together to create a human wall to block the entrance to the compound. None of them were holding weapons.

The hundreds who had gathered in a pretend protest threw off their cloaks and stormed the gate. Their only weapons were the metal clubs that they had been hiding. They waved the batons threateningly, letting the Regenesis Guards know what was coming.

Kellen and Tenzig looked down from above to view the beginning of the end of Regenesis.

The first wave held the people who were the most able to do physical battle. Like a medieval army invading a castle, they stormed into the teeth of the enemy. They charged the gate, screaming and waving their batons, fueled by years of pent up anger and frustration.

With their weapons useless, the Watchers could only fight back with their fists. Some fought valiantly, throwing punches and sacrificing their bodies by flinging themselves in front of the oncoming wave of invaders, but they were hopelessly outnumbered.

Several of the invaders went for the Covian Cubes. They climbed the towers and bashed at the devices with their bats, smashing the glass lenses that focused the insidious light as they mangled the black cubes beyond repair.

The same scene was unfolding at every gate. The invaders quickly overwhelmed the Watchers who had been standing guard. Several of the Watchers didn't even try to fight back. Whether it was because they welcomed the Tyrian League, or they realized that without their weapons it would be a losing battle, they put their hands on their heads in a sign to show that they would not resist.

The first phase of the invasion was a complete success, but it was only the beginning. Overthrowing Regenesis on Tyria wasn't simply about storming the gates. The Tyrian League needed to take command and control of the compound, and The Core.

The plans for the invasion had been created years before. The invaders were divided into groups, each with different goals. Upon hearing the "Strike!" command, those waiting in the basements flooded out onto the streets. Once the gates were cleared, this second wave could engage.

The first wave stayed at the gates inside the compound. They were charged with capturing and holding the Watchers in case they had any thoughts of a counterattack.

Joining them were the Essen-Tet police. For years they had been ruled by the Regenesis Watch. Now, they could once again do their job, which was to uphold the order of law. Laws that had been instituted by the people and their elected representatives, not Regenesis. Their first task was to transport the captured Watchers out of the Regenesis Compound and directly to the various jail cells around Essen-Tet that they'd prepared for this occasion. Within minutes of the attack, Regenesis Watchers were being led out of the compound with their hands strapped behind their backs. Some were bloodied from the attack and would receive medical attention. That too was expected as doctors in hospitals all over the city awaited casualties. Another group of doctors entered with the second wave to treat the less-seriously injured inside the compound.

Hover-trucks arrived at the gates to transport the third wave of invaders deeper into the compound, and ultimately to The Core. These trucks did not draw their power from the Regenesis grid. It was yet another example of how the invaders had the advantage. The trucks were loaded quickly with hundreds of invaders and sped them directly to The Core. They passed the powerless monorail, as well as the beautiful homes of the Regenesis elite.

Several people fled from their mansion-like homes, desperate to escape what was sure to be a reckoning. They wouldn't get beyond the gates, for that was the mission of the next wave of invaders.

This fourth group was charged with finding and arresting the senior church officials. They would search The Core and the opulent mansions that were their homes. The massive wall that had protected Regenesis from the masses became the walls of their prison.

The first to be arrested were the members of the Regenesis Ministry. The remaining five were Kobain's lieutenants. With them gone, leadership was as good as destroyed. Regenesis was rudderless.

The hover-trucks carrying the third wave arrived at The Core and the invaders went directly to level D and the tech floor. The fear was that the technicians who were forced to work for Regenesis would come up with a way to counter the Chrysalis and restore power to the grid. That possibility had to be taken away.

As the group hurried toward level D, they were met with resistance from a few Watchers, but the guards were overmatched. They were quickly overrun, captured, and shuttled out to the waiting police. Like Beck, not all the Watchers were happy that they had been forced to be the strong-arm of Regenesis. A few tossed off their uniforms and surrendered peacefully.

On level D, the tech floor was locked down. Heavy steel doors had been manually closed to protect the heart of the Regenesis network against just such an attack. The invaders were prepared for this. They brought sledgehammers and crowbars and quickly went to work to tear down the doors.

It didn't take long to break through. When the steel doors were peeled back, the invaders were met by a few terrified Watchers who they quickly captured. Beyond them were the hundreds of technicians who huddled together like frightened rabbits. They didn't fight back, there was no point. They were all herded out of the tech floor and shuttled back to the gates.

A splinter group went to the tower that held the dish antennas that transmitted the power throughout the Regenesis world. These had to be controlled in case the power was restored. It was a long climb to reach them since the elevators were useless. Once there, the group cut all power lines. The antennas weren't destroyed but instead they were disabled with no hope for a quick fix.

The well-coordinated attack wasn't only about the Regenesis Compound. All over Essen-Tet, the Tyrian League worked to ensure that the overthrow was complete. The entire operation had been planned, refined, and practiced for years in the hope that it might actually happen one day. That day had finally come. The workers in Factory B rejoiced. While some who remained loyal to the church quietly stole away, most of the workers turned the Covian Cube assembly line into a disassembly line. They battered the cubes that were under construction and destroyed those that were complete.

Vail Kobain's Covian Solution was no more.

The same scene unfolded at Regenesis factories across Essen-Tet. The factories that constructed harmless and necessary items were left untouched, but those that manufactured Regenesis weapons were torn apart.

The Capital Building that was once the center of government in Essen-Tet sat mostly empty for decades. The only staff were the few people who were needed to keep Essen-Tet functioning, but under the stern guidance of Regenesis. It was a government in name only.

Now, only a few hours after the beginning of the attack, a lone transport vehicle flew over the city, making its way toward the domed building. Hundreds of people were gathered outside in anticipation of this momentous event. The Essen-Tet police force was there to keep the order, but they weren't needed. It was a peaceful crowd. A joyful crowd. When they saw the transport-vehicle appear over the dome, a cheer went up. The people waved and shouted with joy. Many cried.

The transport vehicle touched down at the base of the steep steps that led up to the capital building. The crowd kept a respectful and safe distance.

The vehicle's engine powered down and a hatch opened. Two figures stepped out that were dressed all in black. Each carried old-school, non-Regenesis rifles. Nobody feared them for they knew who they were and why they were armed. A moment later, a tall, elderly Black man stepped out of the vehicle. At the sight of him, the crowd went berserk. It was Barron K-Deere, president of the Sandoor Federation. He was the last legitimately elected official of the Sandoor Federation who had been in exile once Regenesis gained power. Seeing him was the most dramatic sign that their nightmare might actually be over.

K-Deere waved to the crowd and climbed up a few steps in order to be seen by all. He stopped and turned back to wave once again. The crowd cheered ecstatically. K-Deere smiled and shed a tear. He finally held up his hands to quiet the crowd.

"My friends," K-Deere said in a strong voice. "Words cannot adequately express the joy I have in my heart. From what I see, you are all feeling the same way. If there's one sentiment we can take away from today, it is that we should all commit ourselves to the concept best expressed by two simple words: Never again."

A cheer went up that lasted a solid minute before K-Deere could speak again.

"Together, we will restore Sandoor to what it once was: a federation that was founded on the principals that all people should be treated equally; and that freedom of thought, speech and religion are the bedrocks of a healthy, prosperous society. The rules of law that guided our federation since its will once again prevail. No one is above the law. Not anymore. If you allow me, I will be honored to help lead us all back into that wonderful light."

The crowd went wild, cheering K-Deere on as he climbed the steps to re-take the reins of his office and restore sanity to a world that had gone mad.

At the Regenesis Compound, a lone invader climbed to the summit of Tower 3. There, he brought down the rising-sun flag of Regenesis and hoisted the flag of the Sandoor Federation.

On the ground, the invaders looked up to see the Sandoor flag snapping in the wind. They applauded, they cheered, they hugged, and they cried. The rebellion was relentless and swift, but complete victory could not be claimed until one final challenge was met.

The Bishop of Regenesis had to be found.

Kellen and Tenzig flew into the compound on Kellen's aerobike and headed straight for The Core. It was a victory lap of sorts since the invaders cheered him as they flew past.

Kellen wasn't ready to celebrate. Not yet.

Vail Kobain was dangerous. She was the senior Bishop of Regenesis, and not only on Tyria. She was the ranking member of the church throughout its entire empire. Kellen knew that while retaking Essen-Tet was a huge victory, it was only the beginning. To completely bring down the bogus church on all the worlds it had conquered, they had to have Vail Kobain.

When Kellen and Tenzig entered The Core, they were approached by several invaders along with a captured church official. He was a short, round little man in a bright blue suit with hair that was parted in the middle and slicked back. He was pushed in front of Kellen where he bowed humbly.

"This one says he's chief counsel to Kobain," the invader said.

"My name is August C-Bonn," the man said. "I surrender to you with no animosity."

He looked up at Kellen, their eyes met, and he went pale.

"You!" he exclaimed, stunned.

"Chief Counsel?" Kellen said. "That's a nice promotion from rat."

"I liked Misha," August said, frantically. "I was only following orders."

"I expect to hear that excuse a lot," Kellen said. "I don't buy it."

"But it's true!" August wailed. "I'm glad it's over. Kobain is a horror!"

"Where is she?"

"In her apartment," August replied. "The top floor of Tower C. But it'll be hard to reach her. The whole floor can be sealed off."

"How many are guarding her?" Tenzig asked.

"Usually no more than two. If you like I could help you--"

"What about the mother of the boy from Earth?" Kellen asked. "And the other Earth kid? Where are they?"

"With her," August replied.

That wasn't the answer Kellen wanted to hear. Having those two could give Kobain bargaining power.

"Keep him here," Kellen said to the invaders. "He could be useful."

"I will be!" August declared. "I'd be happy to tell you anything you need to know."

Kellen walked past him.

"Still a rat," Kellen said to no one.

He and Tenzig walked quickly across the atrium through a flurry of activity and confusion. Many Regenesis Watchers were on their knees with their hands tied behind their backs, being guarded by invaders. Others were being pulled out of hiding places by force. Many civilians who worked in the compound sat against the walls, crying. They had put their faith in the church and in spite of the hardships it caused, they were devasted by the fact that their faith had been misplaced.

"We could have a hostage situation," Tenzig said.

"I know," Kellen replied. "This isn't over."

They went to the stairs beneath Tower C, the tower that held Kobain's apartment. There they met the team that was prepared for this exact situation. There were two beefy men and a woman, the same group who tore open the steel doors that sealed the tech sector. They had their tools ready to do the same if there was trouble entering Kobain's apartment.

"We need more bodies," Kellen said, and pointed to two more of the invaders. "You and you, come with us. Elevators are out so, we climb."

The group of seven went straight for the stairs and began the climb to the top of the tower, and a rendezvous with the Bishop of Regenesis. It was a long climb for all of them, but for Tenzig it was near impossible. He didn't complain, but it was clear that he wouldn't make it on his own. Without being asked, the larger of the four men hefted him up on to his shoulders and continued the climb.

"Normally I'd refuse the offer," Tenzig said. "But I'm not missing out on this."

"It's my honor," the large man said.

The climb took more than half an hour. When the group reached the floor beneath the apartment, they stopped to rest and gather their strength for the task ahead.

Kellen sat down on the stairs, taking deep breaths to get his heart rate back to normal.

Tenzig joined him.

"Worst case," Tenzig said. "She won't release them unless we make her an offer."

"No deals," Kellen said with certainty. "If we let her go, she'll move on to another planet and pick up where she left off here. Her reign has to end now."

"And if she threatens to hurt Bodie? And the mother of the boy we owe everything to?"

It was a torturous dilemma for Kellen.

"I get it," he said. "Sacrificing either of those two makes us no better than Kobain. But letting her go could mean we're sentencing thousands to suffer. What would prevent her from re-building the Covian Cube on another planet? She could put together an army and return to Tyria."

"I'm afraid you're right," Tenzig said. "I have no doubt that whatever assurances she offers she'd eventually be looking to re-group and no doubt seek revenge."

"What would you do?" Kellen asked.

Tenzig took a tired breath and said, "I'd pray that it doesn't come to that, because the right choice isn't the easy one."

Kellen nodded in agreement, then slapped his knees and stood up.

"Let's go," he called to the group.

The final flight of stairs led to a corridor, at the end of which was the vault-like steel door they expected to find. Kellen approached the door, not sure of how to go about opening it. He scanned the frame, then gave up and banged his fist on it.

"Kobain!" he called out. "This is Kellen A-Quiss. The compound and The Core are under the control of the Tyrian League. You already know that we've destroyed your power grid. The Regenesis Watch is no more. Several of your church elders have been arrested, along with your Ministry. Barron K-Deere is back in the capital and has re-taken control of the government. The Essen-Tet police force is providing security. You are no longer in power. You can save yourself a world of trouble by opening the door and surrendering to us."

There was no response.

"Do you think she heard you through that heavy door?" Tenzig asked.

Kellen banged on the door again and called out, "Do you hear me?"

Again, no reply.

Kellen turned to the men and woman with the tools.

"Break it down," he commanded.

The three tore into the job with glee. As they did on Level D, they hammered at the steel with sledgehammers, over and over, until they battered a hole in the surface.

"I'm afraid of what we may find inside," Tenzig said, voicing exactly what was on Kellen's mind.

Kellen continued staring at the door, fearing that their triumphant day could end in tragedy.

The workers used heavy crowbars to peel the heavy sheet metal away from the door, exposing the locking mechanism.

The woman who was banging away approached Kellen and said, "We're almost there. A couple of hits on that lock with shatter it and we'll push it open."

Kellen looked to the two men he had recruited at the last second.

"I'll go in first," he said. "You two come in right behind. There may be some Watchers in there protecting Kobain. Be ready for them."

The two men clutched their metal batons.

Kellen nodded to the woman, who waved to her teammate with the sledgehammer.

The guy wound up like he was going to swing at a fastball, brought the heavy hammer around and nailed the locking mechanism, square on. The lock was crushed, the door disengaged, and with one push he slid it open.

Kellen ran inside. The two men were right behind him. Kellen was ready to fight. He stopped inside the door and scanned the room. There were no Watchers.

"Kobain?" he called out.

His voice echoed back at him.

Tenzig joined him, looking around the apartment in awe.

"I've never seen such luxury," he said.

"Wait, listen," Kellen said.

There was a thumping sound coming from somewhere deeper in the apartment.

Kellen ran toward the sound. He hurried past the dining room through to a second sitting room. The others followed, still primed for a fight. But when Kellen entered this second room, he saw something that was both a relief, and made no sense.

Bound to a chair with her arms behind her, was Tessa. A gag was tied across her mouth, preventing her from yelling out. She had been bouncing the chair against the wall to get their attention. Kellen ran to her and pulled the gag off.

"She's gone," Tessa yelled, frantically. "She took Bodie with her. We have to stop her."

Kellen motioned for one of the invaders to cut her straps.

"When did she leave?" Kellen asked.

"Moments before the power went out. She was watching what was happening on monitors. I saw it all. Donovan and Issa were flying. In a dog fight. They crashed. I thought they were dead, but they survived and—"

Tessa was losing it. Her words spilled out in rapid fire.

"They were attacked on the ground. Watchers were flying at them, shooting. It was horrible, but—"

Kellen knelt down in front of her, trying to calm her down.

"Okay, I get it," he said softly. "Take a deep breath. Did she give you any idea of where she was headed?"

"No," Tessa said, defeated.

"She must be trying to leave Tyria," Tenzig said.

"And she took Bodie," Tessa cried.

"Why?" Kellen asked surprised. "Why would she take the kid from Earth when she had the mother of a scion?"

"To get a Chrysalis!" Tessa shouted with desperation.

"I don't understand," Kellen said.

"My God, Kellen. It was right in front of us," Tessa cried. "If Regenesis has a Chrysalis, they can crack Misha's code and protect their grids on every other planet."

"I know that, but they'd have to track down another scion."

"Exactly!" Tessa exclaimed. "They have!"

"What!" Kellen exclaimed. "Where?"

"Right here. On Tyria."

The news hit Kellen so hard that he had to stand up and take a step away.

"Another scion is here?" he exclaimed, stunned.

"Yes! It's Karter Two. He came home."

"But...when? How?"

"You brought him here, Kellen," Tessa said.

"No, I didn't!"

"But you did. It's Bodie. Bodie is a scion. And now Kobain has a Chrysalis."

CHAPTER 34

Issa and I walked with our new best-pal, the former Watcher named Beck, toward The Core. Since my earbuds had gone south, there was no way to know what had happened after the Chrysalis fried the grid. All we could do was make our way back on foot and hope that the Tyrian League had won. Or at least hadn't been wiped out.

I wasn't sure how I should feel about what I'd done. Though I'd only learned about it a few days before, bringing the Chrysalis back to Tyria was my destiny. It may have taken a minute for me to accept it, but I did. Now I was left with a strangely empty feeling. I'd experienced something completely new. I felt needed. I had purpose. What was I supposed to do now? Go home to my old life? There was no one on Earth I cared about or who cared about me. But I didn't feel like I belonged on Tyria, either. In my heart, Earth was home.

Then there was my mother, and a father who may or may not be alive. I wasn't sure how I felt about them. I know how I wanted to feel. I wanted to be part of a family. But for that I'd have to stay on Tyria. And that would only happen if Regenesis had been overthrown. Let's not forget that.

So many questions, with no answers in sight, except for maybe one.

"Look," Issa exclaimed. She stopped and pointed to the towers of The Core that rose above the trees in the distance.

"What am I looking at?" I asked.

"The tower," Issa said. "That's not the Regenesis flag. Is it? Tell me I'm really seeing this."

"Seeing what?" I asked.

"You're seeing it," Beck said with awe. "It's the flag of the Sandoor Federation.

"They did it," Issa said with growing excitement. "They really did it!"

It was like having a weight lifted off my shoulders. I laughed. Issa did too, and Beck joined in. It was a moment of absolute joy and total relief.

"I can't believe it," Issa said through happy tears.

She picked up the pace with so much energy that I had to work to keep up. Made sense. She ran cross country and was in great shape. That, and she now had every reason to believe that that nightmare had finally ended for her, and for everyone else she cared about. Let's not forget that.

Once we made it out of the forest we found ourselves in another neighborhood of mansions with perfect lawns where several people were being dragged out of their homes by the Essen-Tet police and loaded onto floating trucks.

"They're arresting the church principals," Issa said.

"Great," Beck said sarcastically. "I'll be next."

"No you won't," Issa said with confidence. "You saved us. And you're a Tyro. We'll vouch for you."

"But you might want to take off that uniform," I said. "No reason to put a target on your back."

Beck tossed his hat and dumped his jacket.

"It's a new day," Issa said.

Beck looked ahead to The Core towers that loomed above us with the Sandoor Federation flag flying.

"Yeah, I think maybe it is," he said.

We finally arrived at The Core to see how things had already changed. There wasn't a Watcher in sight. Hundreds of people were milling about, talking and laughing. They were the invaders who had overthrown Regenesis and from the looks of it, the battle was already over. Better still, when people spotted us, they broke out in applause or held up six fingers. It was a way different vibe than when we left the basement. Back then, these same people were tense and scared. Their hopes were pinned on us.

And we came through.

People ran up to us to shake our hands. They were all smiles while saying things like "Thank you, Six!" and "You did it!" I don't think I registered most of what they said because it was a mad jumble of emotion. I felt like a rock star, or a Super Bowl champion.

Issa was getting the same treatment. She moved through the grateful crowd with a glowing smile. We made eye contact, and I knew what she was thinking because I was thinking the same thing: "How cool is this?"

Beck trailed behind awkwardly. It was a good thing he dumped his uniform. People didn't question him. If he was with us, he was okay.

We made our way through the crowd slowly, which was okay by me because I was soaking it all up. I could get used to being adored. Finally, we arrived at the entrance to The Core, having been escorted by dozens of grateful Tyrians.

I wish I could have frozen that moment in time because I didn't think things could get any better.

And I was right. They didn't.

Waiting for us at The Core's entrance was Tenzig. He stood alone, with his arms folded. He wasn't smiling.

"Hey!" I called to him with a laugh. "What's new?"

"There's a problem," he said dourly.

And that was the end of the celebration.

Tenzig looked to Beck with suspicion and said, "Who is he?"

"He saved our lives," I said. "If not for him, we never would have uploaded the Chrysalis."

"He's a Watcher?"

"Former Watcher," Issa said. "He's a Tyro."

Tenzig thought for a moment, then said, "All right, c'mon."

He led us inside and across the atrium to a door that was being guarded by two Essen-Tet policemen. With a nod from Tenzig, they let us enter into what looked like a meeting room. A big conference table with chairs around it filled most of the space. Kellen was looking out of a window while my mother sat at the end of the table, looking glum. They saw us and my mother broke out in a huge smile. She jumped up, threw her arms around me and squeezed me so tight I could barely breath.

I'd never experienced anything like that before. Ever. But I knew what it meant. She was showing me genuine affection. I didn't think too hard about why. I just did what felt right. I hugged her back.

"It's okay," I said softly. "We made it."

Tessa reached out and drew Issa into our hug. I don't think I'll ever forget that moment. For the first time in my life, I felt loved.

"I saw the way they attacked you," she said. "If not for that Watcher who protected you--"

"That's him," I said, gesturing to Beck. "He's a Tyro."

My mother pulled away from us and looked to the former Watcher who stood there looking awkward.

"Thank you," she said.

Beck nodded.

Issa went over to Kellen and said, "Am I dreaming?"

"No dream," Kellen said. "The attack was overwhelming. The hospitals are filled with battered Watchers. It wasn't a bloodless coup, but as far as I know there were no deaths."

"Incredible," Issa said.

"The Essen-Tet police are in control. Regenesis leaders are being arrested. President K-Deere has returned to the capital and is re-forming our government."

"So then what's the problem?" I asked.

Kellen didn't answer. Bad sign.

I glanced around the room to realize someone was missing.

"Where's Bodie?" I asked.

My mother took my hand and gently said, "Sit down. Both of you."

Whatever news was coming wouldn't be good.

"There were no casualties, right?" I asked. "That means he's okay."

Kellen stepped up to the conference table. For a guy who just had a complete and total victory, he didn't look so hot.

"Kobain escaped and took Bodie with her," he said.

"Why?" I asked.

Kellen and Tessa exchanged dark looks.

"There's more to it, isn't there?" Issa asked.

"Turns out Bodie isn't just along for the ride," Kellen said.

"What does that mean?" I asked.

"His real name is Karter."

"What!" Issa exclaimed as she jumped to her feet.

"No, it isn't," I said. "It's Willard. Bodie Willard. Junior."

"That can't be!" Issa said.

"What am I missing?" I asked, totally confused.

Tessa took my hand and said, "Bodie is Karter Two. He's a scion."

My reaction was to laugh.

"That's, uh, that's a joke, right?" I stammered.

"It's not," Tessa said, dead serious. "They scanned him and discovered his Tyrian genetics."

"But he's not," I argued. "He's a rich kid from Earth. From Connecticut. He lives with fancy parents who think he's going to be president or something. He may be a lot of things but he's not a scion."

"Did he ever mention that he was adopted?" Kellen asked.

"No," I shot back quickly. "Why would he? We're not friends. Was he adopted?"

"You didn't tell me you placed Karter Two on Earth," Issa said.

"Because I didn't," Kellen said. "Arri G-Kove is Karter's mother. She left me with Donovan on Earth to bring her son to the planet Tensor. That was the plan, anyway. They never made it, and I never saw them again. I figured she decided the best way to protect him was to disappear. Even from us. She was smart. I never thought to look for them on Earth, in the exact same place I left Donovan."

"So she hid him in plain sight," Issa said.

"And now Kobain has him, which means she's got a Chrysalis," Tenzig said. "If she gets the Chrysalis to another Regenesis planet, they'll dissect it and develop a firewall. The revolution may begin and end on Tyria."

"She hasn't left the planet yet," Kellen said. "The police have been monitoring all arrivals and departures. We have to find them before—"

"I know where she is," Beck said.

All eyes went to the guy who had been standing back, quietly.

Kellen finally focused on him and said, "Who is this kid? Why is a Watcher in here?"

"Because he saved our butts," Issa said. "He held off the Watchers who were attacking us and gave us time to upload the Chrysalis. Without him, the attack would have failed."

"It's true," Tessa said. "I saw it all on the monitors."

Kellen wasn't convinced. I guess it was hard to forget that a Watcher killed Misha.

"My name is Beck D-Ward," Beck said.

Kellen straightened up. The name meant something to him.

"I wasn't a Watcher by choice," Beck said. "I'm a Tyro. I've been working with the Tyrian League. I can give you all my contacts to prove that. My sister is a scion."

"Pasha Four," Kellen said.

I wonder if he remembered the baby girl named Pasha who he dropped off…somewhere. It looked to me like he was having trouble getting his brain around what he'd just heard.

Issa said, "His parents were taken by Regenesis right after—"

"I know what happened!" Kellen snapped. He took a breath to calm himself then looked to Beck and said, "All right, kid. If anybody has a right to be here, you do. Where is Kobain?"

"I've been on her security detail," Beck said. "There's a plan in place to get her away in case of emergency. A tunnel runs below the compound, under the wall and out to a building in the city. If she was ever in danger the plan was for her to escape through the tunnel and contact the Regenesis space-fleet."

"Regenesis has a space fleet?" I asked, incredulous.

"Who do you think attacked us when we left Earth?" Kellen asked.

Oh. Right. Them.

"She'll stay in hiding until a cruiser picks her up," Beck added. "That has to be where she went."

I could sense the wheels turning in Kellen's head as he calculated the possibilities.

"How long ago did she leave here?" Kellen asked Tessa.

"Three hours. Maybe more."

Then to Beck he asked, "How long would it take for a cruiser to get here?"

"Depends on where they're coming from," Beck replied. "It could several hours, or a couple of minutes."

"You said flights are being monitored," Issa said to Kellen. "There are no reports of a Regenesis cruiser arriving? Or leaving?"

"None."

"Then she's still here!" I exclaimed. "And so is Bodie."

"Where's this tunnel?" Kellen asked.

"Four flights down beneath this tower. There's a monorail but it won't run without power."

"Is the tunnel wide enough for an aerobike?" Kellen asked.

Beck nodded. "Absolutely."

"All right then," Kellen said. "We'll take two of our bikes that aren't connected to the grid. Issa and Donovan on one, I'll bring Tenzig on a second."

"What about me?" Beck asked. "She'll be protected."

"All right, three bikes," Kellen said.

"I'll ride with Beck," Tessa said.

"No!" Kellen and I said at the exact same time, though probably for different reasons. I let Kellen give his.

"We need you here," Kellen said. "If we're not back in a few hours, alert the captains as to what's happening."

"I'd rather go with you," Tessa said.

"I know," Kellen said with sympathy. "But you can't. Please don't argue." He looked at the rest of us and said, "We go. Now!"

He strode out of the room. Tenzig and Beck were right after him, leaving Issa and me with my mother.

"I'm in shock," Issa said. "I had no idea about Bodie."

"Good thing," I said. "Or you would have been his guardian angel too, and I'm not good at sharing."

I think Issa blushed. She gave me a little smile and ran after the others.

Tessa said, "I can't begin to tell you how proud I am of you."

"Yeah, well, it's not over yet. There's still time for me to mess up."

Tessa smiled. I liked her smile. It looked like mine.

"You won't," she said. "And when this is over, we're going to find your father."

Those words gave me a rush of excitement. Was he okay? What was he like? Did I look like him? What if I didn't like him? What if he was a pain in the ass like me?

"You'll like him," she said, as if reading my mind. "He's kind of a pain. Just like you."

Well, that answered that.

Tessa gave me a kiss on the cheek and said, "Go get Bodie."

Kellen rounded up three aerobikes outside of The Core that had been flown in by invaders. He quickly loaded two metal baton-weapons on each. Issa didn't need one. She strapped on her backpack. I sat behind her on one bike and wrapped my arms around her waist.

"You know how to drive this thing?" I asked.

"Do you really have to ask?"

I didn't, especially after seeing how she flew that jumper jet.

Beck floated by us slowly and called out, "I'll lead."

He accelerated and flew toward the building, followed by Kellen and Tenzig and then by Issa and me. He led us into a loading dock used by delivery trucks. Once inside we floated down ramp after ramp until we arrived at a set of double doors with no markings. Beck got off his bike and opened up both doors.

"Put on your headlights," he said. "It's a straight shot but the lights won't be burning."

He remounted, turned on his headlight and flew through the door. Kellen was right on his tail with his light trained on Beck. Issa and I followed quickly. The tunnel was maybe wide enough for a single monorail car. Our headlights reflected off of the single, silver track, giving us some guidance in an otherwise pitch-black tunnel. The whine of the engines was deafening in the narrow space.

There was no way to tell when we passed underneath the wall of the compound or how far away this emergency building was, but it only took a few minutes to get there. The tunnel widened out and we soon came upon a miniature monorail train that was parked at the end of the line. We all pulled ahead of it and killed our engines. After the annoying whining sound, it was a relief to hear absolutely nothing.

"From here we're on foot," Beck said. "If they followed procedure, there should be two Watchers protecting her. One will be on the other side of the door to the tunnel, the other will be with her."

He pulled the baton from his bike and added, "I'll take out the first one."

With Beck in the lead, the rest of us followed close behind. Three of us held metal batons. The fourth held her backpack. If things got nasty, my money was on the girl with the backpack.

When we reached a set of double doors, Beck turned back and motioned for us to be quiet. He grasped his baton, reached for the door, and threw it open.

As he predicted, a Watcher stood with his back to the door. I doubt he even saw who we were because Beck clocked him before he could turn around. The guy was unconscious before he hit the floor.

"This is good," Beck whispered. "She's still here."

"You weren't positive before?" Kellen asked.

"No," Beck said. "But it wasn't like you had a better plan."

plan."

That made me laugh. Kellen shot me an angry look. I smiled and shrugged. I was beginning to like Beck.

"Let's go say hi," Kellen said.

Beck stayed in the lead as we went through the door and into a short corridor. A flight of stairs on the far end led up. The five of us moved silently, trying not to tip off our arrival. We climbed the long flight of stairs until we reached what felt like the ground floor.

"What kind of building is this?" Kellen whispered.

"It's the Regenesis Cathedral," Beck replied quietly.

At the end of another short corridor was a wooden door. Beck opened it to reveal a sight that took my breath away.

It was a cathedral, all right. The place was cavernous with an arched ceiling that looked like something out of medieval times. On Earth. The pews were highly polished wood, with three separate aisles leading to the altar in front. This place could easily seat a few thousand people.

At the front of the cathedral was a gigantic stained-glass window that depicted the rising sun of Regenesis. It was the same design as the one on Earth, but five times the size. I had to wonder if there was ever a time that they could fill this church with people who believed in Regenesis and their God they called the Regent. Right now, it was empty except for a single person.

Standing at an ornately carved wooden podium beneath the stained-glass window was Vail Kobain. She wore a bright blue robe, against which her long red hair seemed to glow in the filtered light.

"Glory to the Regent," she announced. "We gather here today to worship him and honor his kindness."

At first I thought she was talking to us, but she was looking out over a sea of empty pews.

"This is crazy," Issa whispered. "She's holding a service."

"For nobody," I said.

Beck motioned for us to keep moving. We crept quietly along one wall, past heavy stone pillars that held up the soaring ceiling.

"The disturbing events that occurred today are of no matter to the Regent," Kobain said. "He has given us a test. A test of our faith and resiliency. All that matters now is how we will respond."

Kobain's words may have been confident, but she looked anything but. Her hair was a mess and her voice shaky. The closer we got to her, the worse she looked.

"We have to ask ourselves, what kind of future do we envision? Regenesis has provided so much for so many. We cannot allow the non-believers to destroy what the Regent has given us."

We neared the front of the cathedral, staying in the shadows.

"This is not a crisis," Kobain announced. "It is an opportunity to re-affirm our faith, honor the Regent, and purge those who are disloyal."

Kobain was unraveling. Her eyes were wild as she glanced back and forth as if looking for invisible threats. She nervously rubbed at her lips with one hand while clutching the podium with the other as if she might fall over if she let go. I'm no psychiatrist, but it sure seemed like she'd lost it. She woke up that morning as the powerful Bishop of Regenesis. Now she was preaching to an empty cathedral.

What we didn't see was Bodie.

"I know you are all upset, but I am here to assure you that the church is strong throughout the galaxy. It will rise again in Essen-Tet. Woe to the non-believers who have perpetrated such a sacrilegious act, for they will suffer the wrath of the Regent."

Who did she think she was talking to? Did she imagine that the cathedral was packed? I might have felt sorry for her if she wasn't a monster. Let's not forget that.

I looked out onto the rows of empty pews to see that the place wasn't empty after all. There was a lone man sitting front and center. He was a little guy dressed in a suit and tie who wore round, wire-rimmed glasses. His dark hair was slicked straight back. I'm not sure he was paying much attention to Kobain because he seemed more interested in the tech-pad he was holding. He'd glance up at Kobain every so often, then back to his pad to make entries like he was taking notes on her speech.

Kobain hadn't gone totally crazy. She was preaching to an audience of one.

"Always remember," Kobain went on. "You are either with Regenesis, or against Regenesis. There can be no doubt, no hesitation, no questioning. The Regent will see over us and—"

"Enough," the little man said impatiently. His voice was high-pitched and squeaky, which would get annoying real fast.

Kobain fell silent and held on to the podium. She looked to be trembling.

"You've been using different versions of those same, tired lines for years," he said to Kobain. "It's no wonder your effectiveness has diminished."

The man spoke with no passion. He wasn't angry, he was just stating facts. But his words were hitting Kobain like punches.

"I will do better upon my return," Kobain said, her voice cracking with tension. She was trying hard to convince him. "What happened is still so fresh and--"

"Yes, it is," the man said with a smirk. "Fresh. And there lies the problem you didn't foresee. This threat should have been eliminated long ago."

"My ministers have been working against me," she said. "They will be replaced with loyalists. Tyria is not lost forever. We will recover."

Kellen couldn't take it anymore. He grasped his baton and walked boldly out of the shadows to announce, "The service is over!"

Kobain's knees buckled and her shoulders fell. This was the last thing she was expecting.

"I couldn't agree more," the little man said. He didn't look surprised at all.

"Who are you?" Kellen asked.

The man cleared his throat and stood up. He was a skinny little dude who looked about as bland as gray paint. He's the kind of guy you'd pass on the street and never give a second look, and probably not even a first.

"Hello Kellen," he said. "I've been looking forward to meeting you for quite some time."

"How do you know me?" Kellen asked.

"I know you all," the man said with a smirk. "Issa K-Hew, the traitorous Beck, the doctor Tenzig, and of course the infamous Donovan Six. Welcome home. I congratulate you all on your success today."

We were all pretty much stunned speechless.

The man chuckled as if he was enjoying our confusion.

"Of course, you're wondering how I could possibly know you all."

He bowed his head slightly and said, "Regenesis is my church. I created it. I am the Regent."

CHAPTER 35

The five of us stood staring at the little man who seemed so strange because there was absolutely nothing strange about him.

"There is no Regent," Kellen said with disdain. "It's a hoax."

"Why would you say that?" the man asked. "Perhaps you were expecting me to have a long gray beard and flowing robes? Maybe even a halo? That is one of the more widely accepted images of God. Most notably on Earth, am I correct Donovan?"

"I may not know a lot," I said. "But I'm pretty sure you're no God. You're just some...guy."

"Indeed, but one who created a movement that has amassed billions of followers in multiple worlds. If that isn't a God, what is?"

"You don't have followers, you have slaves," Tenzig said.

"There are those who reject the church. Or do not have the wisdom to excel within it. You choose to focus on those who have failed and ignore those who have prospered."

"You offer nothing but false promises," Kellen said.

"What I offer is hope. So many people refuse to accept the realities of life. They search for higher meaning. A greater purpose. An explanation for why things are the way they are. It's far easier to blame a higher power for their troubles than to take responsibility for themselves. But if someone thinks that a higher power can give them a better life, they'll gladly accept it."

"For a price," Tenzig said with disgust.

The man shrugged. "This is a business after all."

"Exactly," Kellen said angrily. "You're pretending to be a God when all you're doing is running a business using slave labor. That's worse than criminal. It's immoral."

"Is it?" the man asked. "People are rewarded according to their value. Is that so wrong? If they add value to Regenesis, they will prosper. If they prove to be nothing more than replaceable cogs in a machine, they become expendable."

He held up his tech-pad and waved it. "The bottom line, is always the bottom line."

This guy was more like an accountant than a God. He probably knew where every cent came from and went to.

"But you've ruined millions of lives," Issa said.

"And I've made some people very rich."

The faint sound of an engine broke the silence.

"Ahhh," the man said with delight. "The transport has arrived. I've decided to give Bishop Kobain a second chance. Though she failed here on Tyria, she has also provided the church with the means to finally squash the threat created by Misha K-Soo."

"Bodie," I said under my breath.

"I can assure you that what happened here on Tyria will not be repeated elsewhere," the man said. "Enjoy your freedom while it lasts."

I couldn't take it anymore. This smug, ratty little guy had pushed me over the edge, and I lashed out the way I knew best. I clicked into linebacker mode.

"You're not going anywhere," I said.

I charged the guy, ready to drill him. He didn't flinch or brace for impact, which was weird. But it didn't stop me. I lunged, leaving my feet. But rather than spearing the guy, I passed right through him as if he wasn't there. I landed on the floor, bashing my elbows and knees.

The Regent stood there looking down at me with a smile. For that one moment I thought he might actually be some kind of supernatural being after all.

"I'm sorry to disappoint you," he said. "What you see is a projection. I'm actually standing comfortably in my office a few light years away. But I'll make sure to be here in person when Regenesis returns. I look forward to that day, and meeting you all again."

With that, he disappeared.

We all stared in wonder at the spot where the Regent had been, trying to understand what had happened. The sound of the incoming transport cruiser grew louder, rocking us all back to reality.

"It's landing on the roof," Beck said.

I looked to the podium. Kobain was gone. We were all too focused on the Regent to notice.

"How do we get up there?" Kellen asked.

Beck's answer was to take off running toward the front of the church. The rest of us instantly followed. After quickly climbing a steep flight of stairs, we broke out onto a vast expanse that was the cathedral's roof. The shadow of a transport ship crossed overhead as it cruised to a landing spot on the far side, at least fifty yards away from us.

"Kobain must be up here," Issa called out.

"And Bodie!" I shouted.

Nobody else was on the roof but us as the Regenesis cruiser came in for a landing. The ship gently touched down and a hatch opened, ready to take on passengers.

"There!" Beck shouted.

A Watcher came out of a door on the far side of the roof, pulling Bodie along with him. Bodie struggled to get away as the Watcher roughly pulled him toward the waiting ship.

"Bodie!" I shouted.

"We won't get to him in time," Tenzig said.

"Yeah we will," Issa said.

She ran toward the two. There was no way she was going to get to them before they entered the ship, but that wasn't her plan. As she ran she pulled off her backpack, dropped to one knee, wound up, and fired the line. The long line shot toward the Watcher and wrapped around his legs, tripping him up.

"Yes!" I shouted and took off after them.

The Watcher struggled to free himself. It was all the time I needed. I zeroed in on him and this time I didn't hit air. I nailed the guy square in his chest with my shoulder. He let out a pained grunt as I landed on top of him, knocking out the rest of whatever air was left in his lungs. I rolled over the guy and got my legs wrapped up in Issa's lasso.

"Donovan!" Kellen yelled.

I looked across the expanse of roof to see Kobain hurrying for the waiting ship. I couldn't stop her in time because I was tangled in Issa's line. The others were too far away to catch her before she reached the ship. Kobain was going to get away. Unless…

I give Bodie loads of grief, most of which he deserves. But there are some things I don't give him enough credit for because that's not what I do. But he deserves it.

He's got guts. He may whine and complain, but he doesn't give up. He keeps coming back no matter how hard he gets hit. More important in that moment, he is fast. Crazy fast. He wasn't the QB just because his parents wanted him to be.

"Go get her…Two," I commanded.

He didn't have to be told twice. Without a second of thought, he jumped to his feet and took off after her.

"Hurry!" Issa screamed.

The ships engines were already powering up, ready to lift off.

Kobain was a few steps away from boarding the ship when Bodie tackled her like, well, like I would have. She let out a yelp of surprise as she was hit by the freight train that was Bodie Freakin' Willard.

"Get off of me!" she screamed.

Bodie pinned her to the ground and though she struggled like a trapped animal, he wouldn't let her up.

I was afraid some Watchers would come out of the ship to help her. I also thought back to how easily Kobain had snapped the plastic handcuffs off of my wrists. Bodie needed help, so once I freed myself from the line I ran to them. Kellen and Beck ran there too. There was no way we were going to let her get on that ship.

We didn't have to bother. The ship's hatch closed, and within seconds it lifted off.

"You can't leave me here!" Kobain screamed in despair.

"Looks like they just did," I said.

The ship rose quickly, accelerated, and shot toward the sky.

Bodie stood up, leaving Kobain lying on the ground sobbing. Beaten.

"Nice hit," I said to him.

"Yeah, well, this time it's live, right?"

"Yeah it is," I said with a laugh. "You okay?"

Bodie took a breath and gave a thoughtful answer.

"Physically? Yeah. Past that, I'm not so sure."

"I hear you. We'll figure it out."

The others ran up and we stood together over Kobain, who was a mess of red hair and tears.

"They'll be back," she said through gritted teeth. "This isn't over."

"You think? Seems kind of over to me," I said.

"My flock will not abandon me,"

"You have no flock," came a high-pitched voice.

Standing on the spot where the Regenesis ship had just lifted off from, was the Regent. Or his projected image. He still held his trusty tech pad.

"After your failure here, the only value you had was to deliver that dangerous technology to me."

Kobain got up, smoothed her hair and tried to show that she was still in control.

"There are other scions that carry it," she said. "We will track them down."

"Agreed, but I'll place that task in more capable hands,"

Kobain took a step toward the Regent. She was growing more desperate by the second because her power, her whole world, was slipping away.

"I've dedicated my life to Regenesis," she cried. "I control three different worlds. I now have a foothold on Earth. How can you cast me aside after all I've done for the church? For you?"

"You are more than welcome to continue working for the church," the Regent said.

"I am?" Kobain said, sensing a glimmer of hope.

"Of course. There are any number of menial labor positions that I'm sure you are suited for. That is, if you can free yourself from the clutches of these cretins."

And just as quickly, her hopes were crushed.

"Good-bye, Vail Kobain," the man said. "Thank you for your service."

His image winked out and was gone.

Nobody moved. The hollow sound of wind blowing over the rooftop added an eerie touch to the last moments of freedom for the former Bishop of Regenesis.

"He's wrong you know," Kobain said, sounding stronger than she did just a few seconds before. "I didn't come this far by accident. Or luck."

She turned to us, and I saw that the dark fire in her eyes was back.

"Perhaps the Regent should be worried about his own future," she said with icy calm.

I chill went up my spine. She may have lost this battle, but she was definitely not done.

Kellen said, "Vail Kobain, in the name of the people of the Sandoor Federation, I place you under arrest. You will be brought to trial and answer for your crimes against humanity."

Kobain stood straight, looked Kellen square in the eye, and burst out laughing.

"You have no idea what you're up against," she said.

She pushed past us, boldly headed for the door back down into the Cathedral. Kellen and the others exchanged quick, unnerved looks, and ran after her. If she thought she was going to get away that easily, she was mistaken.

"What just happened?" Bodie asked. "I thought we won."

"We did," I said. "She's just trying to be cool."

Issa didn't look convinced.

We watched as Kellen and Beck caught up with Kobain and each held one of her arms to lead her to the stairs. She went willingly, which made me nervous. Why wasn't she more upset?

"What're you thinking?" I asked Issa.

"I'm thinking we haven't heard the last from the Regent. And probably not from Vail Kobain."

CHAPTER 36

The word "party" wasn't big enough to describe it. When word got out that Vail Kobain had been arrested, it was the final proof that Regenesis had been crushed. All over Essen-Tet, people left their homes and took to the streets to celebrate. Crowds gathered in every neighborhood to share their joy. There was music and laughter and dancing and a crazy amount of hugging and happy crying. Some even did the line-dance I saw at the party. If anybody was upset that Regenesis had been squashed, they weren't showing it. Or they were in jail.

I watched the craziness from the rooftop of Tenzig's apartment building, along with Tenzig, Issa and Bodie. As much as I wanted to be part of it, most everybody knew who I was and wanted a piece of me. The idea of jumping into that mosh was a little scary.

"It's time," Tenzig said.

"For what?" I asked.

"Utility teams have been working to re-connect the city's power grid to the solar farms that haven't been used since Regenesis took control of the energy industry." He glanced at his watch and said, "This is why I brought you up here. To see it. Should be any second now."

It was night. The dark city was even darker than usual since the Regenesis grid had been knocked out. Even the Prestige Manors were dark.

"What's going to happen?" Bodie asked.

His answer came a second later as electricity surged back into every last building. Full electricity. The city lit up like it was Christmas. Lights shone from most every window, streetlights burned, traffic lights flashed. It was a complete rebirth. It was breathtaking.

The dead city had come back to life.

People in the streets below us cheered.

We all laughed with pure joy.

"D-Ray," Tenzig said to me.

"Huh?"

"D-Ray. You asked if Tenzig was my first name or last name. It's my first name. My last name is D-Ray."

"Oh. I think I'll just call you Tenzig."

Beyond all the excitement, there was an unanswered question. I didn't want to kill the mood, but I had to ask it.

"How did they find me?" I asked.

Bodie tensed up. He wanted to know too.

"They got lucky," Tenzig said. "Before they brought Regenesis to Earth, they scanned the planet for biological issues that might be a problem for them. They didn't find any, but what they did detect were Tyrian genetics. That led them to you. To both of you, actually. They didn't realize there were two of you."

"Lucky me," I said.

"My mother was supposed to take me somewhere else?" Bodie asked.

"That was the plan. We think she wanted to disappear. From everyone, including the Tyrian League. So she hid you in plain sight, near another scion. At least that's what we think she did. Only she knows for sure. Nobody has heard from her since she left Kellen on Earth with Donovan."

Bodie stared at the joyful people in the street below, his mind was a million miles away. (Or however many miles there are between Tyria and Earth).

"You had no idea?" I asked him.

"Not until you told us about the dreams," Bodie said. "I've had 'em too. I still have 'em."

"Why didn't you tell us?" Issa asked.

"Because I didn't want to believe it. And I was scared. I still can't get my head around it."

"It'll get easier," I said.

"It will?" Bodie asked.

"No, but it's a nice thing to say."

Truth was, it was going to be a lot harder for him than it was for me. He was lucky. He got adopted by richie-rich parents while I…didn't. He stood to lose a whole lot more than I did, seeing as I pretty much had nothing. Bodie definitely had some adjustments to make.

"I want to go home and pretend like none of this happened," Bodie said.

Issa gave a worried look to Tenzig.

"We beat Regenesis on Tyria," Tenzig said. "But they're still powerful elsewhere."

"They know who you are now," Issa added. "They know about the Chrysalis and what it can do. They'll try to get it."

"So download it from my brain the way you did with Donovan," Bodie said.

"We didn't download it from Donovan," Tenzig replied. "It wouldn't let us. What we did was upload it to the grid, just as it was designed to do."

"So then what am I supposed to do?" Bodie asked with frustration. "Regenesis wants it, and you can't get it."

"But we *will* get it," Issa said. "When we need it."

"You mean when you go after Regenesis on another planet," Bodie said. "Then you'll need me."

"Yes," was Tenzig's no-nonsense reply.

"I'm not a weapon," Bodie exclaimed, exasperated. "Or a computer."

Issa put a comforting hand on Bodie's shoulder but didn't tell him what he wanted to hear.

"I want to know what happened to my mother. And father," Bodie said.

"And I want to find my daughter, Teever," Tenzig said. "Teever Five. And my wife."

"Hey, maybe your father's with mine," I said to Bodie, trying to sound positive. "They probably can't stand each other, just like us."

I thought that would get a smile out of Bodie.

It didn't.

"What you do is your choice," Tenzig said. "But it's safe here on Tyria. I can't say the same for Earth. We can protect you here, and when the time comes—"

"You'll ask me to do what Donovan did," Bodie said.

Nobody said anything, which confirmed Bodie's fear.

Kellen A-Quiss wasn't the kind of guy who would run around screaming and shouting to celebrate a victory. He'd definitely earned it, but that wasn't him.

We left Tenzig's building and met him at the same crummy bar where he'd told us the history of The Tyrian League. I expected him to be as drunk as he was that day. Again, he'd earned it. Instead, he was totally clear-eyed. It was hard to picture him as the drunken waste-case who flew us away from Earth.

Tenzig, Issa, Bodie and I were the only other people there, other than the sleepy bartender. It felt more like a funeral than a victory party.

Part of me wanted to scream: "Tyrian League! Yah!" But that wasn't the vibe.

Kellen said, "It means a lot to me that you're here."

We all mumbled various versions of: "No problem," but I was starting to think I should have taken my chances at one of the crazy street parties. It might have been dangerous, but a lot more fun.

Kellen sighed and turned for the bar. Waiting for him was a double-sized shot glass filled with amber liquid. Seemed as though Kellen's sober period was about to end. The shot glass sat next to a well-worn notebook with a black cover. Kellen picked the book up and held it reverently, as if it was a rare special edition.

"I wish you were here," Kellen said while gazing at the book. "But this moment isn't about me."

It took a second for me to realize who he was talking to. His voice quivered as he struggled to keep it together.

"One of the many terrible things that happened, is that you can't be here to enjoy this," he said as his voice cracked.

He flipped through some of the pages, buying time to get control of his emotions. The pages were filled with notes and mathematical symbols. What little I saw, I recognized because much of it had lived inside my head.

"When the history of Tyria is written, you will be remembered as the brilliant savior who stood up for its people and liberated our world. Your parents would be proud. I know I am. Wherever you are, I hope you know the good you've done, and it makes you happy. Now you can rest, my love."

Kellen gently closed the book and placed it on the bar. He took the shot glass and lifted it up to toast.

"To Misha T-Soo," he said proudly, with tears in his eyes. "Founder of The Tyrian League, savior of Tyria."

"To Misha!" we all said.

Kellen didn't drink. He offered the glass to Tenzig.

"Seriously?" Tenzig asked with surprise.

"It's quality stuff," Kellen said with a twinkle in his eye. "Don't want to waste it."

Tenzig was genuinely moved. He took the glass and said, "I'm not worthy, but it's not a proper toast unless somebody drinks, right?"

"That's right," Kellen exclaimed.

Tenzig knocked the shot back in one gulp, coughed, and slammed the glass down on the bar.

"To Misha," he declared.

We all cheered and broke out in applause while Kellen, who was re-living the best and worst moments of his life, finally smiled.

I'll never forget that moment.

He picked up the notebook and left the bar without so much as a "good-bye." I didn't think anything was wrong, I just figured he was having trouble keeping it together and wanted to be alone. He didn't say where he was going or when he'd return, he just left. I hoped he hadn't gone off the deep end and would start drinking again. Nothing good would come of that.

There was another issue that had to be faced.

Me.

What was I supposed to do? My situation wasn't the same as Bodie's. The Chrysalis was out of me. I was of no use to The Tyrian League anymore, and no threat to Regenesis. The bogus church was done with me, unless they wanted revenge. I wouldn't put it past those goons but with Vail Kobain in jail, it wasn't likely.

My scion days were over.

Also, unlike Bodie, I didn't have a family to go back to. Nobody would miss me, though I suppose a couple of social workers would wonder what became of the annoying kid who couldn't catch a break.

But Earth was home. I liked TV and football and pizza. Could I give that up? Where would I live? What would I do? I had lots of questions and no answers so I went to the one person I hoped might help me make sense of it all.

Tessa T-Shay. My mother.

The next day I visited her in her apartment, where she made me lunch: a grilled cheese sandwich and tomato soup. It was like being on Earth, except nobody on Earth ever made me a grilled cheese sandwich and tomato soup.

We ate at her small kitchen table. It was pretty awkward since we didn't really know each other. After re-living the events of the rebellion for the thousandth time, I finally got up the guts to ask the important question:

"What do I do now?"

Her answer surprised me.

"You figure out who you are," she said. "Don't worry about what other people think or want from you. You were given an immense responsibility, unfairly. But you triumphed and for that you should feel proud. You're at a crossroads, but it's not about deciding whether you should return to Earth, stay on Tyria, or move on to any number of other planets. Not yet, anyway. You first have to understand yourself, and what makes you happy."

"Easier said than done," I said.

"True. It's not a simple answer, for anybody. But if you can be honest with yourself about what's important to you, then the decisions about what to do next will be a little more clear."

"I don't even know where to start," I said.

"That's okay," she said. "There's no rush. No schedule. It's just life."

The realization that I didn't have to make a huge decision right away actually made me feel better.

"How many homes have you had?" she asked.

"None," I replied without hesitation. "I've lived in exactly seventeen different places. I kept count. None were homes."

That answer made her wince, and I felt bad for being so cold about it but hey, she asked.

"You don't know me," she said. "And you may hate me for what your father and I did, but maybe you could try to look at this like a second chance."

"Second chance for what?"

"To have a home," she said. "A real home. Here. With me. Essen-Tet was once a beautiful city. I have no doubt it will return to what it once was. Soon. From here you can go anywhere and do whatever you want. But until then you'll have a safe place where you're welcome."

I didn't realize it until that second, but that was the very thing I wanted to hear.

"I want to find my father," I said.

"I do too," she said with confidence. "You'll like him. Like I said, he's kind of a pain, just like you."

I don't know why, but I felt tears growing in my eyes.

"You don't really know me either," I said. "You may not like me."

"Too late," she said. "I already love you. I never stopped. Now that I've gotten to know you a little, I like you too."

She leaned forward, put her arms around my shoulders and hugged me tight. If that had happened even a few days before, I would have pulled away. Instead, I buried my head on her shoulder, and cried. I'm not ashamed to admit it. There was no way to know what would happen from there, and what living on another planet would be like, but for the first time in my life I felt like I might be home.

Bodie's decision wasn't as easy. It took him a few days of thinking, but he finally made his choice.

He was going home. To Earth. He didn't want to give up the life he knew, no matter how unreasonable and demanding his adoptive parents were. I can't say that I blamed him.

Issa, Bodie and I sat together on the monorail headed toward The Core in the Regenesis Compound. From there we'd go to the transpo center where a Jump Ship was waiting for Issa to fly him back home.

"What are you going to tell everybody?" I asked. "About where you've been for the last few weeks."

"I'll make something up about hitting my head when the locker room was attacked and not knowing where I was until I finally came to. You know, I'll play dumb."

Issa and I exchanged doubtful looks.

"That's like, ridiculous," I said.

"Worse than saying I was abducted by aliens who were battling against an interstellar crime church?"

"That's fair," I said, and shut up.

"We'll be watching you," Issa said.

"Are you going to be my guardian angel?" he asked.

There it was again. I felt a twinge of jealousy.

"No," Issa said. "It'll be Tyros that Regenesis doesn't know about."

Bodie looked disappointed. Too bad.

"So what are you going to do?" Bodie asked her.

"I'm going to track down my sister and the other scions," she said. "And my parents."

With that one conversation, I saw how our paths were going to split. The team that had come together to help defeat Regenesis on Tyria was about to break up.

The monorail arrived at The Core, and it was a short walk to the launch pads near the transpo center. Walking through the compound was much different than before Regenesis fell. People were talking and laughing like it was a regular old day. There were no Watchers lurking around. No tension. No fear. The recovery had begun.

"I'm getting a message," Issa said as she checked her wrist band. She read it and frowned.

"What's the matter?" I asked.

"I don't know," she said. "It's traffic control. I'll meet you at Launch Bay 22."

She took off running for the control tower while Bodie and I walked the rest of the way on our own.

"Want to race?" Bodie asked.

It took me a second to realize he was joking. It was a reminder of the race we had after football practice before finding our entire team was lying unconscious in the locker room. A lifetime ago.

"Nah, I don't want you to lose and feel bad on your last day here," I said.

We walked in silence, but I could tell Bodie had something he wanted to say.

"What?" I finally asked.

"There's no way I could have done what you did," he said. "It's making me nauseous to think that someday I might have to."

I don't know what hit me harder: facing the truth that this war wasn't truly over, or the fact that Bodie had given me a compliment.

"I got lucky," I said. "To be honest, I think you rolled with this better than me. You'll be fine."

"What if I'm not?" he asked.

"Then I'll have your back," I said. "We aliens have to stick together."

He gave me a genuine smile, but he still seemed troubled.

"I'm sorry about the Mutt thing," he said. "That was total douchery."

"It was," I said with a laugh. "But I get it. We come from two different places. Or so we thought."

That gave us both a laugh. We walked past a line of silver Jump Ships until we arrived at Launch Bay 22. It was the only empty bay.

Issa came hurrying up, out of breath.

"Where's the jump ship?" Bodie asked.

"Headed in," Issa replied.

"Why can't we take one of the others?" Bodie asked.

"I don't know," Issa said. "The controller said to take the one that's coming in now."

A silver orb appeared high in the sky that grew larger as it dropped closer. It was amazing to see these globes flying around with no obvious engines or propellers, like big silver bubbles. What other wonders would I be seeing from then on? I was beginning to think that living on Tyria might be pretty cool. Maybe I'd become a pilot. Though I'd still miss pizza.

The ship hovered over the launch bay and settled down gently. No sooner did the whine of the engines die then the hatch opened, and the pilot stepped out.

"Kellen!" Issa yelled with surprise.

Kellen gave us a smile and a big wave. We hadn't seen him in days. I was thinking the worst, but here he was looking sober and strong. He'd even shaved. He strode from the Jump Ship with a pack slung over his shoulder.

"Where have you been?" Issa called out. "We were all going crazy wondering if you were okay."

"I'm sorry about that," he said. "But if I told you what I was doing and it didn't work out, there'd be hard feelings. It was better you didn't know."

"What were you doing?" I asked. "And did it work out?"

"I was making good on a promise," he said. "And yes, it worked out."

He turned back to the Jump Ship. We all looked to the open hatch, wondering what to expect.

Two people stepped out, tentatively, holding hands. It was a man and a woman who looked around Kellen's age. I had no idea who they were.

But Issa did. She let out a gasp and her eyes went wide. She looked to Kellen, questioning. He smiled and nodded "yes."

The couple stood outside the hatch, looking our way. They squinted in the sun as if they hadn't seen it in a long while. Issa slowly walked, no, floated, their way.

"Is it them?" I asked Kellen.

"I found their names on a shipping manifest a while ago," Kellen replied. "They were working in a mining colony on the planet Winder-Ten."

Issa approached them tentatively, as if they were two deer who might run off if spooked. The man put his arm around the woman for support. Though we stood far away from them, I could see tears in their eyes. Issa stepped up and stood facing them. I couldn't hear what was being said, and that was okay. It was their moment. Then, as if a flood of emotions had suddenly broken loose, Issa jumped forward into her parent's arms. The three stood there, hugging and crying.

Issa was no longer an orphan.

"That's awesome," Bodie said, laughing.

"And I'm going to find their daughter, Saree," Kellen said with conviction. "I'm going to find them all."

Issa looked back toward Kellen. With tears of joy streaming down her cheeks she mouthed the words: "Thank you."

"Guess she won't be taking me back to Earth right away," Bodie said.

We both gave him an annoyed look.

"I'm joking!" Bodie said. "I can wait."

Kellen hitched his pack up on his shoulder and turned to walk away.

"Now where are you going?" I asked.

"To sleep for a week," he said. "Oh, almost forgot."

He pulled off his pack and reached inside.

"I picked something up on Earth. It's a strange alien thing. I don't get it, but whatever."

He pulled out a football and tossed it to me.

Bodie laughed.

The feel of catching a football and having it in my hands was a familiar one, like putting on a favorite pair of sneakers.

"Thanks," I said.

"See you around, boys," Kellen said and strode off.

I didn't know Kellen before Misha T-Soo died, but I'd bet the guy we watched strolling off with a confidant swagger was about as close to his being that guy again as possible.

"Do you think he can do it?" Bodie asked. "Find the scions? And the parents?"

"Yeah, I do," I said. "And we can help him."

"How?"

"C'mon," I said. "You've got time."

We walked off, leaving Issa and her parents to start healing some very deep wounds.

Being a celebrity-hero-world saver has its advantages. I was the triumphant scion. Donovan Six. Nobody questioned if I wanted something.

And I wanted to see Vail Kobain.

Bodie and I had no trouble convincing the Essen-Tet police who were guarding the Regenesis prisoners to allow us into the wing of The Core where they were being held. The policeman led us down a long corridor of cells with glass walls. Each were occupied by people who didn't look very happy to be there. There were former Watchers still in uniform, older men and women in blue suits the color of Kobain's scarf who looked like they should be in a business office rather than a jail cell, and on the very end in the last cell, was the Bishop of Regenesis.

The ex-Bishop of Regenesis.

"Let me know if you need me," the policeman said and held out his hand to shake. "And thank you."

I shook his hand and said, "No problem. Thank *you*."

"I can't believe I met you," he said, giddy. "My wife's gonna be jealous."

The guy was treating me like a rock star, which was weird but kind of fun. I could get used to that. Or maybe it would get old real quick.

He left Bodie and me alone.

"I thought he was gonna ask for your autograph," Bodie said with a chuckle.

I focused on Kobain, who sat on the far side of her cell on a metal chair with her head drooped over. Her wild red hair fell down like a fiery waterfall.

She was a mess.

"Can you hear us?" I asked.

Kobain slowly lifted her head, revealing dark sunken eyes. I was afraid her mind had snapped. It's not that I felt sorry for her, but I needed her to focus. I wasn't sure she even knew who we were. She squinted, as if digging through her memory to try and figure out who these visitors were.

"Have you come to dance on my grave?" she asked in a raspy voice.

She knew us all right. But the confidant woman who was feared on multiple worlds, was gone.

"No," I said. "We came to help you."

There was a spark of surprise in her eyes.

"You destroyed me," she hissed angrily. "Why would you help me now?"

"We want information," I said. "Bodie's father. And my father. Tell us where they are, and we'll try to get the Sandoor Federation to cut you a break. It wouldn't be much. It may not be anything, but at least you'd know you did the right thing. For once."

"You're offering me absolution?" she cackled.

"I don't know what that means," I said. "But they owe me. And Bodie. If we can get them to go easier on you, even a little, wouldn't that be worth it?"

"You tear down my life's work, plunge Tyria into chaos, put me in prison, and now you expect me to help you in exchange for what? A crumb of mercy?"

Bodie and I exchanged looks. He shrugged and said, "Yeah, pretty much. What d'ya say?"

Kobain looked me square in the eye. It felt as though the temperature had dropped ten degrees. She may have been a wreck, but her steely gaze proved the fire still burned. It may have been buried deep, but it was there. I suddenly wanted to be somewhere else, even though there was a thick wall of glass between us.

"I am genuinely thrilled that you're here," she said.

Her voice grew stronger.

"Yeah? Why's that?" I asked, though I didn't really want to know the answer.

She gathered herself, got up slowly, and stood straight. It was a chilling sight to see her in that long blue robe with flaming red hair against the white walls of the cell. It was like something out of a horror movie.

"Regenesis is more powerful than you know," she said. "Tyria is one small cog in a vast, complicated machine."

"Everybody knows that," I said. "But messing up a small part of a big machine could destroy the whole thing."

"Or not," Kobain said. "Congratulations. Celebrate. Enjoy your victory while you can."

"I don't think you're in the best spot to be making threats," I said.

Kobain laughed. It was chilling. She was sounding way too confident for somebody who was headed for a lifetime in prison.

"It does seem that way, doesn't it?" she said. "It's true. The Regent has thrown me aside. But he isn't aware of the vast support I have within the church. My people know what I've done for them. They won't abandon me, no matter what the Regent wants."

"You sure look kind of abandoned to me," I said.

"Do I?" she said with a smirk that didn't sit well with me. "How can I be abandoned when my people are everywhere? They may have stepped back into the shadows but trust me, they're out there."

She slowly walked closer to us. Though she was safely behind a couple inches of glass, Bodie and I both took a step backward.

"Maybe," I said. "But they can't help you in prison."

"I agree," Kobain said. "That's why I'm happy that you're here. You'll be the first to understand."

She stopped when she reached the glass wall.

"Understand what?" Bodie asked.

She took another step forward and walked right through the glass wall as if she was a spirit.

"Whoa!" Bodie exclaimed.

Kobain was out of her cell and standing right in front of us.

"Don't be frightened," she said. "I can't hurt you. I'm not even here."

The realization hit hard. She was a projection, just like the Regent in the cathedral.

"Where are you?" I asked.

"On a ship that's light years away from your little celebration party," she said.

"How?" Bodie asked, stunned.

"I told you, I have supporters you know nothing of. But you will learn. And since you asked, I do know where both of your fathers are."

"They're alive?" Bodie asked.

"Very much, though given their situations I'd imagine they both would prefer not to be."

"Where are they?" Bodie asked with desperation.

"And what do I get in return for that information? Mercy? That was such a generous offer but, no thank you. I won't be needing it."

"This doesn't change anything," I said boldly. "What happened here is the beginning of the end of Regenesis."

Kobain stalked toward us. Though it was only an illusion, it still made my heart race.

"You can tell yourself that, but I promise you, I will find the remaining scions, I will destroy every last Chrysalis and put an end to your Tyrian League."

She shot out a hand to grab Bodie by the neck. Bodie threw himself back against the wall, but her hand passed through him harmlessly.

"And then I will implement the Covian Solution," she said.

She leaned over until we were nose to nose. Or nose to projection.

"Please send my regards to Kellen A-Quiss. I look forward to seeing him soon, in the flesh. And you too, Donovan Six."

With that, she winked out, and was gone.

Bodie and I stood shoulder to shoulder, too stunned to move.

"I'm not going home today, am I?" Bodie asked.

"Sorry, Junior," I said.

"So what do we do?"

"We've got to find the other scions before she does," I said. "Without them, without *you*, the Tyrian League won't stand a chance against the rest of Regenesis."

"This was only the beginning," he said, then looked at me and added, "You're pretty calm after what just happened."

"Hey, I said with a shrug. "I don't get mad, I get even. Let's not forget that."

TO BE CONTINUED

Also by
D.J. MacHale

Pendragon – Journal of an Adventure Through Time and
Space (Series)
Morpheus Road (Trilogy)
The SYLO Chronicles (Trilogy)
The Monster Princess
The Library (Trilogy)
Trinity
Voyagers (Book #1)
The Equinox Curiosity Shop (Audible exclusive)
The Green Grabber (Guys Read - Other Worlds)
The Scout (Redux) (Don't Turn Out The Lights Collection)
Beyond Midnight (Short Story Collection)
The Paper Trail

ABOUT THE AUTHOR

D.J. MacHale has created, written, directed, and produced many award-winning television series and movies for young people including *Are You Afraid of the Dark?; Flight 29 Down* and Disney's *Tower of Terror* along with many others.

As an author he has written the bestselling series *Pendragon – Journal of an Adventure Through Time and Space*; the spooky *Morpheus Road* trilogy; and the sci-fi thriller trilogy *The SYLO Chronicles* along with several other titles. D.J. lives with his family in Southern California. Visit him at djmachalebooks.com as well as on Facebook, Twitter, and Instagram.